Damn the Man

by

Michelle L. Witvliet

Damn the Man

Contact Information: info@thewildrosepress.com

Cover Art: *Angela Anderson*

The Wild Rose Press
PO Box 706
Adams Basin, NY 14410-0706
Visit us at www.thewildrosepress.com

Publishing History
First Champagne Rose Edition, June 2007
Print ISBN 1-60154-093-0

Published in the United States of America

"Last night was as real as anything you'll ever find in this lifetime, Maggie."

She nodded. "Yes, it was," she agreed. "When it's just the two of us behind closed doors everything is perfect and wonderful. It's out here—" She gestured to their immediate surroundings. "Where it all falls apart."

"We'll work on that."

"Why, Nick? Nothing has changed. My life is here and yours is wherever you park your truck. Last night you just happen to park it in my driveway."

He stared at her for a time, searching for the right words. When he realized there were no right words, he said whatever came to mind just to shatter the silence. "Okay, fine, Maggie. You win. I'm leaving." He scooped his keys from the counter and headed for the front door. As he crossed the threshold, he rested his hand on the doorframe, and looked at her over his shoulder with a piercing sadness. "Tell me something, Maggie. When did you know?"

"Know what?" she choked.

"When did you first know you didn't love me anymore?"

Maggie flinched and closed her eyes against his candor. She couldn't give him an answer—at least not a truthful one. She lowered her head instead, staring at the floor as if the mysteries of the universe were written in the black rubber scuffmark etched on the tile beneath her toes.

"I'd really like to know," he prodded. "Was it a gradual thing or did it happen suddenly, like one minute you loved me and the next you didn't?"

Maggie shook her head, her voice barely above a whisper. "It's not that simple."

"You got that right. This thing between us is anything but simple." He drew a long, tortured breath. "Hating you for ripping my heart out would be simple. Hating you for giving me one night of false hope would be simple. But since that's not going to happen any time soon, I guess I'll have to do the next best thing."

"What?"

"What I should have done four years ago—make a life without you and hope the hate comes later."

Dedication

This one is for all the Saturday night Dreamers and Believers.

Chapter One

"Mom, come quick!" Son number one screamed from
the front yard in what Maggie recognized as an urgency
not emergency tone. Twelve years of mothering times two
was how she always knew the difference. She might on
occasion have difficulty telling their voices apart, but she
never had trouble distinguishing the level of necessity.
She counted, "One, two, three…" as she waited for the
inevitable follow-up.

"Mommmm!"

There it was, right on cue. Since the day he entered
the world three minutes after his brother, Davey never
did anything too far behind his identical twin, Danny.

Plopping the last of the hamburger patties she was
forming onto a waiting platter, she washed and dried her
hands and reached for the aluminum foil. Looks like the
rest of dinner would have to wait. This wasn't the first
time her active sons had put a hold on their evening meal.
Come to think of it, it wasn't even the first time that
week.

The rumble of a revving engine reverberated off the
plaster walls, filling the house and her head with its
echoing vibrations. It was like standing in the middle of
pit row on any given Saturday night at the local stock car
track, Illiana Speedway. The engine sounded peculiar,
however, like something wasn't quite right with its
timing.

As she slipped the foil wrapped plate of burgers into
the refrigerator, she tipped her head and gave a
concentrated listen, mentally chastising herself for not
recognizing the problem from the onset. Boy was she
slipping. Used to be she could tell what brand of spark
plugs a driver used just from the pitch of his engine at
ignition. It almost sounded like duel engines.

Icy fingers of suspicion tickled and stiffened her
spine. "He didn't," she sputtered as she slammed the

1

refrigerator door. "No, no, no! He didn't, he didn't, he didn't!" Maggie strode from the kitchen, through the foyer and yanked open the front door.

He did.

In spite of her realized misgivings, she couldn't help but chuckle at the scene she discovered in the yard. Wearing the widest, toothiest grin she'd ever seen on her firstborn, Danny sat in the seat of a shiny, brand-spanking new go-kart. And right behind him sat an equally ecstatic Davey in a second equally spectacular machine. Then of course, who could blame them? These weren't just any average, run-of-the-mill, frame and axle go-karts. Oh no. These were state-of-the-art racing go-karts complete with fiberglass bodies custom painted, decaled and numbered to look just like the racecar of the boys' favorite NASCAR driver, Nick Chapparelle. Who, by a stroke of sometimes regrettable coincidence, also happened to be their father.

If it weren't for the looks of pure delight on their beaming faces for these early birthday presents from their famous dad, she might have said something downright pithy to dampen this charming Kodak moment. But she stopped herself, having learned a long time ago to bite her tongue and bide her time when it came to anything concerning Nick Chapparelle. She'd eventually have her say and her way. She always did.

Just the thought of Nick made him materialize. A six-foot-two tight denim and snug t-shirt clad, older, though not always more mature, version of Danny and Davey strolled from around the corner of the house. Wearing his own toothy, dimpled grin, he hooked his thumbs into the front pockets of his snug jeans and leaned a muscled shoulder against the brick, casually crossing one tan booted foot in front of the other.

Maggie's breath hitched. Damn, the man looked good.

Before she realized what she was doing, her eyes traveled from the tip of his tooled cowboy boots to the top of his tousled, sun-streaked head. It was then she noticed he'd acquired a couple of new wrinkles around the eyes. Correction, they were only wrinkles when they showed up on her face. On Nick they were appealing laugh lines.

"Hey, Boomer," he drawled, bright blue eyes flashing

with a spark of mischief she knew could be big trouble.

Maggie bristled and clenched her teeth till her jaw ached. How she hated that nickname. She'd cringed from the first time he and his buddies had tagged and tormented her with the moniker when she was only fifteen. But back then any attention from the cocky twenty-year-old stock car driver she worshipped was better than nothing.

To this day she suffered with the handle because no amount of asking or demanding ever convinced him to stop. She'd learned over the years to prioritize her battles and this one wasn't anywhere near the top of her list. Nick would forever be Nick. That thought in itself was all it took to make her stomach do a crazy tumble. Maybe if he had changed after the divorce she might not still feel like this.

"Hello, Nick," she said, acknowledging her ex-husband with a thin-lipped smile. "What next? Matching Mustangs when they turn sixteen?" Her birthday gifts for the boys paled by comparison. How could she hope to compete with something like this? She couldn't, she reminded herself, and for that reason alone she refused to even try. Someone needed to give their sons a sense of reality and keep them grounded, and it looked like she was the only parent up to the task.

"Maybe," he said with a devilish dimpled grin and a sideward blue-eyed wink. "So, what do you think?" He swept a hand toward the go-karts.

"What I think is the neighbors are going to start a petition to run us out of Cartwright Corners." Maggie turned to address the boys. Raising her voice over the din, she said, "Guys, take those things into the garage and turn them off." The neighborhood children were already swarming around the karts like yellow jackets to an open can of orange soda. "They're not for driving on anything but a regulation go-kart track. No taking them on the street—ever. Is that understood?"

"Aw, Mom," Danny whined, disappointment clearly visible on his adolescent face. "Just to the end of the street and back?" His bright blue eyes pleaded. Davey nodded his blond head vigorously in concurrence. "Dad even got us regulation racing helmets just like his." He

3

held his up proudly.

"Come on, Mom." No big surprise that this came from their father, with an equally boyish blue glint and a lippy pout. "Just to Cartwright Drive and back?"

Adding to her flipping stomach her heart skipped a couple of normal beats. This, too, came as no real surprise. As much as she promised herself Nick wasn't going to affect her like this anymore, he always managed to get to her in one way or another. How many more years was it going to take before she grew immune to his damnable charms? Was just one lifetime a reasonable timeframe? She didn't think so.

Maggie shook her head. "It's not going work this time, fellas." Inasmuch as she wanted to relent, she forced herself to remain firm and managed to screw her sternest parental expression into place. No amount of whining, pleading, pouts, or pairs of puppy-dog eyes were going to shake her resolve. "Not even to the end of the driveway." A choir of disappointed groans emanated from the surrounding children, each obviously hoping for their own turn on the magnificent miniature racecars.

At least Nick, if not his sons, responded, "You heard your mother." He spoke with a great deal more firmness than Maggie was accustomed to hearing.

"When are we gonna take them to the track, Dad?" Danny asked. As the older twin, he had been the official spokesperson for the pair since he babbled his first words.

"We'll decide that later. Now, move it!" Nick spoke with unyielding authority.

Maggie watched her sons. The boys, unaccustomed to hearing their father so much as raise his voice to them, cast each other a bewildered glance but moved without uttering another word.

"Thanks for backing me up on this, Nick," she said, giving the dimpled devil his due, all the while keeping an interested eye on her sons.

Much to her surprise, they maneuvered the karts over the front lawn and onto the driveway with incredible precision and synchronization. Although she knew they'd gone recreational go-karting many times with their father over the years, Maggie also knew these karts had much more horsepower than the run-of-the-mill track supplied.

She was duly impressed with the boys' expertise. She was also suspicious. They didn't just learn to drive like that in the last five minutes. They've been practicing, and from the looks of it, one heck of a lot.

"Stay for dinner, Nick?" Maggie asked. "Nothing fancy, just burgers and potato salad but you're welcome to join us." She stood in the doorway, waiting for his reply.

"You're inviting me to dinner, Boomer? What's the catch?"

Inwardly cringing at his continual use of the name, she still managed to cast him a sweet, benign smile. If he so much as suspected the real reason behind her overt hospitality, he'd be out of there in record-breaking time.

"No catch, Nick. I'm hurt you'd even think such a thing," she feigned, palming her hand against her chest. "The boys would never forgive me if I let you dash off. Consider it an early birthday celebration..." She paused just long enough for effect, and then added, "...especially since you can't be here for their party on Sunday." She turned and made her exit, allowing the storm door to swing on its hinges in her wake.

Nick was hot on her heels. "I'm not going there today, Maggie." He yanked open the door before it had a chance to settle in its frame and followed close behind. "It's not my fault Brickyard always falls around the same time as the boys' birthday. So you can forget about making me feel guilty for something I can't control."

She stopped dead in her tracks and whirled around to face him. Her action caused his boots to slip and skid on the kitchen quarry tiles. He reached for the island counter to keep from slamming into her. Toe-to-toe, they stood inches apart, and she gave an indignant sniffing huff. Big mistake. Men who worked around cars were supposed to smell like grease and fuel, not Lagerfeld. Any other time she might have allowed herself a moment to enjoy the aromatic interlude. She gave a mind-clearing, derisive guffaw instead.

"When have you ever felt an ounce of guilt about gallivanting all over the country doing what you do?" She waved her hand at him in an effort to emphasize her point. "You've had years of practice, Nick. Ignoring your family should be second nature to you by now."

"Trying to earn a living for my family is a far cry from ignoring them! I did what I did for all those years because I had a wife and kids to support. I had to go where the races were."

"You were making a name for yourself," Maggie corrected. "The fact that you made a few bucks doing it was just sweeter icing on the cake." Maybe if he hadn't been so good at what he did in the first place, she wouldn't have had to do what she did in the second place.

"The bigger the name the bigger the paycheck, honey," he shot back. "Maybe you haven't taken a good look around lately, but you and the boys aren't lacking for one damn thing."

"The money was never that important," she murmured, stung by the fact that he ever thought differently. "You know that."

"Must have been important enough not to send the support checks back!"

With a silent gasp, Maggie stumbled back as if she'd been punched. Her recovery was slow and shaky.

"Damn!" Nick cursed under his breath as he lowered his head to meet his hand. Rigid fingers sliced through his hair and settled at the base of his skull.

She stared at him in utter disbelief. This was a first. They'd had some heated arguments over the years—before, during and after the divorce. They both had tempers when provoked, but never once had he ever used money in any form as a weapon. If anything, his generosity had been overwhelming after the divorce.

She held up her palms, as if to ward off any further verbal blows and expelled a slow breath. "Maybe dinner wasn't such a good idea after all."

"Mags," he said in a hoarse whisper. He took a step closer and wrapped his fingers around her shoulders to prevent her from moving away. She felt the heat of his touch beneath the thin white cotton knit. "I didn't mean anything by what I said."

"Then why did you say it?" she asked, more curious than angry. "This argument isn't a new one, Nick. It's the same fight, just a different round. Something must have triggered the money angle this time."

"You should know better than to listen to anything I

say when we're fighting." He cupped her face, her chin resting in the curve between thumb and forefinger, and forced her to look at him. He stared long and deep into her eyes. "You're the last person on the face of this earth I want to hurt. Why is it you always seem to be the first?"

A bittersweet laugh burst from her lips as she broke free from his grip. Propelled by the powerful need to place some distance between them, she moved to the other side of the kitchen. How far did she have to go to sever the connection? Halfway across the room and she still felt his incredible touch warming her skin. "Irreconcilable differences, isn't that what our lawyers called it?"

"For lack of anything better," he grumbled, sounding every bit as bitter as he had the day the divorce was finalized. "I'll be out of here as soon as I say goodbye to the boys." He headed for the sliding glass door leading to the backyard deck and detached garage.

For whatever the reason, she didn't want him to leave—not like this. There was already too much animosity stacked between them. She wasn't looking to add to the pile.

"Start the grill as long as you're heading that way," she said. "We'll never eat if you don't get the burgers started." Maggie pulled the hamburgers from the fridge and handed the plate to Nick along with a long-handled spatula and a forgiving smile. Some things were better left unspoken.

Without a word, Nick took the plate and spatula and headed for the gas barbeque grill as he expelled a slow, low whistle under his breath.

Maggie barked a short laugh, recognizing the audible expression as one he always used whenever he thought he'd just dodged a .357 Maggie, as he called it. She smiled, knowing she was still fully loaded and able to pull the trigger whenever the next opportunity presented itself.

He was still in the process of adjusting the flame when she joined him, barefooted and carrying a longneck bottle of beer, which she offered by waving it in front of his face.

"Thanks," he said. Pressing the icy cold bottle to his lips, he tossed back his head and took a long swallow.

Maggie dragged a redwood deck chair closer to where he stood by the smoking grill. Perched on the edge of the cushioned seat, she rubbed her palms together in slow circles, glancing down, as something weighed heavily on her mind. After a long silence, she asked, "Nick, are you having financial difficulties?"

"No," he said as he placed the meat patties on the heated grate. "Why do you ask?" he questioned over the sizzling hiss of the juicy burgers.

"What you said before about the money, it got me thinking. If you're having a cash flow problem, I'll try to help any way I can. I've managed to save a little. It's yours if you need it."

He lowered the lid on the grill and gazed at her, a thoughtful, curious expression came over his features. "Thanks, Mags, but everything's fine. Chapparelle Racing Team Corporation couldn't be better. So stop worrying."

She gave an easy, husky laugh. "That's easier said than done, Nicky. Worrying about you is a habit I just can't seem to break." She stood and hurried down the deck steps into the yard before he pressed for further clarification.

"Danny, Davey," she called. "Time to shut the garage and wash up. Dinner in ten minutes."

Chapter Two

Maggie smiled and sat back, her hand wrapped around a fresh tumbler of raspberry iced tea as she watched her beautiful sons interact with their handsome father. All through dinner Nick and the boys filled the kitchen with corny jokes, teasing wisecracks, and raucous laughter.

She would be forever grateful to her ex for not allowing his ambivalence toward her affect his relationship with their sons. In all likelihood, they saw their father more now than before the divorce. Like so many divorced dads, Nick made a greater effort to keep in touch and stay involved. He had been spreading himself so thin during their marriage that none of them received the attention they deserved. Something was bound to break under the strain. Their eight-year marriage wound up being the casualty with Maggie calling the time of death.

"When are you leaving for Indianapolis, Dad?" Danny asked, shoving the last of his second double cheeseburger into his mouth.

"Tonight," he said, shooting an unhurried glance in Maggie's direction. "No later than tomorrow morning for certain. Practice starts Thursday."

"How do you think you're gonna qualify?" Danny asked his father.

Nick shrugged with his typical 'we'll see' attitude. He pushed the oak captain's chair away from the table, leaned back and stretched his legs, crossing them at the ankle. His forearms rested on the curved chair arms. Another nearly empty beer bottle dangled from his relaxed fingers. "If the car runs as well as it did during testing, I expect to place somewhere in the top half of the field."

Talk of the upcoming race was Maggie's cue to leave the dinner table. She stood and began scraping and stacking the dishes. As she worked her way around the table, she couldn't help but notice how Nick's muscled thighs stretched and strained the taut dark denim with every subtle shift of his body. Her stomach did a tumbling lurch when her gaze settled on the nicely shaped bulge between his legs.

Damn, the man still looked mighty fine in tight jeans.

Further consideration of his assets forced her to eye the luxurious head of tousled blond hair and washboard abs. Weren't thirty-five year old men supposed to start developing a paunch or at the very least a couple of visible love handles? There should be at least the beginnings of a gut to show for his fondness of beer. Then again, Maggie reminded herself, Nick rarely did anything like normal men. Why should growing older be any different?

Catching sight of the bottle dangling from his fingers, she dragged her attention from the man and followed her instincts. Glancing into the recycling bin on her way to the sink she counted enough empties to know Nick had more than reached his limit for the night.

"I've got double fudge brownie delight, caramel pecan fudge swirl, chocolate chip brownies or chocolate-chocolate chip cookies for dessert," she offered, reaching for a scoop, spoons and bowls to serve their selections. "Name your poison, gentlemen."

Danny and Davey quickly placed their orders, requesting caramel pecan fudge swirl with chocolate-chocolate chip cookies on the side.

"Geez, Maggie, think you got enough chocolate there?" Nick teased as he pushed himself out of the chair and moved to stand across from her at the island counter.

The icy slick carton slipped through her fingers and landed on the granite with a hard thud. "You know me and my love for the stuff," she said, casting him a weak smile. "How about a nice foamy mocha cappuccino with your dessert?"

He shuddered. "I'll pass. No dessert for me either." He pitched the empty beer bottle into the recycle bin and pulled another cold one from the fridge.

Taking the bottle from him before he had a chance to twist off the cap, she offered, "Then how about a regular cup of coffee instead?" Sliding the bottle out of his reach, she situated herself between him and the refrigerator and held him back with a palm planted firmly against his warm, hard chest.

"I don't think driving to Indy tonight is such a good idea," she said, low enough for only Nick to hear.

"Why? Because I've had a couple of beers?"

"That," she said, jerking a thumb at the bottle she'd placed on the counter behind her. "Would have been number seven."

Bracing himself with one hand against the edge of the counter, he planted his feet on either side of hers and slowly leaned forward in a sneaky attempt to reach around her. "Come on, Maggie. You know I can hold my brew."

"In fact, I don't want you driving anywhere tonight." She studied him with a keen eye and had to admit he didn't appear the slightest bit intoxicated. But that much alcohol had to have some adverse effect on his reflexes didn't it? "Give me your truck keys."

With a sly grin, he dangled the keys in front of her nose, trapping her against the counter between his hip and free arm. "That sounds like an invitation to spend the night."

Snatching the keys, she ducked under his arm and out of his reach. The very fact that she was able to take the keys without any effort was all it took to convince her that his reaction time was indeed compromised.

"Sort of looks that way, Nicky," was all she offered as she side-stepped any further advances. She'd deal with informing him her invitation extended only as far as one of the twin beds in the guest room later.

"Coffee?" she asked, handing him a steaming mug of straight, unadulterated Colombian, which he took with a reluctant grunt.

"When are we going to the go-kart track, Dad?" Danny asked, shoving a heaping spoonful of gooey ice cream into his mouth. He swallowed and wiped his sticky lips with the back of his hand.

"Looks like we need to find time to work on your table manners, young man," Maggie interjected, handing him a paper napkin.

She might as well have saved her breath. Not one of her dinner companions was the least bit interested in working on their social skills. Now, if she knew the secret of how to shave two-tenths of a second off their lap time, she'd have their undivided attention.

She dug into her bowl of double fudge brownie delight and savored the creamy rich chocolate and chewy brownie bits like a deprived addict. Resisting the temptation to wipe her mouth with the back of her hand, she licked her sticky lips and reached for a napkin to finish the task.

"What do you think the karts will do in the back straightaway?" Davey asked, helping himself to another fistful of cookies.

Maggie made a mental note to start taking more money to the grocery store. The boys were eating double helpings of everything lately.

"Listen guys, you know you need a lot of practice before trying anything fancy in the back straightaway." Nick tried to sound parental and firm. He failed miserably. No matter what he said, the tone of his voice was a dead giveaway. She knew he was just as eager as the boys to see what the go-karts could do. What she found even more interesting was the way the three of them opened the door and ushered her to the threshold. All she had to do was walk on through. It was true, she thought, good things did come to those who waited. Her opportunity had finally arrived.

"Gee, Nick," Maggie chimed in. "How much practice do you think they're going to need, over and above what they've already had?" Raising her brows, she sipped her coffee, glancing at each of them over the rim of her cup. "Once around the track maybe?"

All three stopped what they were doing—a cookie, a spoon, and a coffee mug hovered in mid air between hand and mouth. Looking very much like a trio of deer caught in high beam headlights, they turned their wide-eyed gazes toward Maggie, all waiting for the other shoe to fall. There was always another shoe.

Maggie chose not say another word, deciding instead to let silence and the tension of the moment work its own particular brand of magic. She'd often heard that patience was a virtue. Well, she was about as virtuous as she was ever going to get as she waited for one of them to crack and confess. Her money was on Davey. Danny might be the spokesperson but Davey was her informant. She tapped her fingers in a quick tattoo against the tabletop. And the winner is...

"Busted," Davey mumbled around a mouthful of cookie, crumbs flying from his lips.

"Shut up, Davey!" Danny hissed, knuckle-punching his brother on the arm.

"Oww," Davey responded, rubbing the spot.

"Danny, stop," Maggie warned, raising her hand to block another attack.

"Okay, I admit we haven't been totally above board with you," Nick interjected. "We've been going to the track a little more often than you've known about."

"How much more often?" she asked, shooting him an inquisitive stare. Although she could pretty much guess what his answer was going to be, she waited to hear what he had to say.

Wide-eyed and attentive, Danny and Davey also watched their father, looking just as curious as she as to how he was going to respond.

"Well, actually..." he began on a tentative note. "Uh, you see what we were trying to..." he started again, glancing at the boys who appeared to hang onto his every word.

Maggie watched an amazing transformation come over Nick. He sat up straight, drew a deep breath, slapped his palm on the table, and let the words fly. "Damn it Maggie! They needed extra practice. Because you insisted they wait to race until they were twelve most of the kids in the same age class have two to three years experience on Davey and Danny. After carefully weighing their options I did what I thought was best for them under the circumstances.

"So go ahead, get it over with—tell me again how irresponsible I am. It's not like I haven't heard it all before. But before you do, I just want to add that as their father I should be allowed to make a decision about the boys and their activities without always checking with you first."

13

Where did that come from? It wasn't that Nick didn't stand up to her—quite the contrary. Only God and a host of His angels knew how often they butted heads, but when it came to making decisions about the children he always deferred to her. He was just full of surprises today, first the crack about the money and now this.

"Let me see if I'm understanding this," she said. "What you're trying to tell me is this all comes back to being my fault?"

"Okay, sure," Nick agreed.

"Amazing, utterly amazing," Maggie remarked. "You've managed to turn your deceit and duplicity, for who knows how long..." She hesitated, searching. "Help me out here, guys. How long has this been going on?"

"Since April," Davey offered without hesitation.

"Way to go, Davey." Danny gave his brother another jab. "Get dad in more trouble."

"Your dad is not in any trouble," Maggie assured her son.

"He's not?" Danny, Davey, and Nick asked in unison.

"I mean I'm not?" Nick corrected.

"No, Nick. You're not," she confirmed. "You made some very valid points just now. And you're right, I haven't been fair by making all the decisions about the boys and their activities.

"However," she continued.

"Uh oh, here it comes," Danny said.

"However," she repeated, casting Danny one of her famous *mother* glares. "I will not tolerate the three of you lying to me again. Is that understood?"

"All right!" the boys cheered, slapping each other an exuberant high five. They leaped out of their chairs and started hopping around the table, waving their arms in the air in what could only be interpreted as their version of an end zone victory dance.

It was a well-known scientific fact that twelve-year-old boys were not the most coordinated creatures on the face of the earth. Their arms and legs were growing faster than their brains could compute or react to their ungainly actions. As he pulled back his arm and swung it around, Davey hit his ice cream bowl in mid back swing. The bowl appeared to have an onboard guidance system as it tipped and teetered, spinning and skittering across the table on its way to its final destination. Like a heat-seeking missile it found its target and made a direct hit on Nick's outstretched lap.

Helpless to prevent the incident, Maggie watched the sequence of events with eyes and mouth wide open. No doubt about it, she observed, Nick's reflexes were most definitely compromised. His attempts to push away from the table to dodge the gooey mess were clumsy and way off their mark. She bit her lip and covered her mouth to stifle herself from laughing out loud. He looked like Bambi on ice, his legs moving but not getting anywhere as his boot heels sought traction without success against the tile floor.

Half sitting, half standing, Nick stared at the sticky mess dripping melted caramel and fudge over his stomach, crotch and thighs. Spills were such a common occurrence in their house the whole incident barely fazed Maggie. Unfortunately a combination snicker/giggle escaped through her fingers.

"This isn't funny, Maggie," Nick stated.

"Yes it is!" She burst out laughing. "You think it's funny too, don't you, boys?" She jumped up, grabbing a dishtowel and a handful of paper towels and started blotting the mess from the floor and table.

"Yeah, Dad!" said Davey. "You look real funny."

"We'll call it NASCAR ala mode," Danny observed with a hearty laugh.

"Maggie, do something!" Nick pleaded.

"I'm cleaning it up. What else would you suggest I do?" She was still chuckling as she wiped part of the mess from the front of Nick's shirt. The rest of it further south would be his to clean off. She tossed the dishtowel into his lap.

"You could help me take these pants off for starters," he drawled. It wasn't so much what he said but how he said it.

"OooOOOooo," Danny and Davey chirped in pre-pubescent unison, giving each other devilish, sideward glances and elbow nudges. Their behavior convinced Maggie the time had come for that next level sex talk. Since Nick was so eager to be a part of the boys' lives, maybe she'd let him handle this one.

"Enough of that, you two. It's time to hit the showers." In spite of the fact that she was having difficulty keeping herself from laughing, she spoke in a tone that brooked no arguments. She glanced at Nick. He, too, appeared to be having trouble keeping a straight face.

The second she was certain her sons were well out of hearing range, her shoulders began to shake and the laughter erupted without further restraint. Nick's hearty chuckle accompanied her.

"Those two are really something else." Nick wiped the tears of laughter from his eyes and shook his head. "I don't know how you keep up with them."

"It's not easy. They're clones of you," she said on a semi-serious note. "The older they get the more I see it."

The laughter died from his lips. "You okay with that?" he asked. He picked up the towel she had tossed at him earlier and attempted to wipe more of the mess from his lap.

"Of course," she answered, somewhat confused. "Why would you ask something like that?"

He shrugged. "Some divorced women resent the kids as much as the father."

Maggie bristled. "The only thing I resent is you even thinking such a thing."

"This isn't working," he grumbled, tossing the towel aside. "I've got to get out of these." He unbuckled his belt and popped the brass button at his trim waist.

He was just about to pull down the zipper when Maggie interrupted, "Uh, what do you intend on wearing while I wash those?"

The gaze he leveled on her was a sensual mixture of tease and heat. The look sent hot shivers rippling through her body. "Not a thing, darlin'," he drawled. Lower and lower the waistband slipped without a hint of boxer, brief, or bikini on the horizon. Nada, zip, zilch, zero, nothing!

Damn, the man was going commando! He was about to bare his tight cheeked ass and there wasn't a thing she could do but watch the show. Nick's moves were every bit as provocative as the male stripper her friends had taken her to see shortly after the divorce. Maybe more so, she was already familiar with the package he was unwrapping. Whoever said great things come in small packages had never seen her ex naked. Was it getting warm in there?

"You're enjoying this far too much," she finally said, her voice dropping several octaves into a husky range she found alarming. Could she be coming down with a cold, she wondered, dragging her gaze away with every last ounce of willpower she possessed. With a great deal of effort, she forced herself to direct her attention elsewhere and busied herself with clearing the dessert dishes from the table.

"You bet I am," he retorted.

"There's a box of your old clothes in the basement. There must be something in it you can put on."

Sliding the pants back up, he headed for the basement door and grumbled, "Spoil-sport."

"You bet I am," she mumbled.

He returned a few minutes later bare-chested this time but wearing a pair of snug faded to pale jeans, worn thin in the knees and left back pocket where he always kept his wallet. "Looks like I've gained a few pounds since I last wore these," he remarked, patting his tight abs as he carried his soiled clothes to the laundry room. The boots he added to the rest of the family's footwear piled by the service door. "You'd think we had a half a dozen kids from the number of shoes sitting here."

"Did you also happen to notice how large those shoes have gotten?" Maggie poked her head around the doorway. "Their age and shoe size seem to be in direct correlation to one another." She took the dirty clothes from Nick and tossed them into the washer along with some of the boys' things from the hamper.

"They're getting big all right," he agreed. "They're such great kids, Maggie. You've done a good job with them."

"I'm not raising them by myself, you know."

He shook his head and sighed. "I can't take any credit for the way they're turning out."

"Don't sell yourself short, Nick. You've stayed involved in their lives. That's important." She placed an open hand on his back in a comforting gesture of reassurance. "You're a wonderful father. Don't ever think otherwise." His skin was warm and supple beneath her palm and she received much more than the consoling touch was intended to convey.

He must have felt it too, she realized, too late to stop the course of events that followed. At the same intense moment he ceased breathing and turned, casting a hooded gaze so forceful it knocked the breath right out of her and caused her fingers to flex and withdraw from the powerful jolt of hot desire shooting up her arm. It settled in her body with a fierce aching she found hard ignore yet impossible to act upon.

With a determined frown, Maggie pushed the unsettling feelings aside, refusing to examine them, afraid of discovering the naked truth buried beneath.

"It's gotten awfully quiet up there." She turned and started to walk away, adding, "I'd better go see what those two are up to."

"Mind if I come?" Nick asked, acting hesitant to intrude.

"Of course not," she answered, surprised by his reticence.

Nick followed her up the staircase to the second floor. He couldn't help admiring the rear view afforded him as he walked behind her, and he smiled with unabashed appreciation. Smoothly curved calf muscles flexed and relaxed as long, lean thighs and nicely rounded feminine hips and butt shifted and swayed with each stair she climbed. She'd put on a few pounds, he noticed, but they only seemed to add to her luscious curves and feminine form.

His fingers clenched the banister as he silently congratulated himself for keeping his mounting libido in check when all he really wanted to do was regress to the base instincts of a Neanderthal, grab her by the hair and drag her off so that he could touch and caress every enticing, delicious curve to his horny heart's content.

Emotionally kicking and mentally screaming against the harsh intrusion into his fantasy world, Nick was dragged back to reality the moment they reached the upstairs landing. He hadn't been up there since the divorce almost four years ago. In some ways it seemed like only yesterday that they'd lived there together. Yet, in so many other ways it had been an unbearable eternity.

His gaze was drawn against his better judgment to the door at the end of the hall. So many memories connected to that room flooded his consciousness, some passionate and playful, others less pleasant and regretful, and a few downright awful and agonizing. Fractured flashes of their past popped and danced in his head much like a slide show gone berserk. Nick felt a stinging burn behind his eyes and he fiercely rubbed against the cruel intrusion with thumb and forefinger, realizing too late what a mistake it was to come up there. It left him feeling exposed and open to a whole new batch of hurt.

Maggie pushed on the boys' partially shut bedroom door. The hall light shed enough illumination to see into the darkened room and the trail of wet towels and cast off dirty shirts and shorts leading from the door to where their sons lay sleeping, curled in almost identical positions.

"They still share a room?" Nick whispered.

She nodded. "They insist they like it this way," she returned. "I figure they'll come to me when and if they're ever ready for separate bedrooms. Although at the rate they're going I don't expect it to happen until after they graduate college. I am hoping it'll be before they get married."

Nick gave a soft chuckle and leaned against the doorjamb, watching her step lively over the obstacle course and adjust the blankets over each of their sleeping sons as she brushed back their hair and kissed each on the forehead. How he cherished these few and far between moments. His chest tightened as he wondered how something so right one minute could go so wrong the next.

Chapter Three

"It was a good day, Mags." Reacting to the moment, Nick hooked his arm around her neck and pressed a quick kiss on the top of her head. The lingering feel of her silky curls against his cheek and lips teased his already rubbed raw emotions as he steered her through the kitchen toward the adjacent family room. "Thanks for the invite."

"You're welcome," she croaked as she eased out from under his embrace and moved to sit in a chair clear on the other side of the room. She cast him a weak smile. "The boys really enjoyed themselves tonight. In case you haven't noticed, they like having you around."

Her intentional severance from his side sliced through him like a fragment of sharp sheet metal and caused him to inwardly flinch from her painful slight. Under most circumstances he would have made some snide remark about it to really piss her off, which in turn would have prompted her to show him the door, beer goggles or no beer goggles. It came as a bit of a surprise that no spiteful response came immediately to mind and made him wonder if his lack of reaction was a sign that his heart was catching up to what his head kept trying to tell him on a daily basis. Alarmed by the thought, he tossed it aside like a piece of unsolicited mail and diverted his attention to the assortment of photos scattered on the mahogany shelves of the entertainment unit. One picture in particular captured and held his interest. He picked it up and studied the recent photo of Maggie and their sons.

"What about you, Maggie?" he asked, focusing on her smiling image. He rubbed his thumb across the photo as if the repetitious strokes could summon a genie that would put him back in the picture. "Are you okay with having me around?" He replaced the photo and turned his interest to a stack of compact disks. He picked up a CD case and flipped it over to read the play list on the back.

"It's getting easier. You are, after all, the father of my

children. If for no other reason, you will always be welcome in this house for that."

His expression somber, Nick turned to her. He watched her lift a remote from the collection on the coffee table and aim it at the stereo. The savory rich alto sax of Dave Koz flowed like rough silk from the sound system's speakers. "I can remember a time not so long ago I didn't feel very welcome for any reason."

"I know, Nick. I'm sorry for that. It's just that…" She stopped in mid sentence. It made him wonder what it was she kept herself from saying. "As long as you're here, I've got a stack of mail for you again." She uncurled her legs and started to stand.

"I'll get it," Nick told her. He hitched a thumb toward the front of the house. "Your office?"

She nodded and sat back down. "One of these years the mailman is going to figure out you don't live here anymore."

"Probably all junk anyway. The bills *always* manage to find me."

"You want that cappuccino now?" she called after him.

"Sure," he said, heading down the hall for Maggie's studio/workroom. He'd agree to thumb screws and a full body wax if it would prolong their evening together.

He walked from the kitchen and into the largest room off the main foyer. It was by original design a formal living room and adjoining dining room separated by an archway, but shortly after they moved in Maggie had taken the—in her own words—unused space and converted it into a workroom for her growing quilting enterprise, claiming the basement was too far removed from the everyday activities of two young boys. It had proved to be a practical solution and one she never found reason to change.

Unprepared for how these rooms would affect him, he stood in the doorway to give himself a chance to adjust to the sensory deluge as he scanned the room and everything in it. Sturdy wood shelves held baskets of supplies and colorful bolts of fabric. Several sewing machines, a large worktable, and a quilting frame wrapped with an intricate geometric patterned quilt filled a good part of

21

the larger room. An L-shaped desk sat in one corner of what was once the formal dining room and held a computer and four-in-one printer.

Her essence lingered like a benevolent spirit, enticing and inviting. He closed his eyes and breathed deep, overloading his senses to sustain him through the dark days ahead. Looks like his heart still had a lot of catching up to do.

"Did you find them?" Maggie called from down the hall. "Everything's in the big manila envelope on my desk next to the printer." He heard the hollow clang of the washer lid closing and the tumbling start of the dryer.

The lilt of her voice and the everyday sounds of domesticity nudged Nick back to the here and now. He didn't return with a willing heart. He cleared his throat and called back, "I got it."

Finding the envelope, he snatched it from between the printer and monitor, eager to get back to her. In doing so, a stack of loose mail fell out and scattered across the desktop and floor. Kneeling, he began the task of gathering it together. A good many of the envelopes were addressed to Danny and Davey. Birthday cards, he assumed, recognizing several return addresses. Two of them were from his mom and two more were from Maggie's mother, the latter taking him by surprise since the woman had never accepted their elopement let alone the birth of her grandchildren. It made him wonder if Janelle Thornton was attempting to heal the rift she'd created with her estranged daughter. He hoped so for Maggie's sake.

Curiosity got the best of him and he read the cards from his mother. Aside from the standard children's birthday greetings, his mom had written a personalized message to each of the boys saying how much she loved them and missed them and hoped they would come visit her in Atlanta real soon.

The notes got Nick to thinking. He'd last seen his mom just a few months ago when he raced down there in the spring, but he couldn't recall when the boys had last seen their grandma. He decided right there and then to take them for a visit just as soon as racing season was over.

Nick stuffed the cards from his mom into their envelopes and shuffled through the remainder of the stack to see who else had been thoughtful enough to remember his children on their special day. He stopped when he came across a name he didn't recognize. The cards were signed: Fondly, Joel. He didn't know any Joel, at least none that would be sending greeting cards to his sons. But Maggie and the boys did. And fondly, no less. Four angry fingers and a twitching thumb curled around the colorful cardstock, crumpling it as easily as if it were a sheet of tissue paper.

Gripping the crumpled wad in his fist, he strode down the hall, pushed and bullied every step of the way by a very large, overbearing green-eyed monster.

He found Maggie curled up in one corner of the couch clutching an oversized yellow cup. Not even the sight of her licking the creamy cappuccino froth from her upper lip with a lazy swipe of her dusky pink tongue could distract him from his purpose.

Tossing what was left of the card into her lap, he demanded, "Who the hell is Joel?"

Lifting the wadded mess of primary colors with thumb and forefinger, she removed it from where it had perched itself between her thighs as she explained, "Joel is the principal at the junior high where Danny and Davey are going this fall."

"Why is he sending *fond* birthday greetings to my sons?" Nick crooked two fingers on each hand, doing the quotes gesture to emphasize the word.

She gestured right back in similar fashion. "Because he's a *thoughtful* man."

"Does he send birthday cards to all the children who are going to his school?"

"I haven't the faintest idea. Frankly, the topic has never come up. But if you're really all that interested I'll be happy to ask him for you the next time I see him."

"Anything else come up between the two of you?" He never meant to ask that, not in that suggestive tone anyway, because he really didn't want to know the answer, but the beast at his back was making him do things he wouldn't ordinarily do. At least that was what he tried to tell himself.

Nick recognized the annoyed sigh she expelled, telling him she was starting to lose her patience. Not that she had much to start with when it came to him.

"Joel is a friend," Maggie explained. "I've known him for years."

"Years? Just how long has this been going on?"

"There's nothing *going on*," she insisted.

"Than how come this is the first I'm hearing about it?"

"Maybe because none of us thought it was worth mentioning. It's just that Joel doesn't have any family in the area. I've had him over for dinner a few times. Taking the boys and me to a couple of movies and a Cubs game this summer has been his way of repaying us for our hospitality." She omitted the part about Joel being a recent widower. She wasn't ready to explain the extent of her relationship with Joel, not yet anyway. She hadn't even told the boys yet. They would all find out soon enough.

"What a cozy family picture that must have made," he bit out.

"They don't call Wrigley Field the *Friendly Confines* for nothing." She struggled against the maddening impulse to scream.

Nick crammed his hands into his pockets and grumbled, "Just because he doesn't have a family of his own doesn't give him the right to horn in on my wife and kids."

"Ex-wife," she corrected.

"Not by choice," he countered. "I'm not the one who wanted the damn divorce."

"Now I see where you're going with this. Since you didn't initiate the divorce, you don't think you have to play by its rules, is that it?" Maggie questioned, all the while asking herself why she wasted her breath. There was no reasoning with Nick when he got like this and her patience with the man was stretched to its limit. But, she insisted, since he'd tossed down the gauntlet she was honor bound to pick it up and slap some sense into him with it.

Exhibiting an outward calm she was far from feeling, she set her cup on the coffee table as she collected her final thoughts on the subject and stood. "Okay, Nick, if that's how you want it, fine. I'll be happy to answer any questions you have about my relationship with Joel as long as you extend me the same courtesy."

"I don't understand," he said, not only sounding confused but looking the part too. "What do you mean?"

"It's very simple, really. Tit for tat, quid pro quo, I'll show you mine if you show me yours... You know what I'm talking about, Nicky. You first."

"You want names or just a grand total?"

"Grand total?" she gulped, stricken by the image of Nick surrounded by a bevy of bodacious lovelies. "How many have there been?" She'd swung the gauntlet at him so hard she got caught in the backlash and she flinched from the sting.

"None. There haven't been any, Maggie."

"I beg your pardon?" Maggie was certain she hadn't heard him right. If she thought he looked confused a moment ago, then she must look downright dumbfounded. "Would you mind clarifying that?"

"There haven't been any other women since we split up. Is that clear enough for you?"

"I don't believe it," she breathed, more to herself than for his benefit. "I've seen for years the way women look at you. You've never been propositioned by any of them?"

"Propositioned? Yeah, sure," Nick admitted with a shrug of indifference.

"But you've never been tempted?"

"Tempted? Of course, lots of times."

"Yet you can stand there and tell me you've never taken any of them up, most recently with that Pamela Anderson knock-off, Mandy Morgan?"

His posture stiffened at the mention of his sponsor's daughter and business manager. "My relationship with Mandy is strictly business."

"Business??" Maggie choked on the word. "I can't stand in a grocery check-out any more without seeing the four of you staring back at me from the pages of one tabloid or another."

Her implication dawned on him and he chuckled. "Oh, you mean me, Mandy and *the girls*?"

"Yes, Nick. Any pair that big deserves to be

recognized as separate entities—maybe even separate zip codes."

Nick smiled when realizing his green-eyed buddy was nipping at Maggie's ass for a change, and he loved every second of it. "I've got to admit. There are certain advantages to doing business with Mandy."

"I'd sure like to know what kind of business requires her hanging all over you in a Houston nightclub till four in the morning." Oops. Maggie stopped, clamping her mouth shut. She had the right not to incriminate herself. She'd already said more than she ever intended. That she followed Nick's escapades through the tabloids was nobody's business but her own.

"No matter how it looks, it's still just business, Boomer." He placed a hand over his heart and raised choirboy blue eyes heavenward. "I swear."

Leveling a narrow gaze on his pious performance, she collapsed into the supple leather cushions of the sofa. "Come on, Nick. This is me you're talking to. Abstinence was never one of your strong suits, which kind of makes me doubt that you've lived celibate these last four years." She couldn't make herself believe it. To do otherwise would nullify the years they'd been apart. The divorce had been his ticket to freedom. What did he hope to achieve by lying to her about it now?

Unsure how to respond, Nick was subdued, stunned in fact. Somewhere along the line this had stopped being funny. The very thought of Maggie in the arms of another man left him reeling, as if he'd been physically assaulted, and he found himself wondering why her reaction to the idea of him with another woman wasn't similar to that of his own. The emerald-eyed monster was back in his corner with a vengeance.

He pulled her to her feet. "Why is my fidelity so difficult for you to believe? Is it because you'd rather think the worst about me than give me the benefit of the doubt?

"Just because I could never keep my hands off of you doesn't mean I can't practice restraint with anyone else. Yes, Maggie, I've had offers—lots of them. But I need more than just a hard dick and a willing place to put it.

"All I've ever wanted was you," he confessed, his breath a gentle wind across her skin as he sealed his

26

words with a possessive kiss. His lips softened, opening to release a tongue searching for its mate. A trilling, desolate moan escaped from her when he broke the intimate contact.

"Do you really want me doing that to another woman?" he taunted. "Or this?" His hands were like a master sculptor's, molding and pressing her body to conform to the peaks and valleys of his own. "Or this?" His hands slipped beneath the hem of her shorts and cupped her bottom, pressing her into his hardening arousal.

Maggie was helpless to do anything but cling to him as if her very existence depended upon it. Maybe it did, and the thought terrified her. She returned his kisses with an unfurling passion only he could set free. The thin fabric of her shirt did nothing to protect her from the searing heat of his hot flesh or stifle the beat of his pounding heart.

Breaking the kiss with a gasping moan, Nick continued to hold her tightly against him, dragging his lips to her ear. "Feel how perfectly we still fit together?" His voice was ragged, a grating whisper that rumbled down her spine.

Unable to catch her breath, Maggie struggled against the painful longing and heart-stopping memories he stirred. Tears pooled and distorted his features into a blurred swirl of hazy warm colors. He couldn't possibly want her any more than she wanted him.

"I know every inch of your body. I know every mole, every freckle, every crease, every curve. I know where your buttons are, Maggie, and I know when and where to push them." His gaze softened and turned tender, causing more tears. "No other man will take the time or make the effort to know you the way I do." He kissed her again.

Desire coiled deep inside her. "Nick, please..." She wanted him to stop—she wanted him to never stop. It wasn't supposed to be like this anymore. Why was he doing this to her? She'd given him his freedom. Why didn't he take it and run?

"Please what, Maggie?" His lips left a trail of warm, wet kisses down her neck, sending a flood of hot lava through every nerve. His hands touched her in places that hadn't been touched in a very long time. Secret places, warm places, aching places, places she had forgotten were still a part of her until he awakened them. "Tell me what you want."

He knew what she wanted. He always knew. "Please...please love me...Now," she murmured against his shoulder as she pressed moist, nibbling kisses against the bare flesh. Starved for his touch, craving it more than Nick could ever imagine, every last shred of her defenses crumpled under his familiar embrace.

"Now and forever," he replied, his voice nothing more than a raspy whisper.

Common sense, be damned. The voice of reason, the one Maggie always relied on to keep her out of trouble, couldn't shout loud enough. All the usual warning bells and whistles were muffled and silenced by the frantic beating of her starving heart.

Deft fingers crept slowly under her shirt and found her eager breasts, waiting, wanting, needing only what he could give her. She helped him push the tee up and off, equally frustrated by its constraints. Her bra was disposed of in short order, leaving her standing before him half naked beneath his lazy, wandering gaze. The mere thought of him touching her was enough to cause her nipples to grow taut, aching with expectation.

"They remember me," he said, grinning, revealing dimples that creased his cheeks with adorable deep furrows.

"Oh yeah," Maggie managed to mutter, kissing and tongue tickling the tight flesh of his chest. She trembled against the warm pressure of his hand as he cupped her breast and trapped the tight nipple between his fingers, eliciting from her a gasping moan of pleasure.

Breathing hard and heavy, they stood in the middle of the room and tugged at the remaining fabric separating them, groping each other like eager teenagers.

One last vestige of sanity burst from her lips, "Nick, stop, we can't do this!" She placed restraining palms against his heaving chest.

Crazed and confused, "Huh?" was all the response he could manage.

"We can't do this," she repeated.

"We can't?"

"Not down here. The boys."

Relief washed across his features. "Minor detail," he said. Sweeping her into his arms, he carried her through the foyer and up the stairs. Destination: Bedroom at the end of the hall.

Lifting her hips, Nick stripped her of her shorts and panties with expedience. His too tight jeans were another experience altogether. They bunched around his calves and ankles and he found himself doing a frantic jig of pulling and stepping, pulling and stepping, until he freed himself of the clinging denim. With a husky laugh, he fell onto the bed beside her.

As he ran his hand down her body, she arched into his caress, asking, "When did you stop wearing underwear?"

His mouth followed the path of his hands and he murmured against her belly, "Four years ago." His words vibrated her flesh as his breath washed across her. "It was either go commando or go broke buying new underwear all the time." He cuddled close, intertwining his limbs with hers, and cupped the swell of her breast. Even after all this time the perfection of the fit never ceased to amaze him.

"Why would you need to buy it all the time?" she pursued. "You know how to use a washer."

"Maggie, honey," he growled. "Now is not the time to discuss my underwear. So drop it, huh?" he added, lowering his head to return to what he was doing.

"Looks to me like you already did," she giggled, squirming against him.

He drew lazy moist circles around the nipple with his tongue, causing her to arch against his mouth, seeking more. His lips curled into a smile as she responded to his suckling the dusky bud between his lips.

The familiarity of the moment filled Maggie's heart. The days, the months, the years slipped away, leaving only the two of them suspended in cherished time and space. If only for one brief, shining moment, they shared a place where only love dwelled and the past slipped into non-existence.

His scent, his touch, his knowing lips triggered

responses locked away and long forgotten. Every nerve ending sparked and tingled with aroused anticipation. It was true. He did know where all her buttons were, and he found each and every one of them in turn.

Nick paused, his breaths coming in quick, shallow pants, and rolled away. Lying against the pillows, he covered his eyes with his forearm and began a series of slow, controlled breaths.

"We gotta slow down, honey," he said on a ragged note as he raised himself up on one elbow and gazed at her with undisguised heat and desire. "Or this is gonna be over before it gets started."

She caressed his face and scooted nearer, planting slow, lingering kisses on each inch of flesh she encountered on the way. She knew where his buttons were too.

"You know," she said between kisses. "I can think of a couple of ways to take care of that."

"And they are?"

She whispered the first solution in his ear.

"Not funny, Mags," he growled. "My days of flying solo end here and now."

"Then let's get this over and done with so we can better concentrate on coming attractions." She pushed him onto his back and straddled him.

"Now you're talking!" He lounged against the pillows, resting his hands on her hips, and let her have her way with him.

Bracing her hands against his chest, she lowered her hips, impaling herself on his erection, and moved with slow, controlled lifts and thrusts. Rocking her hips against him, her full pale breasts swaying with each deliberate move, she tightened around him and felt herself flying into the storm of her climax only moments before he cried out in sweet release as his body tensed and trembled beneath her. Embracing him with every muscle she possessed, she drew him tightly against her body with a fierce possessiveness she found alarming in its dependency.

Loving Nick had never been the problem.

Chapter Four

No. No. No. He wasn't going to do it. Nick refused to take the chance by opening his eyes. He wasn't ready to let go of what might be nothing more than a vivid dream. His dreams were all he had left.

Every nerve running the length of his body could still feel her—the weight of her arm lying across his chest, the wispy tendrils of her hair tickling his neck, the steady rhythm of her breathing washing over his skin—it all felt so unbelievably real. There had been so many nights like this, where he'd felt Maggie asleep in his arms only to have her vanish come morning, leaving him empty and heartsick over and over again. He surrendered to the fantasy and drifted back to sleep, back to the time and place before she stopped loving him.

Awareness crept into the pleasant state of Maggie's unconsciousness like a toothache, nagging and nudging her awake against every single-minded attempt on her part to ignore it. She really hated when reality intruded like this, disturbing her sleep and peace of mind. Not anywhere near ready to face what the morning had in store for her, Maggie settled deeper into the mattress.

Having never grown accustomed to sleeping alone, she frequently woke up on the wrong side of the bed hugging a pillow so it didn't come as any real surprise to find herself there now. What came as a bit of a shock and caused her eyes to fly open was discovering the usual cool cotton and feathers she snuggled with had turned into warm flesh and blood.

Lifting her head from the cradle of his shoulder, she peered at the man sleeping so peacefully beside her. Their night together had been a passionate one. He was more than likely exhausted to the point of unconsciousness than just sleeping. Whichever the case, he was incapacitated, giving her a much better chance of slipping out of bed without waking him.

How many times had they lost themselves in each other's arms—each encounter more passionate and poignant than the last? However many times it was, judging from the soreness between her legs, it was a new personal best for her and the man who kept mumbling something about making up for lost time.

Tossing back her side of the quilt that had somehow managed to find its way from the closet shelf to cover them, she scooted to the edge of the bed and hesitated, casting a lingering glance over her shoulder before pushing herself off the mattress and scurrying to the bathroom.

Hoping it would pummel the courage she needed to get through this business with Nick again, she cranked the showerhead to hard pulse and stepped under the pelting spray. It was not the wisest decision to make under the circumstances. All the pounding jets did was heighten the sensitivity of her already tender, manhandled flesh and urge her to hasten through the rest of the shower with a quick head to toe lather and rinse.

After brushing her teeth, she scrunched a palm full of mousse through her shoulder-length curls, coaxing the strawberry blonde waves to behave without the added taming aids of a brush and dryer, which she didn't dare start up since the aging appliance sounded like the neighbor's leaf blower. Taking a shower had already risked waking him.

Simple white cotton underwear and her old terry bathrobe was all she put on before leaving. She cast a passing glance at her reflection in the vanity mirror. Well, the look wasn't as frumpy as she might have liked but it was close. Better still it wasn't sexy or the least bit alluring, the very last things she wanted to be the next time she faced Nick.

Averting her gaze from the bed and more important the man in it, she focused instead on the door and making a clean getaway. She held her breath as she placed one foot and then the other into the hallway, not allowing herself to breathe until she closed the bedroom door behind her. So far, so good, she thought, as she padded barefooted past the boys' room and down the carpeted stairs, finally slipping into her workroom when reaching the dark foyer.

She stood there, motionless, deciding what to do next. She reached for the desk lamp. The sudden brightness blinded her until her pupils adjusted. It was then she noticed the scattered cards and envelopes lying on the floor, the abandoned manila envelope that held Nick's misdirected mail, and it all came crashing down around her. She collapsed into the nearest chair, an aged oak rocker that had belonged to her beloved grandmother. For four long years she'd managed to keep Nick at a safe, untouchable distance. How did she let this happen?

She'd just destroyed everything with just one night of...Maggie hesitated, unable to finish the thought, and wondered, *of what*? What did she call what happened between her and Nick? Lust? Desire? Desperation? Jealously? Passion? Love? Was it all or none of the above? She honestly didn't know.

The room wasn't cold but she shivered nevertheless. Tugging at the antique quilt draped over the back of the rocker, Maggie drew up her knees and sought solace in the soft, faded folds of lovingly sewn pieces of calico, batting, and cotton. Minutes passed as she let her mind wander like a tortured soul searching for a final resting place. She rubbed the quilt in lazy, aimless circles, feeling Nell Thornton's delicate stitches beneath her own skilled fingertips, the whole time reminding herself of all the reasons why she ended her marriage in the first place.

Tossing grandma's quilt aside with a soul-weary sigh, she left the room, restless and confused, and no closer to knowing what to do than when she had entered.

Like an aimless sleepwalker, Maggie felt herself moving toward the back of the house, out the sliding glass door, down the deck steps, and across the lawn toward the garage. There was just a hint of dawn creeping around the edges of the still dark early morning sky and the summer-dry grass crunched beneath her bare feet, a harsh reminder of how desperately the drought stricken region needed rain.

She opened the service door, perturbed that the boys hadn't locked it as she reached around the doorframe for the light switch. A flicker of hope momentarily lightened her mood. What were the chances of someone stealing both the go-karts?

Not very good, she realized, squinting against the harsh brightness of the bare bulb hanging from the center of the ceiling, throwing deep shadows into every corner. Half hidden behind her Jeep, Maggie's green eyes riveted on the miniature replicas of Nick's racecar.

She stepped around the hood of the blue Cherokee and walked to where the twin racing go-karts sat side-by-side gleaming red and new, taunting her. Why was every generation of men in her life so hell-bent with the need for speed and making her life miserable in the process?

"Damn you Nick and damn those cars!" she said aloud, swinging a bare foot at one of the tires. When she made contact she cried out at the stabbing pain and hobbled around on the injured foot's heel until the throbbing ache in her big toe subsided. She stared long and hard at the source of her self-inflicted pain, and her heart gave a sudden lurch.

The smells of gas, and oil, and grease grew more pungent, filling her nostrils with the repulsive stench. A wave of nausea churned her stomach and she clamped a hand over her mouth as a spasm of dry heaves convulsed her body. Cold beads of sweat dampened her hair and body and caused her to shiver in spite of the balmy August night.

All the same old uncertainties rushed up and swirled around her, dragging her into an eddy of renewed memories and fresh heartache. "I can't go through this again," she whispered. Letting him go the first time had been hard enough.

Her heart was breaking all over again. Hot tears spilled down her cheeks as her legs gave out from under her. She fell to her knees, and clutched her arms around her middle as she rocked back and forth on the gritty concrete floor.

Maggie used the sleeve of her robe to blot her eyes and wipe her runny nose. She sniffled, each breath shuddering deep in her chest as she struggled to get a grip on emotions still too raw and fragile to be faced. She'd pull them out and examine them when she was better able to cope, she told herself, wondering when exactly that might be. Four years hadn't been long enough.

"Maggie honey, are you out here?" Nick questioned, pushing open the garage door. Showered and dressed, he stood in the doorway to give his eyes a chance to focus. "I saw the light on and—" When he found her on the floor beside the go-karts he rushed to her side.

"Maggie!" He dropped to his knees, sat back on his booted heels and gathered her into his arms, nestling her into the cradle of his thighs. With a touch so tender it caught her by surprise, he pushed the mousse-stiffened tendrils from her flushed face. "What happened? Your knees are bleeding."

"I tripped," she lied, glancing at her wounds for the first time. A trickle of blood oozed through the bits of dirt and gravel clinging to the abrasions. She shrugged the scrapes off as nothing and tried to stand.

He held her firm as he determined the extent of her injuries. Once satisfied that she appeared otherwise unharmed, he inquired, "What were you doing out here?"

She had hoped her bloody knees would have been enough of a distraction to keep him from asking that. Her reasons for being there could not be easily explained. "I heard a noise," she blurted. Not a great excuse, but adequate on such short notice, and hopefully enough to satisfy his curiosity.

"And you thought you could battle burglars in your bathrobe?" Although she detected a hint of amusement in his tone, nothing close to humor carried over to his features. Deep furrows erupted between his eyes and the corners of his mouth turned down in a ponderous frown.

She just shrugged in response.

For lack of anything better, Nick wrapped a portion of her robe hem around his fingertips and blotted the bloody scrapes. His gentleness and caring overwhelmed her. Fresh tears welled up and blurred her vision when her gaze fell upon the hand tending to her wounds. How had she missed it? He may not be wearing it on his left hand, but it was the same chunky gold band she had scrimped and saved for months to buy for their second anniversary.

Guilty with the knowledge her own wedding band was tucked away in her jewelry chest, she took his hand in hers and fingered the ring. "Why do you still wear it?"

He seemed embarrassed to answer. "Superstitious, I guess. The only time I crashed was when I didn't have it on."

Maggie remembered. It was shortly after the divorce was finalized. "Talledega," she whispered. Why would a man wear a symbol of a failed marriage as a good luck charm? She couldn't begin to answer that question.

In an abrupt effort to change the subject, he said, "Come on, Mags. Let's get you inside and get those knees cleaned out before they get infected." Nick's demeanor brooked no arguments. He took control of the situation and had her on her feet before she could utter a solitary objection to his suggestion. Placing a guiding hand on the small of her back, he prompted her to start moving. She walked in silence toward the house with Nick following close behind.

"Sit," he said, pointing to the nearest kitchen chair. "You still keep the first aid stuff in the cabinet by the sink?" Swinging open the cabinet door, he answered his own question and gathered the necessary medical supplies.

"Nick, this really isn't necessary," she insisted. "I'll take a hot bath and soak for a while. That should take care of the knees. And a few other tender areas," she added under her breath, wincing as she adjusted herself in the hard wooden chair.

He studied her pained expression. "Did I hurt you last night?"

"Nothing that a few days of abstinence and a good night's sleep won't cure," she said as she gave his arm a reassuring pat. "One thing for certain, Nicky, the makers of Viagra won't be asking you for your endorsement anytime soon." Maggie was determined to keep her tone light.

His expression of concern evolved into one of sheepish contrition. "Yeah, well, about last night…"

"No need to say another word," she interjected. She shoved out of the chair with a great deal more force than necessary and walked away, hoping Nick would take the hint and not pursue the subject. She didn't want him pressing her for a commitment she wasn't able to give.

What she needed to do was find a way to discourage Nick, to keep him from thinking their night of reckless passion was anything more than just that. How convincing could she be?

Maggie proceeded to attempt to separate a coffee filter from a stack she pulled from a canister. Her fingers didn't seem to work any better than the rest of her that morning. "Screw it," she muttered near tears, tossing the filters onto the counter. "I'll have tea."

In spite of her obvious attempt to distance herself from him, Nick wasn't about to let her shut him out. Not this time. He made that mistake once.

He got to his feet and came up behind her, resting his hands on her shoulders. The tension he felt beneath his fingers emanated with a force he found alarming. He kneaded the tight flesh, working at the knots, as if doing so would exorcise whatever it was that caused them.

"Shouldn't you be leaving for Indy," she said.

"I'd rather go back to bed instead," he stated, nuzzling and kissing her neck. "I feel a fever coming on." His hands crept around her waist and worked their way up her ribcage to her breasts. Delighted to find nothing but the robe covering them, he gave a deep-throated growl and cupped them in his palms. Not even the weight of the terrycloth could disguise the way her nipples responded to his diligent thumbs.

"What are you talking about? There's nothing wrong with you."

"I was thinking that maybe I'd skip Brickyard and hang around with you and the boys for the rest of the week." He felt her go rigid in his arms.

"You can't do that," she sputtered, pushing out of his grasp. "This is an important race for you."

"Not as important to me as last night," he countered.

He watched her curls bounce around her cheeks as she shook her head. "Let's not talk about last night."

"I think we need to talk about last night, Mags."

"Why?" she challenged. "It happened. What more needs to be said?"

"I'd say a lot, judging from your behavior. Talk to me, Maggie," he urged. His fears and frustrations were mounting.

"Why is this so important to you?" she returned with a sharp rise in the pitch of her voice. "What is it you want from me? Do you really need to hear me say how great the sex was?"

His hands dropped to his sides and he took a startled step back. "My god, Maggie, is that all last night was to you?"

"Isn't that all it was to you?"

"I don't give a damn about the sex!"

"Oh, really?" she challenged.

"Okay, sure, it's important," he conceded. "But that's *not* what this is about, Maggie. Can't you see that?" Frustrated beyond words, he rubbed his palms against his freshly shaven cheeks and expelled an exasperating breath. "Why do you keep looking for reasons to push me away?"

"Don't you see what's happening, Nick? If I don't push you away now, it's going to start all over again. Do you really want to go back to that? I know I don't." Her words tumbled out like marbles from a broken bag. "How can we even consider putting ourselves through that again?"

"I don't remember it being as bad as you make it sound."

She looked incredulous. "You really don't, do you?"

"Last night was as real as anything you'll ever find in this lifetime, Maggie."

She nodded. "Yes, it was," she agreed. "When it's just the two of us behind closed doors everything is perfect and wonderful. It's out here—" She gestured to their immediate surroundings. "—where it all falls apart."

"We'll work on that."

"Why, Nick? Nothing has changed. My life is here and yours is wherever you park your truck. Last night you just happen to park it in my driveway."

He stared at her for a time, searching for the right words. When he realized there were no right words, he said whatever came to mind just to shatter the silence. "Okay, Maggie. You win. I'm leaving." He scooped his keys from the counter and headed for the front door. As he crossed the threshold, he hesitated, resting his hand on the doorframe, and looked at her over his shoulder with a piercing sadness. "Tell me something, Maggie…When did you know?"

"Know what?" she choked.

"When did you first know you didn't love me anymore?"

Maggie flinched and closed her eyes against his candor. She couldn't give him an answer—at least not a truthful one. She lowered her head instead, staring at the floor as if the mysteries of the universe were written in the black rubber scuffmark etched on the tile beneath her toes.

"I'd really like to know," he prodded. "Was it a gradual thing or did it happen suddenly, like one minute you loved me and the next you didn't?"

Maggie shook her head, her voice barely above a whisper. "It's not that simple."

"You got that right. This thing between us is anything but simple." He drew a long, tortured breath. "Hating you for ripping my heart out would be simple. Hating you for giving me one night of false hope would be simple. But since that's not going to happen any time soon, I guess I'll have to do the next best thing."

"What?"

"What I should have done four years ago—make a life without you and hope the hate comes later."

"Loving you has nothing to do with this!"

"Yes it does. It has everything to do with it. Two people who love each other are supposed to fight to stay together, no matter what." He drew a ragged sigh. "Somewhere along the way you stopped fighting for me, Maggie, and I'm getting tired of fighting this battle all by myself."

Then he was gone, leaving Maggie to stare at the space he had occupied only moments before through a blur of unshed tears. She heard the truck door slam, the engine turn over and spark to life. Tires squealed and spun as he peeled away from the curb, causing an awful racket in the quiet neighborhood so early in the morning.

She was rooted to the floor. If questioned as to how much time had passed between his departure and her eventual attempt to force her leaden limbs to move, she couldn't have ventured to guess. Seconds, hours, minutes, years? It didn't matter. All it did was define a small piece of the eternity she would live without him.

Some day, she told herself. Maybe some day he'd realize why she did what she did and understand that she never stopped fighting for him. Everything she ever did was for him.

****

Nick drove only as far as the end of the street. He pulled over and pounded the steering wheel with the heels of his hands before gripping it with such force his entire body shook from the rage and frustration coursing through him.

He knew better that to get behind the wheel in this frame of mind. It was as bad as or worse than driving under the influence. He needed to calm down and focus on the three-hour trip to Indianapolis—not an easy task considering what he'd just been put through. But that's what he did for a living—drive.

So drive he did in spite of the hole in his chest where his heart used to be.

Chapter Five

After a resounding rendition of "Happy Birthday" sung by a chorus of changing adolescent voices, Maggie shooed the birthday boys and their guests outside while she sliced the cake, an ability she had never quite successfully mastered. She knew it, what's more, so did her sons.

Danny hustled his guests toward the sliding door like a fireman from a burning building. "We don't want to be anywhere near here when she starts hacking into that thing," he stage whispered.

"Yeah, its not gonna be pretty," Davey interjected, adding a horrified shudder for effect.

Maggie didn't understand where she went wrong. She was a skilled seamstress with nimble fingers. It was beyond her comprehension why every cake she tackled came out looking like she'd used a chainsaw instead of the special knife she ordered whose only function was to "*cut cake like a pro*" according to the ad. But this cake met the same fate as every other cake had over the years. She was 0 for 12. After only a few swipes with the knife, she was up to her wrists in frosting when the phone rang.

Holding up her hands in a helpless gesture, she asked, "Would you get that for me, Joel?"

Two boys could be a handful at times. Adding eleven more to the mix had left her wondering if the house would still be standing by the end of the day. It had taken all of five seconds for her to accept Joel's offer to help with crowd control. As principal of a large junior high, Joel had amassed scads of experience dealing with pre-pubescent boys and the havoc their antics created. His presence alone appeared to keep all the boys within the boundaries of their best behavior.

"Chapparelle residence," he answered, sounding every bit the professional he was as he cradled the cordless phone against his ear. He cast Maggie a warm smile and a quick teasing wink. He listened for a moment then said, "This is Joel Hubbard. Who is this?" His demeanor made a startling transformation from cheery professional to stern authoritarian.

Puzzled by his sudden switch in tone and attitude, Maggie motioned in a questioning manner as she licked gooey butter cream from her fingers before passing her hands under a running faucet of warm water.

Joel punched the bridge of his steel-rimmed glasses with his index finger as he handed her the phone. "Nick," was all he said.

She took the phone with an eagerness that caught her by surprise. "Thanks, Joel," she said, perhaps a bit too engaging but nonetheless sincere. However much she tried to deny the simple fact, she had been looking forward to hearing from Nick again. There, she'd admitted it, if only to herself.

Her smile faltered then slipped away altogether as she watched Joel retreat to the family room. He gave every effort to appear interested in the pre-race hoopla already blaring from the TV. She felt awful putting her dear friend in a situation where he felt uncomfortable, and she resented Nick for being the cause of it.

Her eagerness to talk to him abruptly turned to annoyance, pure and simple.

"What did you say to Joel?" she demanded in an angry whisper.

"I just offered some friendly advice."

"What kind of advice?" she inquired.

"Important stuff every man needs to know," he said.

"Tell me!" she demanded.

"I just told him how risky it was to tighten his lug nuts with someone else's wrench and for his own safety he'd best keep his tire iron in his trunk where it belonged."

"You didn't!" she sputtered. Suddenly unable to deal with Nick another second, she walked with the portable phone toward the sliding glass door. "The boys are in the garage showing the go-karts to their guests. I'll get them." She motioned to Danny and Davey and held the phone up as a signal that there was a call for them.

"Maggie, wait!" she heard Nick shout.

"What?" she said, terse and impatient.

"Are you watching the race?" Nick asked, changing the subject quicker than his pit crew could change four tires.

"The boys will be watching," was all she said.

"I didn't ask that. I asked if *you* were going to watch."

"You already know my answer, Nick."

"I'm asking you to make an exception, Mags."

"I stopped watching you race a long time ago, why would I start again now?"

"Just this once, please." He sounded inordinately subdued.

Maggie frowned. Nick was usually upbeat before a race. The volatile mix of testosterone and adrenaline started pumping through his veins long before the green flag dropped. This request sounded more like a child's desperate plea for attention. She couldn't help but acquiesce. "Okay sure," she conceded. "I'll try to catch part of it."

"Thanks, Boomer." Inasmuch as he sounded much more like the confident Nick she knew, she felt no less puzzled by Nick's odd behavior as she handed the phone to Davey.

Maggie busied herself with finishing the job of butchering the cake and scooping ice cream onto NASCAR embellished paper plates. She knew they were a little too childish for a twelve-year-old's party, but she though they were so cute and apropos she couldn't help but toss them into her shopping cart. The boys didn't seem to mind. She figured as long as she filled the plates with enough cake and ice cream they could be Barbie or My Pretty Pony. They crowded around the counter waiting for the guests of honor to finish their phone call, each and every one of them eyeing the plates of dessert to see which one held the largest portion.

Knowing full well that she had just fed them massive quantities of pizza, hot dogs, chips and soda less that an hour earlier, Maggie wondered where they were putting it all as she handed out the generously portioned chunks of frosted cake, heaping scoops of ice cream and additional cups of root beer and orange soda.

Lingering longer than necessary in the kitchen after

the boys had settled in front of the TV to watch the race, Maggie busied herself with wiping already clean counters. She really wasn't looking forward to watching even one moment of the race. Her body vibrated with tension and anxiety. Why did she agree to something she had promised herself she would never do again? Watching him race was just a painful reminder of what she had given up, and why. What good was there in putting herself through that?

"Is there anything else I can help you with before I go?" So immersed in her thoughts she hadn't even heard Joel approach.

She looked at him for a brief second before his words registered. "You're not leaving already?"

"You seem to have everything under control now. I really should go."

"Joel, please don't leave on account of Nick and his adolescent threats." She saw the look of surprise on Joel's face.

"He told me what he said," she explained.

"It's not that big of a deal, Maggie, really. I must say, though, no one has attempted intimidation quite that creatively since last fall when I disqualified the captain of our football team from playing for failing grades."

Maggie was appalled. "You were threatened by a student?"

"Oh no," Joel assured. "I was threatened by his mother!"

In spite of the moment, Maggie couldn't help but laugh.

"What I don't understand is why my family jewels are always the point of reference," he added with a deadpan she found impossible to take seriously.

Laughing, she said, "I'm really sorry about Nick, Joel. I should have warned you about him. He's still kind of overprotective."

"Oh, do you think?" Joel inquired, raising a cynical brow.

She laughed again. "I can assure you, he's really quite harmless. Most of his aggressions will be taken out on the track today." She smiled and gave his arm a reassuring pat. "Now, I don't want to hear anymore talk about leaving. I'll fix us a couple of iced cappuccinos and we'll watch Nick and his cohorts chase each other around the track for a couple of hours."

Tall, frosty glasses in hand, Maggie and Joel sat down just in time to see Nick's tanned, handsome face fill the big screen, larger than life. Davey snatched the remote from Danny and adjusted the volume. A voice-over informed them that the following interview had been previously recorded.

Maggie glanced at the DVR to make sure it was running. The boys always recorded Nick's races, but sure as there was mud on the bottom of their sneakers, this would be the one time they'd forget to set it. She relaxed and sat back when seeing the green recording light.

The sportscaster stood smiling beside Nick and announced, "I'm standing on the famous *Yard of Bricks* located at the start/finish line at Indianapolis Motor Speedway. I managed to catch Nick Chapparelle as he was entering the park this morning."

Maggie watched Nick's heirs apparent beam with pride at seeing their father as the featured pre-race interview. Their guests appeared suitably impressed as well. At least they had all stopped eating long enough to watch, which in itself said a lot.

"Hello, Nick. Thanks for giving me and the fans a few minutes of your time."

"My pleasure, Bob." Nick smiled congenially and pushed back the brim of the black NASCAR baseball hat with a bent knuckle, causing a shock of sun-streaked hair to fall across his forehead. Fans of all ages, most of them female, jockeyed for position around Nick and the sportscaster. As the announcer spoke about the race and its history, Nick glanced away, his easy dimpled smile and teasing wink obviously meant for one or more fans off camera. The crystal timbre of feminine giggles and sighs tripped lightly through the announcer's microphone.

Joel leaned close to Maggie and whispered, "Your Nick is quite a charmer."

Staring at the man who had charmed his way into her heart so many years before, Maggie couldn't agree with Joel more. "He does have his moments," she murmured.

A brief flash of their last intimate moments caused a warm rush to spread through her body. It started at her toes and traveled upward, settling somewhere and everywhere between her breasts and thighs. A long sip of her chilled cappuccino did nothing to douse the throbbing heat. She squirmed against the leather upholstery, uncrossing and crossing her legs in an ineffective effort to find a more comfortable position. Damn Nick for doing this to her.

"You okay?" Joel asked, glancing in her direction.

"Fine, just fine," she answered, forcing herself to concentrate on the interview.

"Your time yesterday was the fastest you've ever qualified, Nick. How do you feel about it?"

"I couldn't be more pleased. All the hard work my team has done on this car is finally paying off, Bob. It felt incredibly solid in the turns."

"How comfortable do you feel with a pole position of ninth in a field of forty-three?"

"I'm thrilled. I told my sons a few days ago, I would have been happy to start somewhere in the middle of the pack."

"They called Earnhardt Sr. the Intimidator. What do you think they're calling you these days?"

"Lucky, I think," Nick laughed.

"Your last win a few weeks ago was pretty spectacular."

"It was an exciting finish," Nick agreed.

"How about telling us about it."

"Well, I was running third for 30 laps and couldn't find an opening. Coming into the last turn second place attempted to pass the leader on the inside. They rubbed a little too hard and spun each other out. One went into the wall and the other into the infield, parting like the Red Sea. I shot between them and waltzed across the finish line."

"Before you go Nick, there's been a rumor about you flying around the track this weekend even faster than your car. Care to comment on it?"

Nick laughed easily. "Which rumor is that, Bob?"

"There's talk that you might be retiring."

"There's nothing etched in stone."

"Could this be your last race?"

Nick shrugged and answered with an enigmatic, tight-lipped smile. "Can't say for sure."

"I got to tell you, Nick," the sportscaster chuckled good-naturedly. "You're not giving me much to work with here. You've already racked up four big wins this season and have consistently placed in the top ten. Your points put you into serious contention for national champion. What's prompted this retirement talk at a time when you're beginning to find real success in the sport?"

In order to concentrate on his answer, Maggie scooted to the edge of her seat and leaned forward, resting her elbows on her knees. Placing her palms flat together, Maggie pressed the steeple of her fingers against her lips. Nick looked straight into the camera. She felt as if he was looking directly at her.

"There is no simple answer to that question, Bob."

Nick continued. "Inasmuch as I love this sport and everything connected with it, I've always said I'd know when it was time to quit and walk away, you know, before that luck I was talking about earlier runs out."

"Would this decision also mean an end to Chapparelle Racing?"

"On the contrary, Bob. It will be business as usual for teammates Jess McIntyre and Skip Fowler, as well as the rest of the crew."

"Then there's some truth to the rumor of a merger between Morgan Enterprises and Chapparelle Racing?"

"It's a little premature to comment on anything regarding Morgan Enterprises."

"Is it also too premature to comment on anything regarding you and the CEO's daughter, Mandy Morgan?"

"That, too," was Nick's only response. In spite of his unwavering smile, Nick's frosty tone conveyed no further discussion on the subject of Mandy Morgan would be tolerated. "Now if you'll excuse me, I see my crew chief trying to get my attention."

The announcer turned into the camera with a cheesy grin. "This is Bob Miller for Sports Entertainment News. We'll be right back with more behind-the-scenes racing excitement after these important messages."

Chapter Six

Few viewers, if any, would have paid the slightest bit of attention to the dispersing crowds mingling behind the announcer. If the truth were known, most of them weren't even in front of their televisions, having used the commercial break to make a quick potty run or stockpile food and beverages to sustain them thorough the forthcoming race. Maggie, however, looked past him and watched the brief interaction between Nick and none other than the aforementioned Mandy Morgan.

It couldn't have taken Bob Miller more than ten seconds to wrap up the segment, yet Maggie witnessed what she could only describe as an intimate exchange between two people well known to one another. Mandy may have initiated the embrace, but Nick appeared to be fully cooperative, draping his arm across her shoulders as they walked away looking very much like they were joined at the hip. If what Nick told her a couple days ago was true and there hadn't been anything going on between him and Mandy before, it appeared there was now. He apparently meant what he said about getting on with his life, and wasn't wasting any time in doing just that. What better way to start than with a very rich, very beautiful, very influential young woman?

Maggie never expected it would hurt this much. She gripped the sofa arm to steady herself as the colors around her swirled into nauseating pools of muddy rainbows. The boys' behavior during the commercial break convinced Maggie that they hadn't been paying as close attention as she had, and for that she was grateful. The last thing she needed was a bunch of questions about the woman with their dad.

"You all right, Maggie?" Joel asked, a concerned frown punctuating his question. He gripped her arm and ushered her from the room before any of the boys noticed the greenish tinge to her skin.

Maggie lowered herself into the nearest kitchen chair and leaned back, closing her eyes against the glaring afternoon sunlight streaming through the window. She took a deep breath, feeling somewhat foolish, and accepted the proffered glass of water. She sipped slowly, collecting her scattered thoughts.

Joel pulled out a second chair and positioned it in front of her, their knees barely touching as he sat to face her. "Can I get you anything else?"

Unable to speak, Maggie shook her head.

"That announcement obviously came as a surprise to you?"

"I just saw Nick a few days ago. He never gave the slightest indication he was thinking about giving up racing. I can't help asking myself the same question the sportscaster posed. Why now? What's changed since I last saw him?" Maggie couldn't help wondering, however, if Ms. Morgan was behind this sudden decision.

"Mom!" Davey called from the family room. "The race is starting!"

Mommmmm! You gonna watch or what?" Danny yelled, obviously annoyed at her leaving at such a critical moment. "You heard the announcer. This could be the last time you ever see dad race." Whoever said girls at this age were overly dramatic never met her son.

"I'll be there in a few, guys," she answered, relieved that the boys were focusing their attention on the race and not the preceding drama.

"Maggie, correct me if I'm wrong, but isn't this announcement of Nick's a good thing?"

She was appalled by his assumption. "Why would you think that?"

"I may be myopic but I'm not blind. I know a woman in love when I see one. Since I know I'm not the object of that affection, I just figured..." He left the rest of his sentence unspoken and cocked his head to one side with a know-it-all raise of his eyebrows. "Although you've never come right out and said so, I've always gotten the impression from off-handed comments you've made that Nick's profession was at least in part why you divorced him."

"Oh, it's true I divorced Nick because of his racing. It

was the only way I knew how to keep him from giving it up."

She recognized the look of bewilderment that settled over Joel's features, prompting her to further her explanation. "I grew up watching my father chase his dreams around that half-mile track at Illiana. He was good, really good, but he never managed to take his talents beyond the local legend status and it turned him into a bitter and resentful man. I never wanted to see that same regret in Nick's eyes.

"I was barely fifteen the first time I saw Nick put rubber to asphalt. He had the most amazing instincts I'd ever seen in a young driver." Like a war veteran suffering from flashbacks, she closed her eyes and envisioned that first night with such clarity she felt as if she could reach out and touch Nick's young, handsome face. Her fingers curled into fists ready to do battle against the teasing hallucination.

"Maggie?" Joel touched her shoulder.

Startled, she blinked once and blinked again, finding Joel staring at her wearing the most curious expression. "Where was I?"

"Illiana," he prompted. "The night you met Nick."

"After that I followed him around like a lost puppy waiting for him to toss me a scrap of attention. All I ever got from him and his buddies was teasing and torment on a weekly basis. That's how I got tagged with the handle Boomer. It's short for boomerang because no matter what they did or said I kept coming back.

"The winter I turned seventeen my body went through some amazing changes. I practically blossomed over night. I filled up and out and I went a little wild when I realized what power these things had." She gestured to her breasts. "Guys are so easy. Flash a little cleavage and they'll do anything for the remote chance of getting another peek."

Joel cleared his throat. "Personally, I'm a leg man."

Maggie chuckled. "Present company excluded, of course."

"I did everything I could think of to get Nick's attention and make him start thinking of me as something more than Ben Thornton's kid. I dyed my hair a scary shade of red, triple pierced my ears and got a tattoo."

"You have a tattoo?" Joel sounded more than a little intrigued.

"I can't believe Beth never mentioned any of this to you. She was with me when I got it."

"She never said a word. Where is it? Can I see it?"

She shook her head. "Absolutely not, only two men have ever had the opportunity—Nick and my OB-GYN. Even the tattoo artist was a woman."

"Davey and Danny must have seen it."

"Not that they would remember."

"Come on, Maggie. You can at least tell me what it's of?"

"No!" she exclaimed. "It's not something I'm proud of, Joel. I'm sorry I ever mentioned it."

"If you don't want to tell me, that's fine. I'll just ask Dr. Jansen the next time I see him."

"That's privileged information!" Maggie sputtered.

"I don't think tattoos fall under doctor/patient privilege, Maggie," Joel pointed out.

"Well they ought to," Maggie grumbled, deciding that changing the subject was her best course of action. "Do you want to hear the rest of this story or not?"

"Please, go on," he smirked.

"Well, I showed up at the track one night looking like a cross between Elvira and Olivia Newton-John in the scene at the end of *Grease*—tight black spandex pants, black leather biker jacket, a skimpy strapless tube top and spike-heeled boots, which I nearly killed myself in trying to walk in the gravel at the track. But I was determined to show Nick that I was all grown up."

"I'll bet that got his attention," Joel remarked.

"In a manner of speaking. I was hanging out in the pits with a pretty rowdy bunch after the races when he came over and joined us. He didn't recognize me. Like I said, I'd changed a lot over the winter. I had a cigarette in one hand and was holding a can of beer somebody had shoved into my other hand. I started flirting and coming on to him and he was giving it right back. Then somebody called me Boomer. This real funny look came over him. He knocked the beer and cigarette out of my hands and dragged me off behind a trailer where he proceeded to lecture me about my unacceptable appearance and shameless behavior. I kissed him to shut him up. The relationship heated up pretty fast after that. In fact it was only a week later that we..."

"I get the picture," Joel interjected.

"To make a long story short, by the time I turned eighteen we were married and I was very pregnant. Nick struggled to finish his degree at night, race the circuit on weekends and work long hours during the week at a job he hated just to make ends meet. I, on the other hand, was a frightened, insecure young wife and mother stuck in a little apartment with not one but two babies, feeling neglected and sorry for myself.

"I began to hate anything and everything that took him away and I started to verbalize my resentment whenever he did happen to be home, which was also the only time he had to finish assignments and spend time with the boys. I wanted him to be successful at everything he did as long as it didn't interfere with the time I expected him to spend with me. When I think back to some of the things I said, I'm constantly amazed that Nick didn't walk out long before I asked for the divorce."

"This all sounds like pretty typical stuff for a young couple to go through when they're first starting out," Joel pointed out. "It's not easy for any two people, practically strangers in a lot of ways, to start living together. Throw in children early in the game and there's no telling what can happen. Beth and I had some pretty rough moments in the beginning too. Didn't you have anyone to talk to? A friend? A family member?"

Maggie shook her head. "My mother was drowning in her own self pity and all but disowned me when Nick and I eloped. My Dad? Well, he would have sided with Nick and blamed me the same way he did my mother. I lost my best friend when she went away to college and fell in love with a handsome grad student." She glanced at Joel with a loving yet reproachful smile. "The only person I had left was my Dad's mother, Grandma Nell, but she died when the twins were still babies. I was isolated and very much alone after that."

"Beth always regretted the two of you losing touch

when she went away to school. You were the first thing on her to-do list when we moved back to this area."

"And she came back into my life when I needed a friend the most." Maggie's eyes welled up and she wiped her fingers under them just as the tears started to fall. "She got me laughing again when all I wanted to do was cry." An uneasy stillness settled between them. "I'm sorry, Joel. I know it's still difficult for you to talk about her."

"On the contrary," he assured her. "You're the only person who talks about Beth the way she would have wanted to be remembered—fun-loving and laughing. I'm still having trouble getting past the tubes and needles of her final days." Joel sighed and stood, stretching his legs. "Would you mind if we moved this outside? I could really use a smoke."

"Sure," she said, sounding a little surprised. "I could use some fresh air myself. Let's go out front." She glanced at the boys, who were totally engrossed in the race. They'd never miss her, she reasoned.

If anyone had bothered to ask, Maggie would have admitted that she preferred the front porch to the much larger back deck. The front porch was simply friendlier in her opinion. The back deck always seemed so isolated from the rest of the neighborhood. Although the porch wasn't much more than an expanded covered stoop, Maggie managed to fit a two-seater glider and a small square wicker table to one side of the front door.

She watched Joel retrieve a pack of cigarettes and a lighter from his car and return. "In all the time I've known you, I never suspected you smoked, "she said, pushing off with her foot to set the glider in motion.

"On and off since college," he admitted, adding, "But never at school or around the kids." He leaned against the porch's support column and took a drag. "I started up again when Beth got sick, but I promise to quit for good when the time comes." It was only after he exhaled did he add, "You now have my undivided attention again."

"Well, "she said, starting out slowly. "After Gran died, Nick came up with the brilliant idea that maybe if we bought a house I'd settle into married life. He'd inherited some money when his own grandmother died a couple months before mine and we used it for the down payment.

"I admit it worked for a few years until I discovered I was pregnant again. While Nick seemed happy enough about another baby, I was miserable for nine months. I felt like it was just another link in the chain I'd slipped around his neck."

"I knew you'd lost a child but since you never mentioned it I never wanted to pry. Even now I hesitate to ask what happened."

"Megan was almost four months old, healthy one minute and in less than forty-eight hours she was gone. It was so fast—viral cardiomyopathy—according to the autopsy report. She was so little and when the virus settled in her heart she wasn't strong enough to fight it. There was nothing they could do. Nick was out of town. She died before he made it to the hospital.

"A few days after the funeral Nick told me he was going to give up racing, fully believing I would be thrilled by his decision."

"But you asked for a divorce instead," Joel finished for her.

"I couldn't let him throw it all away on some misplaced sense of guilt. We should never have gotten married. He thought he was doing the honorable thing by marrying me because I was pregnant. It took me years to build enough courage to give him back what he shouldn't have had to give up in the first place. You can see for yourself how successful he's become since we split up. That's why I'm having such a hard time understanding any of this now. It makes me feel like I've done it all for nothing!"

"Nick didn't try to fight the divorce?"

Maggie shook her head. "No, not really. Oh, he tried at first but when he realized how determined I was he gave up. Nick thinks I wanted the divorce because I stopped loving him. I convinced myself that I would after the divorce. It didn't take me long to realize the only thing I stopped being was his wife."

"Well, then, isn't this announcement a good thing?"

"I'm not so sure. I need to know what made him come to this decision."

"What difference does it make how he reached it? He

has and now you can put all this nonsense behind you, resolve your differences, and live the fairy tale life you deserve with the man you love." He flicked the cigarette butt into the street and joined her on the glider. Placing his arm casually across the back of the seat, he sighed and said, "I just love happy endings, don't you?"

Maggie grinned in spite of herself at Joel's expansive simplification and resolution of a situation she'd struggled with for years. "It's a little more complicated than that," she argued. "I can't picture my future with Nick in it. I never have. Nick is destined for something much greater than mediocrity with me in the suburbs."

"So you cut him out of your life to fulfill your own prophesy?"

"Don't try to analyze me, Dr. Hubbard. You majored in child psychology, remember?"

"Your behavior is worse than any child's." Joel sounded angry and frustrated. "The choices, the decisions, you made were irresponsible, maybe even a little irrational given the circumstances, and weren't just yours to make, Maggie."

"You just don't understand!" she cried, stinging from his analysis.

"Then help me understand, Maggie," Joel urged. "You're a dear friend who has always been there for me and Beth, and you're hurting. Was I wrong in thinking you still love Nick?"

She shook her head. "No," she said weakly, almost painfully, "I'm still in love with him. And I'd give anything not to be."

"Maggie, what are you saying? I'd give anything to find someone to love like that again."

"No, no, not this way, Joel." Her voice was ragged and raw. "Don't ever love someone like this." She clenched her fist and clutched it between her breasts. "It hurts so much. Here, deep inside."

"Maggie, I did love like that once," he said.

Maggie just stared at him, his words striking a familiar, responsive chord. Her eyes glistened with unshed tears. "I'm so sorry, Joel. I didn't mean it that way. I know how much you loved Beth."

"I miss her so much."

"I miss her too," Maggie said, leaning into Joel and burying her face against his shoulder.

"That's why you can't waste this time, Maggie. If you really love him, try to work it out."

"It doesn't matter how I feel any more. Nick's involved with someone else."

She pushed herself off the glider and stood, intending to join her sons and their friends. "Right or wrong, I made my choices and now I have to live with them."

Danny suddenly appeared in the doorway, looking stunned and pale. Davey stood silent and equally drained behind his brother.

An icy chill shot up her spine. "What's wrong?" Maggie choked, fearful of his answer.

"Dad crashed."

Chapter Seven

"Why don't they tell us something?" Maggie screamed, directing her pleas to the television.

The crash involved a grand total of thirteen cars, three of which were so mangled the drivers had to be cut out of the twisted metal in spite of all the beefed up safety requirements.

The announcers couldn't or wouldn't release any information about the condition of the drivers who had to be taken away in ambulances, Nick being one of them. Either they didn't know anything and couldn't say, or they knew plenty but wouldn't say. Regardless of which, they weren't giving Maggie much hope. They kept telling her what she could see for herself as they replayed the moments just before, during and after the crash.

She watched in surrealistic slow motion, Nick's red and black racecar get right reared, which spun him into a staggered six pack of oncoming cars trying to get out of the way. He bounced between the wall and three other cars before one final hit broadside flipped and rolled his car into the infield. No amount of safety features or equipment could prevent injuries or predict the outcome from the kind of jarring blows Nick had sustained.

To make matters worse some ingenious editor spliced the accident clip with the segment of Nick's interview where he mentioned how he wanted to get out before his luck ran out.

"I need to get to Indianapolis," Maggie announced. She paced around the family room and through the kitchen as if searching for something. "My keys, I need my keys. Danny, Davey, get in the car."

"Whoa, whoa, hold on, Maggie." Joel came to her side and took her by the arm. "You're in no condition to walk across the street, let alone drive to Indy," he told her. Taking her by the shoulders he guided her to the couch and forced her to sit. In spite of her initial resistance, once she started to bend the rest of her practically fell into the cushions.

"You don't even know what hospital they've taken him to," he pointed out. "I'll drive you there myself the minute we hear something."

Maggie cast Joel a beyond grateful glance. He was everything that she wasn't at the moment. She didn't know how she would have managed to this point if he hadn't been there. His stable, calming presence was the only thing that kept her from shattering into a million irreparable pieces.

"Yeah, Mom," Danny agreed, placing a hand on her back with a reassuring touch she found heartbreaking by his effort to comfort her. She clasped his arm and drew him down to sit beside her, motioning for Davey to join them. They clung to her, and she to them. The same fear that glazed their mother's eyes was reflected in theirs.

"You know Doug'll call as soon as he knows something," Davey reminded her.

"Nick's cell phone!" Maggie exclaimed. "Doug always keeps it in his pocket during a race." She jumped up and ran to the phone in the kitchen. In her haste to tap out the number, she screwed up twice before finally getting it right. She held her breath as she listened for the connection. One ring, two, three, four... It picked up on the fifth.

She heard the automatic voice mail announcement then Nick's personal message. The sound of his voice, warm and husky, struck and snapped the last rational nerve she had left and she lost it. Hot tears spilled down her cheeks. She teetered on the brink of tumbling into a place she didn't want to go.

"Voice mail! I got his damn voice mail!" Frustrated and frightened beyond reason, Maggie flung the cordless phone across the room. It deflected off a chair cushion and landed on the carpet still in one piece, ringing almost simultaneously with its landing.

Joel reached it first and answered. He listened, held his hand up to ward off Maggie's outstretched arm, and shook his head in answer to her pleading gaze. "Mrs. Chapparelle has nothing to say at this time." Joel punched the disconnect button. "Reporter," was all he said in answer to her questioning stare.

"Maggie, listen to me," Joel said. That reporter's call is just the beginning of what's going to become a media frenzy. I'll man the phone while you pack a bag. We'll leave the second you hear something."

She was just about to do what he suggested when the phone rang again. Joel averted her attempts to snatch it from his hand and answered, "Chapparelle residence." She watched his expression, or rather the lack of one. He was stoic and unresponsive as he listened to the caller. "Of course," he said. "She's right here." He handed her the phone. "It's Nick."

Maggie's hand shook as she took the receiver.

"Nicky?" she said. His name escaped her lips with a breathless whoosh. "You okay?"

"Yeah, Mags."

She closed her eyes and let the sound of his voice embrace her and she expelled another short, tension-relieving breath.

"I'm pretty banged up, a lot of bruises and some sprains, and I was knocked unconscious for a while. I've got a concussion and one helluva headache, but the doctors tell me I'm going to be fine." Nick hesitated before adding, "The other two drivers didn't fair as well."

"What? Tell me what happened."

"Mark Katz has some internal injuries. He's in surgery now. Eddie Sutton suffered massive head trauma. They're not sure he's going to make it." He sounded weak and exhausted.

"Oh, Nicky. I'm so sorry." It could just as easily have been Nick, she realized, offering two silent prayers—one of gratitude for sparing Nick and one for the other drivers and their families.

"Do..." She had difficulty finding her voice. "Do you need someone to come get you? I can be there in a couple of hours."

"That's not necessary. They're keeping me here a day or two for observation."

"I can still be there in a couple of hours," she offered again. Please let him tell her he needed her to be there, she silently implored. The last few agonizing hours had given her a whole new perspective on her future relationship with Nick.

"Don't come, Maggie."

"What?" she breathed, hoping she misunderstood, but afraid she didn't.

"I don't want you here."

His rejection stung like a barehanded slap across a cold cheek. A weighty silence hung between them. "You'll need someplace to recuperate when you're released, won't you?

"I've already made arrangements for when I'm released."

There was another long silence before she finally managed to speak. "Okay, sure, I understand," she answered. She really didn't understand at all but what else could she say under the circumstances. "Do you want to talk to the boys?"

"I can't. Not now." His voice trembled. "The pain medication they gave me is kicking in. Tell them I'll call tomorrow."

"Sure," she acknowledged. "Take care of yourself, Nicky."

"Goodbye, Maggie."

Maggie collapsed into the nearest chair. His goodbye sounded so final. She wrapped her fists together and squeezed so hard that the nails of her right hand dug into the tender palm until she drew blood. She never felt it. Nothing inside her seemed to be working. She was cold and numb. A chilling, desperate need to feel something, anything, crept through her like thick molasses.

She didn't have time for this self pity, she chastised, giving herself a mental kick in the pants. Danny and Davey needed her. She looked across the table and saw them standing side-by-side, watching, waiting. She gave them a weak smile. "Your dad's going to be fine. He says he'll call you in the morning."

"We're not going to Indy?" Danny questioned.

"No." She shook her head. "Not tonight. Your dad doesn't want us driving this late." How could she tell her sons the truth—that they couldn't see their father because Nick didn't want to see her? She'd figure out something more plausible to tell them in the morning.

"You guys okay with that?" She wouldn't hesitate to

ignore Nick's wishes if her sons expressed a desire to see their father.

"Yeah," said Danny, subdued, his blue eyes dull and sad.

It was Davey who asked, "Is it okay if we call our friends and let them know dad's okay?"

"Of course, sweetie." She squeezed his hand as he started to reach for the phone. "Why don't you use the line in my office? It'll give you some privacy." They nodded in unison and headed down the hall.

Elbow on the table and lost in her thoughts, Maggie chewed a thumb nail ragged, her fingers itching to make a mad grab for the portable phone lying within an arm's length.

She jumped when Joel touched her on the shoulder, asking, "You okay?"

Maggie waved off his concern. "I'm fine, but I'm not so sure about my sons." She smacked her palm down hard on the tabletop. "Damn! I hate it when Nick does this."

Joel pulled out a chair and sat across from her, quiet and ready to listen, which was all it took to get her started.

"He needs to know that when he shuts me out like this he's hurting the boys in the same process. They needed to hear about his condition straight from him, not secondhand." She came to a decision. "Is that offer to drive us to Indy still open?"

"Yes, of course, but I thought Nick didn't want you to there."

"To hell with what Nick wants. I'm thinking of what my sons need." Maggie picked up the phone and scanned the caller ID to find the number from where Nick called. Knowing she couldn't reach him on his cell phone in a hospital, she hit *69 to activate the automatic call back feature.

"E.R."

She hadn't expected the call to go directly to the emergency room. Startled, she stammered. "Uh, yes, I was wondering if I could speak to Nick Chapparelle. He called me from this number earlier."

"He's not here anymore."

"Do you have the room number he was transferred

to?"

"He wasn't transferred to a room."

"Excuse me?"

"Mr. Chapparelle checked himself out."

"There must be some mistake."

"No, no mistake. I helped him into a cab myself."

"Did he say where he was going?"

"Who is this?"

She never knew quite how to answer that question. Wife wasn't right, but ex-wife always sounded wrong, too, even though that was what she was in fact. The term had fallen into the same often-maligned category as step mom and mother-in-law. In the interest of steps, exes, and in-laws everywhere, she decided to dodge the question altogether and said instead, "I'm calling on behalf of his sons."

As it turned out it didn't matter what Maggie said or what she called herself because the nurse didn't have any more information to tell her. To put it in a language any idiot could understand: Nick had left the building without leaving a forwarding address.

****

Through Davey her informant, she discovered when Nick checked himself out of the hospital he'd checked into a downtown Indianapolis hotel for a couple of days. His whereabouts after that, however, were a mystery to everyone including the boys. No one on his crew would admit to knowing where he went either. That was at least their story and they were sticking to it—staunchly loyal to the very end. And who could blame them? They knew who signed their paychecks.

It was nearly two weeks later as she stood in the checkout line at the grocery store when Nick's covert location revealed itself to her—her and the whole civilized world.

Standing behind an elderly woman leafing through a copy of *Celebrity Expose'*, the teasing tabloid headline jumped off the page and punched Maggie right between the eyes. Leaning forward and a little to the left, she craned her neck to see over the woman's shoulder. Fortunately for Maggie, the little old lady couldn't have been more than five feet tall, which made it that much easier to read the revealing headline.

Her jaw dropped and her eyes grew enormous as she read: **Injured NASCAR Hunk Escapes to Virgin Island Paradise with Morgan Heiress for R & R and T.L.C.** The accompanying front-page photo showed them walking arm in arm across the tarmac from a private jet. When the woman turned the page, Maggie immediately glanced to the rack to find her own copy.

Empty. Glancing over the racks of gum and candy, she peered left then right to see if there were any more copies at the other checkout racks. Empty, empty, and empty. Damn, was the whole town reading about Nick's Caribbean escape? As the line started moving, the woman started to put the paper back. Maggie snatched it out of her hand.

"Sorry," Maggie apologized as she smiled at the somewhat startled woman. "I just can't wait to see what the celebrity chef is whipping up this week."

She tore through the paper like a woman possessed searching for the full article. It was a two-page color photo spread—complete with captions. Nick and Mandy lounging on the private terrace of daddy's villa overlooking Cane Bay, Nick and Mandy on the deck of daddy's yacht, Nick and Mandy sharing an intimate candlelit dinner at a local bistro, and last but not least, and Maggie's personal favorite, Nick and Mandy smiling on the dance floor at an island nightclub.

Who was this guy? Maggie wondered. She didn't know this man in the pictures. Oh, he looked like Nick, and he smiled like Nick, and judging from the way he was flailing his arms on the dance floor, he danced like Nick, but this was not the Nick she knew and loved. This man was a total stranger and she couldn't help wondering which Nick she would see the next time he decided to show up at her door.

Maggie studied the pictures with abject curiosity, wondering what kind of telephoto lens the photographer used to get one particularly up close and personal shot of Mandy Morgan. Amazing. The woman not only had gravity defying breasts, her butt was pretty spectacular, too. It would have to be to get away with the scraps she was passing off as a bikini bottom. Her skin, every exposed millimeter of it, was firm and flawless. Not a single stretch mark, pimple, dimple or spider vein dared to mar the perfection. Maggie peered at the revealing photo with an overly critical eye. Did the woman also bathe in a vat of depilatory? The upkeep on a body like that must be astronomical.

"Plastic?"

Maggie nodded. "You can bet on it," she said absently.

"Excuse me?" The bewildered bag boy questioned.

Maggie dragged her eyes away from the photos. "What? Oh, yes. Plastic will be fine." It was good enough for Nick. She tossed the magazine on the moving conveyor with a half-hearted chuckle. While she was good enough to bear Nick's children, Mandy Morgan got to bare everything else for him.

And to think she had envisioned him holed up alone and miserable in some Indianapolis hotel while he recuperated, ordering room service and watching daytime television until he grew bleary-eyed with complementary USA Todays strewn across the floor. She pictured an assortment of little booze bottles from the mini-bar lying on the bed beside him in a staggered formation similar to the positions of the cars just before the crash for a reenactment of the disastrous event. In the past she'd seen him use sugar packets in restaurants, Matchbox cars at home, even stones in parking lots—why not little whiskey bottles in hotel rooms?

That was what the Nick she knew would have done. Well, maybe not exactly, but it made Maggie feel better imagining that's what he would have done.

Damn the man for going off to an island paradise to recuperate. Wasn't Northwest Indiana good enough for him anymore?

Chapter Eight

As she tackled the task of sorting through their drawers and closet, Maggie decided the boys needed a whole new back-to-school wardrobe. They must have grown two inches over the summer. Jeans and shirts she'd bought them in the spring were already too tight, too short, or just plain worn out.

Danny and Davey were growing up much too fast to suit Maggie. If only there was some magic formula to transform them into five year olds forever, or at least a little longer. At five they had been such sweet, wide-eyed innocent children, eager to learn and equally eager to please. Now they teetered on the fringe of raging hormones and crushing peer pressure. She faced a certain future of backtalk, endless attempts at asserting their independence, and a myriad of attitudes, not to mention endless battles of wills with not one but a pair of teenagers ganging up against her. Maggie quaked at the prospect.

Shaking off such nerve-wracking thoughts, she focused on the task at hand, the one she could control, and sorted each item of clothing into three piles—the good, the bad and the hopeless.

As she sorted her way through their drawers and closet, Maggie realized the most difficult part of this whole clothing process was still ahead of her. The really tough part was getting Danny and Davey to the mall. From the time they were little shopping with the boys had never been a pleasant experience and she dreaded it every bit as much as… as…well, she couldn't think of anything worse than going shopping with the boys.

She pulled a stack of sweatshirts from the bottom dresser drawer and out from between the thick knit folds fell a Victoria's Secret Catalog.

Surprised? Just a little. Shocked? No, not really. A greater concern at the moment was deciding how to break the news to her sons that the women in this catalog didn't accurately represent the female population as a whole. They were in for a huge let down if they thought every woman looked like this in her underwear, or fully clothed for that matter. She slipped the catalog back into the drawer. Let them hang onto their fantasies a little longer. They would be disillusioned soon enough.

"Mommmm!" Davey screamed. "Mommmm!"

Half way down the stairs, balancing a box stuffed with outgrown clothing, Maggie lost her grip. End over end, the box tumbled and thumped down each carpeted step, slinging tee shirts, shoes, jeans, khakis and polos in every direction.

Eyeing the mess, she sighed and started picking up the trail of strewn garments on her descent to meet Davey, who was now joined by his brother. They stood side-by-side eagerly waiting to spill their guts, acting like they were about to burst.

They always seemed to have the latest neighborhood gossip before anyone else although she never knew how they managed it. She had a sneaking suspicion it had something to do with their ability to be in two places at once—sort of a twin twist on the *divide and conquer* theory.

"What's up, guys?" Maggie asked, picking up one last shirt. Folding it, she tossed it into the box and parked herself on the third step from the bottom.

"Guess who's moving into the Cartwright house?" Davey exclaimed.

"Somebody finally bought it?" Maggie questioned.

It was a big, old house left empty since the owner's death seven years earlier. The surrounding property was overgrown and neglected, and the house had fallen into major disrepair, but Maggie looked past all that and saw such abiding promise in the sprawling Craftsman-style bungalow nestled amid enormous oaks and maples. It was the anchor of Cartwright Corners development and one of the reasons she fell in love with the new subdivision when she and Nick were hunting for a place to raise their family.

In spite of her affinity for the place, she was practical enough to know how much time and money would be involved in restoring it to its original stylish beauty. "I pity the poor soul who bought that money pit."

"Dad!" Danny exclaimed.

Amazed at how Danny could flit from one subject to another, she queried, "Dad what?"

"Dad bought it," Danny clarified.

"What?" she half-laughed. "There's no reason for you father to be buying a house, here or anywhere else." Northwest Indiana was wholesome and comfortable, a place to put down roots. Nick never stayed in one place long enough to send out feelers. "You must have misunderstood."

"Nuh uh. He's over there right now with the real estate lady getting the keys." Danny's confidence in his facts never faltered. "It's going to be so cool, Mom. He said we could get four-wheelers and snowmobiles, and he wants to convert the old horse track into a go-kart track for us."

Maggie picked up the box of clothes, her knuckles turning white, and headed for the basement. "The neighbors are going to love that," she muttered, wondering how long it would be before he put in miniature golf and batting cages, too.

Irritated as she was by the thought of Nick pulling something like this, she was equally intrigued at the prospect of finally getting into that house. Nick or no Nick, she was going in.

She wondered if he'd mind her taking an impromptu tour. Oh, who cares if he does or not, she finally decided. Besides, she was just as curious to see how the healing waters of the Caribbean had worked on him. Yeah, right. Who was she kidding? She didn't care about the house or St. Croix. All she really wanted was to see was Nick.

Maggie walked the short block to the house, approaching it with a tentative step. What if he still didn't want to see her? What then? Would he ask her to leave or would he at least try to be civil? Maggie hoped the realtor was still there because it would force him to behave. Maybe.

Two vehicles sat parked next to each other on the gravel drive in front. One she recognized as Nick's big blue truck. The other was a dark green Lincoln Town car wearing a magnetic sign on the driver's door stamped with Marconi Realty in bright yellow letters. Her luck was holding.

Gwen Marconi was the realtor of choice in the area. She was a thirty something, attractive, statuesque blonde, in a flashy, obvious sort of way. She was also one helluva real estate agent. Everyone said so and tolerated her often pushy, brash tactics because she got the job done. Although she had never personally met the woman, Maggie knew of her by sight from the boys' school. Gwen had a daughter in the same class as Danny and Davey.

Taking the front stairs, Maggie was mindful of where she stepped. Wood had a nasty habit of rotting when deprived of an occasional coat of paint, stain, or varnish. Much to her surprise, they appeared in relatively good condition considering how long they had been left unattended.

The front door had been left ajar and she took that as a sign to enter without knocking. As she pushed on the heavy oak panel it gave a low, creaking moan as it swung open. The moment she walked across the threshold, she heard voices echoing through the empty rooms although it was impossible to immediately pinpoint their origin from where she stood.

The place reminded her of Disney's Haunted Mansion. Dark shadowed corners and thick dangling cobwebs added to the creepy atmosphere. The house smelled musty and a cloying dampness permeated the place from floor to ceiling. She would have expected the house to be hot and stuffy from being closed up for so long, yet a penetrating chill crept deep into her bones and caused her to shiver. Rubbing the exposed flesh of her upper arms in an attempt to bring some warmth back where her skin crawled with goose-bumps, she stepped further into the entry hall.

Hearing a woman's throaty laughter, Maggie followed the sound through the dining room and into the huge but outdated kitchen. It was obvious that it had never been touched since it was built sixty plus years earlier. It was there, standing on cracked and peeling linoleum, where she discovered Nick and Gwen near the back door that led to a sagging screened-in porch minus most of the screens.

She cast a dubious glance in Nick's direction, wondering if he had the slightest clue as to what he had gotten himself into. She'd seen him turn battered old junk cars into classic restorations. But a house took a whole different set of tools and talents. Maggie wasn't sure he was capable of tackling a restoration job of this magnitude.

Then she turned her attention to the other occupant and watched Gwen's fluent body language with envious fascination as the other woman touched Nick's arm or shoulder to make a point or redirect his attention to her ample bosom. A teasing hint of cleavage revealed itself at the neckline every time she moved or gestured. The tailored black suit jacket and pencil slim skirt hugged her curves with flawless perfection, and her stance was open and inviting.

Wow! All that and the woman knew the difference between a fixed and an adjusted rate mortgage.

Nick on the other hand, was being, well, Nick. He was his usual charming, laid back self, smiling at all the right places and creating an inviting atmosphere. And he gave every indication that he was listening intently to Gwen's every utterance, but Maggie knew otherwise. She recognized the imperceptible fluttering of his eyelids, indicating his attention span was reaching its breaking point. It was time to come to his rescue, or Gwen's, depending on whose point of view she was deciphering.

Maggie rapped on the doorframe with fisted knuckles. Both occupants turned to the sound. "Hi," she smiled, waving. "I understand congratulations are in order. Welcome to the neighborhood, Nick."

"News sure travels fast around here," Gwen remarked, raising a perfectly arched brow as she stepped back to take a lingering assessment of Maggie the interloper.

"Hello. I'm Maggie Chapparelle. I live up the street." She extended her hand.

"Chapparelle?" Gwen reiterated, shaking Maggie's hand with a perfunctory clasp. "Are you two related?" she questioned as she waggled a perfectly polished index fingernail between Nick and Maggie.

"Sorta kinda," Nick interjected with a dimpled smirk. "Maggie is my ex-wife."

"And the mother of the two boys who were here earlier," Gwen finished making the connection. "Well, Nick, I guess I'll be going now. But please, don't hesitate to call if there's anything else I can do for you." She made her exit with flawless grandeur, turning with a practiced flourish on impeccable stacked heels and graceful, long-legged strides.

Nick waited for the door to shut before turning his attention to Maggie. "Your timing was perfect. I was beginning to feel like she was sizing me up for dinner."

"More like dessert. That woman was ready to cover you with whipped cream and eat you with a spoon." Maggie chuckled.

"Are you kidding? Rumor has it she's an experienced man-eater. She doesn't use utensils!" Nick shared Maggie's laughter.

"So," he said on a more serious note with an expansive sweeping gesture. "What do you think of my new house?"

Maggie eyed the peeling paint and sagging cupboard doors. "New?"

"It will be when I'm finished. I'm remodeling every inch of this place, inside and out. I plan on doing a lot of the work myself." He spoke with ambitious pride as he flipped the house key ring around his finger.

"What prompted this, Nick?"

"I figured it was time to find a permanent spot to park my truck."

She chose to ignore his reference to her previously made remark in an effort to avoid what would undoubtedly become another argument. "Why here?" she questioned. "I would have thought someplace more glamorous than Northwest Indiana would have better suited you these days."

"What's that supposed to mean?" he bristled. "My sons live here. What better reason do I need?"

"You're right," she replied. "There is no better reason."

There had been a time, not too long ago in fact, he would have also mentioned her as one of his reasons. He's doing what you wanted, she reminded herself. And she couldn't deny how wonderful having Nick close by would be for the boys. For her own peace of mind, however, she wasn't sure if having him in such close proximity was such a good idea. But just like everything else concerning Nick, she'd learn to adjust, that's all. It did make her wonder though what other surprises he had up his sleeve. Would there be a new wife waiting to take up residence when he finished the restorations?

Stop right there, her mind screamed. *Don't go any further. Change the subject. Change it! Change it right now.*

"You're looking well, Nick. St. Croix obviously agreed with you." That might have gone better, she mentally chided. Changing the subject to one that didn't include Mandy might have been a better choice.

"Oh, Mags, everything was absolutely perfect," he said with a tad too much enthusiasm she noted. "The weather, the water—I never lifted a finger the entire time I was there. Mandy's staff waited on me hand and foot. And the food! I must have gained ten pounds. As soon as the doctor releases me I need to find a gym and start working it off." He rubbed his stomach with a satisfied, reminiscent smile. "Really, Maggie, you've got to go there some time. You'd love it."

"I'll be sure to add it to my must-do list, right after having the septic tank sucked out and cleaning the gutters."

The reality of the situation smacked her right between the eyes. Although they would be living in the same neighborhood barely a block apart, their lifestyles were greatly dissimilar. How had she phrased it to Joel? *Nick was destined for something greater than mediocrity in the suburbs.* The prophetic words came back to haunt her. The greatest irony was he would be doing it all right under her nose. Damn the man for not having the decency to start his new life elsewhere.

Maggie didn't want to hear another word. "I should be going," she said, backing away. "It's getting dark. Danny and Davey will be wondering what happened to me."

"Hold on," he said, shutting and bolting the back

door. "I'll walk out with you."

"This place is so cool, Dad," Danny announced as he came bounding up the stairs just as Nick and Maggie stepped onto the front porch. "Are you gonna sleep here tonight?"

Nick gave a laugh as he locked the door. "Not tonight, Dan. I don't have any utilities turned on yet."

"Where are you staying tonight?" Davey asked.

"The Holiday Inn Express in town."

"Couldn't he stay with us like the last time, Mom?"

"Last time?" Maggie stammered, remembering the last time all too well.

"Its movie night and Mom's making spaghetti. It's my turn to pick the movie but you can pick if you want, Dad. How about it?"

"I don't know guys. That's a lot of extra work for your mom."

"I ain't that much more work, is it, Mom?"

"It *isn't* that much more work," Maggie said, correcting her son's atrocious grammar.

"See, Dad, mom says so too."

Nick couldn't suppress a chuckle. "Well, I guess. As long as your mother says it's okay."

Wide-eyed and expectant, Danny and Davey looked to Maggie.

"Sure, why not?" Maggie replied, unable to say anything else under the circumstances. *Why not?* Her mind screamed. Why not? She had a hundred reasons and they all started and ended with Nick Chapparelle.

"All right!" The boys leaped down the stairs and started running toward their house.

Giving her hair a haughty flip, Maggie sighed and drawled, "I've given the staff the night off, Nick, but you're welcome to stay as long as you're willing to fend for yourself."

"I'll force myself to endure," Nick replied.

"I'd settle for uneventful," Maggie returned with a grim twist of her lips.

Chapter Nine

"Okay, guys, movie's over. Bed time." Maggie pushed herself off the couch and started collecting popcorn bowls, crumpled napkins, and empty pop cans from the coffee table.

"But its Friday night," Danny pointed out.

"And the only reason you're up this late," she returned as she carried everything into the kitchen. "Don't forget to brush your teeth."

"Where's Dad?" asked Davey, looking around.

"His cell rang about twenty minutes ago," Maggie explained. "He went into the other room to take the call."

"He missed the ending."

"Davey," Maggie stated incredulously. "It's *Days of Thunder*." True to his word, Davey had let Nick choose the movie. What a surprise he selected a film about stock car racing. "Do you really think your dad doesn't know how it ends?"

"No, but he still missed it."

"Can't argue with that," she said, loading the bowls into the dishwasher.

"Sorry about the interruption," Nick said as he entered the kitchen still carrying his phone. He placed it on the counter and glanced disappointedly at the TV. "Aw, I missed the ending?"

"That seems to be the general consensus," Maggie laughed. Nick and the boys were like a pair and a spare. She couldn't help thinking what a nice evening they had shared as a family.

"I'm hungry," Nick said, rubbing his stomach. "How about ordering a pizza?"

"Yeah!" Danny and Davey concurred in unison.

"A pizza?" Maggie reiterated. "At this hour? It'll be after midnight before it's delivered."

"Yeah, you're probably right," agreed Nick. "It'll be quicker if we go out."

Maggie held up her hand in a gesture of both refusal and capitulation. "You and the boys go if you must but leave me out of it. I'm exhausted and I'm going to bed." She started for the stairs then stopped and fixed her I-don't-want-any-arguments stare on Danny and Davey. "Don't make any plans for tomorrow. We're going school clothes shopping."

"Argh!" Danny collapsed and began writhing is pseudo agony. "No, no, anything but that. Dad, please, don't let her do this. You gotta save us!"

"Better you than me, guys," was all Nick had to say on the subject. Needless to say, Nick wasn't fond of shopping either. As a matter of fact, she remembered him behaving almost as badly as Danny once when she remarked that he could use some new shirts. It made her wonder who prodded him to get new clothes when he needed them now. No surprise that he chose to go commando. Running into Wal-Mart for a pack of boxers or briefs was too much for him to handle. If there wasn't a motor attached to it he wasn't interested.

He tossed Davey his keys. "Get in the truck, I'll be right out."

Nick turned to her after the boys left and said, "I can see how awkward this is for you, Maggie."

Shrugging, she chose her words carefully, "I'll never stop you from spending time with the boys."

"Why do you always do that?" he demanded.

"Do what?"

"Make it sound like you're only tolerating me for the boys' sake."

"I didn't mean for it to sound like that. It's just that I don't want you mistaking tonight for anything more."

"You know what I think, Mags? I think you're the one who's afraid of tonight turning into something more." He paused and gazed at her thoughtfully. "Or maybe you're afraid that it won't."

"Don't be ridiculous," she flustered, feeling a warm flush creep up her neck and settle on her cheeks.

"If it'll make you feel any better, I'll sleep down here on the couch."

"That won't be necessary. You can sleep upstairs."

His face brightened and the smile that tugged at the

corners of his mouth was provocative and disarming. "With you?"

Maggie smiled sweetly and shook her head. "Not when there's a perfectly good bed in the spare room." She spun around and headed up the stairs, tossing a wave over her shoulder. "Goodniiiight…" she trilled.

****

After completing her normal nighttime routine, Maggie climbed into bed and reached for the TV remote. No matter how tired she was, she always needed to unwind for a few minutes. Watching a classic Nick@Night rerun or mindless infomercial always did the trick. Flipping on the TV, she surfed through the channels.

Intrigued, her thumb hesitated over the channel selector. What's this? Had she stumbled on some unexpected soft porn channel? But knowing she didn't subscribe to any movie channels, let alone the spicy ones—her sons were growing up fast enough without them coming across the sexual antics of the Busty Coeds—there wasn't a logical explanation as to why this was on her television. Still, she couldn't bring herself to switch it off.

It was the close up shot of a man's naked chest that first captured her attention. It was a *very* nice chest, and she could appreciate a well-built male body as much as the next woman. And this one was about as nice as they came. Tanned and slick with water, broad and well muscled, the camera caressed every inch of smooth, hard flesh.

Her gaze remained glued to the screen as the camera pulled back to reveal more and more of what was connected to that chest. She struggled for more definitive words to describe the beautiful male physique on the screen. The right words escaped her vocabulary. Oh my, he was so…he was…he was Nick! This was not the Nick at Night she'd had in mind.

Except for the heavy linked gold chain around his neck and a fluffy navy blue towel wrapped low on his hips, he wasn't wearing anything else but a provocative smile. Long delicate pink fingernails trailed down his perfectly tanned water-glistened pecs and abs.

A breathless woman's voice purred, "His Chassis is

all I ever need to get my motor running."

Then, if that weren't enough, the commercial flipped to a woman's equally scantily pink towel-clad body, also shimmering with water droplets. It was none other than Mandy, naturally. Nick's husky voice whispered seductively, "And Her Chassis is all I need to rev my engine." The next shot was of his hand running down the length of her bare arm.

The very last thing the viewer saw are blue and pink towels crumpled in a tangled heap around their feet as a disembodied voice-over proclaimed the captivating allure of *His Chassis* cologne for men and *Her Chassis* perfume for women, now enhanced with natural pheromones.

It was the sexiest, most provocative advertisement that Maggie had ever seen. No wonder it was being shown during late night TV. It sure wasn't appropriate for prime time. How could they have crammed so much blatant sexuality into a thirty second commercial? It should come with a warning about not being suitable for young viewers—or ex-wives.

Maggie punched the power button, plunging the bedroom into darkness. Then she punched her pillow. Damn the man for finding yet another way to torment her.

****

Maggie was rousted from a dead sleep when she heard Nick and the boys return from their late night pizza run. She rolled to her side, wrapped a pillow around her head, and tried to ignore their feeble attempts to be quiet. It seemed the harder they tried the louder they got.

"Shhhh," Nick whispered, sounding like he was standing in the same room with her. "You'll wake you're mother."

"Too late," she muttered into her pillow. "They already did."

She heard the door to the guest room open. "Good night guys," said Nick.

"Aren't you sleeping in mom's room tonight?" Danny asked.

Wide-eyed and even wider-awake, Maggie sat straight up at hearing her son's innocent inquiry. Bracing her palms flat against the mattress, she cocked her head as if doing so would help her hearing and broaden the range of her eavesdropping.

"Uh, no, Dan. Why do you ask?" Nick questioned.

"Because you did last time."

Maggie gasped and slapped her hands across her mouth to stifle any further outcry. Losing her balance, she rolled backwards and cracked her head against the unyielding oak headboard. Wincing, she mouthed "Ow," as she massaged the nasty bump rising on the back of her head.

"Yeah, well," Nick stammered. "If you know what's good for you, you'll keep that bit of information to yourself."

Maggie scooted off the bed and crept toward the closed bedroom door. She didn't want to miss a single syllable of the ensuing conversation taking place in the hall.

"Come on, Dad. We're not like little kids anymore, you know. Me and Davey, we're cool with it."

"You're cool with what?" Nick asked.

"That you and mom, you know, had sex that night."

"There's just one other thing I need to know," Nick said. His words were stilted and he paused as if he were having difficulty formulating what he was about to say. "How did you and your brother come to the conclusion that my sleeping in the same room with your mother meant we were having sex?"

"You're kidding, right? You and mom weren't exactly quiet about what you were doing. When I got up to use the bathroom I heard you going at it pretty good."

"Oh!" Mortified, Maggie covered her face with her hands. She felt the tingling warmth of a heated flush creep up her neck. Never in a million years had she imagined her sons had any knowledge of that night with Nick.

"Going at it?" Nick stumbled over the phrase. "Uh, Danny," he began. "Talk like this is okay between us guys but it tends to make moms very nervous, especially coming from her twelve-year-old son. So it's probably best not to let your mother hear you use phrases like '*going at it.*' Okay?"

"Yeah, Dad, sure. I understand what you're saying."

"Hey, Dan."

"Yeah, Dad?"

"Have you ever heard, you know...noises like that any other time coming from mom's bedroom?"

Maggie yanked open the bedroom door with such incredible force she expected the handle to come off in her hand. "Daniel Evan Chapparelle, if you say so much as one more word—"

"Mom, I wasn't—"

"Not a single word," she warned.

"But, Mom—"

"Get in your room. Now!"

Danny backed into the room and shut the door.

"Come on Maggie, you're not being fair," Nick said in his son's defense. "This isn't Danny's fault."

"You're damned right it's not!"

"Then why are you taking it out on him?"

"Because he's your son!" she exclaimed for lack of a better reason.

"Oh, well," Nick intoned. "That explains everything."

"No... no," she shook her head adamantly. "You are not going to joke your way out of this. Not this time. You have stepped way, way over the line, Nick Chapparelle." She turned on him, eyes flashing with contempt. "How dare you? I can't believe you'd stoop to this." Angry tears spilled down her cheeks as she sputtered and stumbled over her words. "Isn't it bad enough that you discuss our sex life with Danny? But to further my humiliation by interrogating him about information that is none of your business. You... You...You had no right!"

"Maggie, I said what I did to Danny because I heard you in the bedroom. It was a just a joke. I knew you were awake."

"Pardon me for not finding this the least bit amusing."

"Come on, Boomer. You know I wasn't serious." He was beginning to sound desperate.

"Save your breath, Nick. I'm not interested in hearing any more of your lame excuses. I want you out of my house and out of my life." Pushing past him, she stormed down the stairs. "And stop calling me Boomer!" she screamed.

Arriving in the kitchen, Maggie stood there for a moment, not knowing exactly what she intended on doing there. She just wanted to get as far away from Nick as possible and the stairs were the easiest route of placing the most distance between them. She braced her palms against the counter and attempted to calm her trembling outrage. More angry tears began to fall.

"You know, if you don't want your sons, or your ex-husband for that matter, thinking of you as a sexual being, you really ought to put a robe on." He draped the terrycloth robe she kept in her bathroom over her shoulders.

In her fit of rage, she hadn't given what she was wearing a passing thought. The cotton lawn nightgown she wore wasn't particularly sexy, but it was sheer, and short. Except for the scattered embroidered pink rosebuds and a pair of bikini panties, she suddenly felt exposed and vulnerable. Slipping her arms into the sleeves, her hands trembled as she gathered the plush fabric around her and tied the belt.

"I never realized you thought so little of me, Nick." Her voice quavered as she blinked to clear her vision.

"I don't understand." He sounded genuinely baffled. "What do you mean?"

"How could you say something like that to Danny? Even in jest?" She pressed the heels of her palms against her eyes to dam the fresh wave of hurt threatening to spill as she gathered her frayed and fragile emotions before attempting to speak again. "Do you really think that I've been parading men in and out of my bedroom since you left?"

"No!" Nick denied. "Of course not. I've never thought that!"

"Inasmuch as your opinion of me doesn't matter much anymore," she said. "My sons' opinion still matters a great deal. When they were born I was so afraid of screwing up those two precious little boys the doctor placed in my arms. But ready or not, I was a mom. And right then and there I made them a promise to be the best mom I could be. I wanted desperately for them to grow up being proud of their mother. I really thought I was doing a pretty good job so far, too."

"You are," Nick reassured. "You're a wonderful mother, Maggie. The best."

She choked a bitter laugh. "Too little, too late, Nick. The damage has been done. In one fell swoop you managed to make me feel like the same insecure, unworthy, pregnant seventeen-year-old I was when you married me. Only this time your teasing humiliation wasn't in front of your pit buddies it was in front of our son. You might as well have called me a whore in front of him. I don't think I can ever forgive you for that."

"Oh god, no, Maggie," he groaned. "Please, please, don't say that. I know what I said was incredibly thoughtless and stupid. It was a bad joke. That's all. I'm sorry."

Maggie studied him intently and she looked him squarely in the face. "I've tried to raise the boys to treat girls—and women—with respect. With that one thoughtless, *incredibly stupid*, comment you've managed to teach them it's okay to make derogatory, off-color remarks about women as long as it's passed off as a joke." Squeezing her eyes tightly shut, Maggie felt the trickle of fresh tears and turned away to regain her slipping composure.

Lifting her chin in an almost haughty tilt, she brushed the tears away and continued, "I never imagined you capable of doing something like this." Her lower lip trembled, yet she maintained an almost frightening calm level of self-control. "I don't think I know you anymore. It makes me wonder if I ever did."

Nick's cell phone vibrated across the countertop. He picked it up, glanced at the screen, and turned it off without answering.

"Go ahead and take it. I'm finished with you."
****

Not entirely sure how she had gotten there, Maggie found herself standing at Joel's front door at four o'clock in the morning. When he answered, she said, "Can I come in?"

"Of course," he said, standing aside. She stepped into the foyer and headed straight for the kitchen. It was such a special place for her. She and Beth had shared so many heart-to-hearts there. Maggie needed that comforting atmosphere more than anything at the moment. The second she sank into the ladder-back chair at the aged oak table, she felt Beth's calming influence wrap around her like a favorite quilt.

Amazed she had any tears left, her red and swollen eyes welled up. "I expected to find her standing here," she said.

"You too?" he asked. Filling a shiny copper kettle with tap water, he set it on the stove and cranked up the burner.

He collected cups and saucers from the oak hutch behind her and placed a tin canister marked TEA on the table next to the Felix the Cat cookie jar already there.

"You want to tell me what's going on?" Joel prompted.

Maggie sighed wearily. "Just another round with Nick."

"In person or over the phone?"

"Up close and personal this time." Maggie rubbed her fingertips across the raised grain of the antique oak tabletop. The gesture was hypnotic and she felt herself relaxing to the point of falling asleep. "He bought the Cartwright house," she mumbled, fighting the heavy weights pushing her eyelids closed. "Can you believe it? He's gonna be my neighbor." Her vocal chords trembled, as if someone had stretched them beyond their limit, and she choked a feeble sob.

Joel took her by the arm and led her to the floral chintz sofa in the living room. After tugging off her shoes, he urged her to lie back as he tucked an oversized afghan around her shoulders. "This couch is very comfortable," he said, his voice low and soothing. "Try to get some sleep."

"I haven't finished telling you about Nick," Maggie muttered, attempting to sit up.

Joel sat on the edge of the couch cushion and pressed her back against the throw pillows. "It'll keep." She was asleep before he could draw the drapes and leave the room. The kettle was just starting to whistle its readiness in the kitchen.

****

In another kitchen across town Nick sat at the table drinking the end of what was his second pot of strong black coffee. If he smoked there would have had been an ashtray overflowing with crushed butts by now too. He tossed back the final swallow and plunked the mug down hard. A crescent shaped chip broke from the bottom edge and shot across the table. That's just great, he thought, just one more thing for her to be pissed at him about. What else could he manage to screw up before she banished him from her life forever? He'd be gone already if she hadn't been the one to take off instead.

Shoving back on the chair arms, he stood and began pacing. Where could she be? Where could she have gone? For her to leave in the middle of the night like this was totally out of character. He knew how much Maggie hated driving in the dark. It only convinced him how desperate she must have been to get away. A painful realization came over him. My god, he'd driven her out of her home. How could he ever forgive himself for that on top of everything else?

After circling the front hall at least half a dozen times he yanked open the door and searched the empty street hoping, no praying, to see her blue Cherokee turn the corner. He was met with the eerie silence of a neighborhood still asleep on an early Saturday morning. The sun was just beginning its morning ritual of changing the sky from black to blue. He was damned worried. She'd been gone for hours.

This wasn't like her. Maggie wasn't the one to walk out after a fight. That was his modus operandi. She was the nurturer, the homemaker, and the nest builder. His glance shifted from floor to ceiling and wall-to-wall. Every stroke of paint, every strip of wallpaper, every stick of furniture was her doing; single-handedly she had made this house a warm, comfortable home. God knows he had never been around enough to help her with any of it. Is it any wonder why she wanted out of the marriage?

He raked his hand through his hair. Think, damn it. Think! Where the hell would she have gone? Lack of sleep and gallons of caffeine seemed to have transformed his brain into nothing more than a hyperactive cauliflower.

"Dad?" Danny said, sounding surprised. "You're still here?"

"You can't be anymore surprised than I am, Danny."

"We're in really deep poop, aren't we, Dad?"

"That's one way of putting it. But I'm afraid your mother has reserved the deepest part of that pile just for me. She loves you too much to stay mad at you."

"She still loves you too, Dad."

Inasmuch as he'd like nothing better than to believe Danny's assessment, Nick shook his head against the very idea. "No, Dan, I don't think so. Not any more. I really blew it this time."

Danny placed a consoling hand on his father's shoulder. "As soon as she calms down she'll realize you were only joking and forgive you. I guarantee it."

Nick turned and gazed at his son with amazed admiration. When had this child of his grown into a caring young man? He wrapped his arm around Danny's neck and pulled him against his chest, hugging him tightly. "I hope so, Danny. I sure hope so."

"What's going on?" Davey asked, coming down the stairs rubbing his eyes at the sight of his father hugging Danny in the open doorway.

"As usual, you slept through everything," said Danny.

"I'm hungry," Davey said. "What's for breakfast?"

"I'm not up to fixing anything this morning, guys. How does breakfast at McDonald's sound?"

Chapter Ten

Maggie woke up groggy and disoriented. It took her a long minute to put together the rough pieces of the previous night and figure out where she was and how she got there. She sat up, pushed off the crocheted blanket, and swung her feet to the floor, immediately cradling her pounding head. It felt heavy in her hands. Her eyes were dry and scratchy and she rubbed them in a useless effort to find some moisture. It came as no surprise that she'd cried herself to the point of dehydration.

The smell of coffee and bacon made her stomach churn and growl. And for a moment she wasn't sure if she wanted to eat or throw up. Hungry, she finally decided. Yes, she was definitely more hungry than nauseous.

With one hand on the cast iron skillet handle, Joel turned away from the stove when she entered. "Morning," he said. "Juice is on the table," he added, turning back to the task of flipping the bacon with long-handled tongs. Standing in sweat socks and a pair of blue and green plaid flannel pants and a navy tee, Joel appeared much less prim and proper than Maggie was ever used to seeing him. He was a button down collar and penny loafer kind of guy.

She lifted the glass of apple juice and took a long swallow.

"Scrambled or fried," he queried.

Maggie shook her head and waved off the offer. "I should be getting home. I've imposed on your hospitality long enough." She hesitated then added, "But I guess I owe you some sort of explanation before I go."

Turning off the stove, Joel set the frying pan aside and pulled out the chair opposite from her. Reaching across the table, he patted one of her hands. "I know you well enough to know you didn't show up at my door in the middle of the night just to be sociable. You needed someplace to go. I'm glad I was here for you."

"Thank you," she said softly. She dropped her head in her hands. "I don't know what to do with Nick anymore. Whenever we're together I find myself either wanting to kick him hard or kiss him harder."

"And last night?"

"I kicked him—*very* hard. Not that he didn't deserve it, but I might have kicked a little harder than necessary. It's just that everything he says or does lately makes me crazy."

"Do you know why I still fix my bacon on the stove instead of in the microwave?"

A puzzled furrow creased her brow. Although not sure where he was going with this off-the-wall remark, she shook her head, curious enough to stick around and hear him out.

"We're all creatures of habit, Maggie. And, good or bad, they're easy to develop but difficult to break."

"What does that have to do with any of this?"

"I think you've gotten yourself caught up in a highly destructive habit of expecting the worst out of Nick. You've made him the fall guy. It's easier to justify the divorce if everything that goes wrong is always Nick's fault."

"There you go trying to analyze me again."

He adjusted his glasses and grinned. "I just can't help myself. You're such a fascinating subject."

"So, in your professional opinion, what do I do now?"

"It's time to stop blaming him for your own mistakes. Let it go, Maggie. Let him go."

Maggie considered Joel's solution with thoughtful deliberation, and came to the conclusion that he was right. If she really believed what she did was best for Nick, then she had to accept it and move on.

Joel jumped up as if his chair had suddenly caught fire. "What the hell!" The pounding paused for a moment, then started up again, louder and longer the second time, accompanied by a constant dinging of the doorbell. Boom, boom, boom! Ding, ding, ding!

Pressing her palms over her ears, Maggie attempted to muffle the incessant racket. "It's Nick. I know it. He must have seen my car parked out front."

"Do you want to talk to him?

85

"No." She shook her head. "I can't. Not now. Not yet."

"Then stay here. I'll take care of him." He opened the door and was greeted by a raised fist, ready to start its assault on the door again.

Nick lowered his arm. "Where is she? Where's Maggie?" He tried to see past Joel into the house. "I've got to talk to her. I have to explain."

Maggie peered around the kitchen doorframe. She couldn't help make a physical comparison between the two men. Both were similarly sized. While Nick was a slightly broader, at six-foot-four Joel held the edge in the height department. Needless to say, they presented a formidable pair standing nose-to-nose and toe-to-toe.

In his aggressive attempt to see around Joel, Nick spotted her. "Maggie, please hear me out." As he attempted to step further into the house, Joel stopped him with a firmly planted hand on his shoulder.

"You need to leave."

Nick grabbed Joel by the wrist and shoved him away. "Get your hand off me. I'm talking to Maggie."

"She doesn't want to talk to you." His voice was low, but firm. Joel stood his ground, planting himself in the doorway with one hand gripping the frame and the other on the door, blocking Nick from any further access.

"Get—out—of—my—way," Nick stressed each word as he punched his shoulder into Joel's chest with a sharp, hard jab. The sudden, unexpected action caught Joel off guard and sent him sprawling.

Maggie ran to Joel's assistance. "Have you completely lost your mind?" she demanded, sending Nick a shriveling glance that would have downed a lesser man. Nick, however, stood his ground and appeared unfazed. Clutching Joel's arm she helped him to his feet. "You okay?"

"Yeah. I just lost my balance." He sounded more embarrassed than hurt. "You got one helluva shoulder jab, Nick. Football or basketball?"

"Lettered in both."

"College?"

"Nah. Only high school. You?"

"Basketball, prep and collegiate."

"Nice." Nick sounded genuinely impressed.

"Scholarship?"

"Full ride."

"Where?"

"Penn State."

"Big Ten. Very nice." Nick reached out his hand and said, "No hard feelings?"

"Don't give it a second thought. Given similar circumstances, I might have done the same thing."

"I hope you didn't hurt yourself when you fell?"

"Just my pride. Used to be I could take a hit like that without so much as a flinch."

Baffled didn't begin to describe the way Maggie felt. Shifting her gaze from Nick to Joel then back to Nick, she couldn't help wonder what just happened here. How did he do it? Nick extracted personal data from Joel even she didn't know, and she'd known him for four years. What next?

"How about a cup of coffee?" Joel started moving toward the kitchen.

Maggie tossed her hands in the air. Slack-jawed and wide-eyed, she stared at Joel with nothing less than astonishment.

"Sounds good," said Nick, following. "You like baseball?"

"You know it. Did you see yesterday's Cubs game?" Joel asked. Their voices grew less distinct the farther down the hall they traveled.

Maggie rubbed her eyes and shook her head as if none of what she'd just witnessed really happened. She'd heard it, she'd seen it, but she still didn't believe it. How was this possible? How could they be sparing partners one minute and bosom buddies the next? Too much testosterone? Not enough?

There was only one thing she knew with absolute certainty, she wasn't going to stand there and listen to them male-bonding for one second longer. She was out of there. To hell with them both.

Chapter Eleven

Danny and Davey spotted Maggie the moment she exited Joel's house. Scrambling out of the truck, they ran to greet her.

Danny threw his arms around her and pressed his head against her shoulder, nearly knocking her down with his enthusiastic bear hug. "I'm real sorry, Mom."

"I know, sweetie." She wrapped her arms around him and hugged him tight, kissing the top of his head. "I'm sorry too."

It was only after she released her remorseful son, did she look at them both with an inquisitive frown. "What are you doing here?" she asked. "Have you been waiting in your father's truck all this time?"

"It's okay," Davey said, holding up a half-eaten egg McMuffin in one hand and a ketchup slathered hash brown in the other. "He left us food and cracked the windows."

"I'd like to crack more than his windows," Maggie mumbled. "Get in my car. We're going home."

"What about dad?" Danny asked.

"Your dad's a big boy. He can find his own way home." She glanced in Davey's direction. "If nothing else, he can follow the trail of crumbs."

Except for the occasional straw slurp, lip smack and bag crinkle from the back seat where Davey proceeded to finish his breakfast with single-minded concentration, the beginning part of the drive home was made in total silence.

Danny sat next to Maggie in the front seat. "Are we still going clothes shopping today?" he questioned.

Maggie cast him a quick, astonished glance before returning her gaze to the road. "You're reminding me about going shopping? What gives?"

"I don't want you mad at me any more."

"I get mad at you guys all the time. It never lasts.

You know that."

"Last night was different. Me and dad both knew it."

"You discussed last night with your dad?"

Danny nodded and looked at her, turning in his seat as far as the seatbelt would allow. "He didn't mean anything by what he said, Mom. Honest. That's just the way guys talk sometimes."

"Oh it is, huh?" She concentrated on her driving to keep from smiling at the seriousness of her son's wise-beyond-his-years demeanor.

"Sure. I know dad's real sorry for everything."

"He told you that?"

"He made it real clear to us that what he did was wrong and if he ever heard me or Davey making deroge..." He stumbled over the word.

"Derogatory?" Maggie interjected. She found it interesting that Nick used the same word with the boys that she had with him.

"Yeah, derogatory. If he ever heard us say anything like that about a girl, we'd have you *and* him to answer to for it."

"Do you understand what derogatory means?"

Davey piped up. "Isn't it kind of like making fun of someone or teasing them?"

"Yes, it's a lot like that, only worse. Teasing girls may seem like fun now, but someday soon they're going to become important to you. Wouldn't you rather they remember you for something nice you once said to them than something derogatory? And trust me, guys, girls can have very long memories." Women too, for that matter, she reminded herself. Maybe Joel and the Beatles were right. It was time to let it go and *Let it Be*.

Pulling into the driveway, Maggie stifled a yawn. "Inasmuch as I know you were looking forward to our shopping excursion, it's just going to have to wait. I'm not up to facing the challenges of the mall right now." Unable to contain this one, she yawned again. Maybe she'd perk up after a shower.

All the shower did was work the knots out of her neck and shoulders and lull her into a near comatose state of relaxation. Donning baggy sweats and a seen-better-days Winston Cup tee shirt, Maggie headed down the stairs to the kitchen. She couldn't sleep until she had something to eat because the growling in her stomach would just keep her awake. She was starving, and regretted not accepting Joel's offer of bacon and eggs.

After a less elaborate breakfast of corn puffs, raisin bagel and orange juice, she wandered into the family room with the paper and curled on the couch to catch up on the local news. Settling against the supple leather cushions, she convinced herself she only needed to rest her eyes for a few minutes.

The way she felt when she awoke translated into much longer than just a few minutes. Stiff and cramped, Maggie stretched and flexed her arms and shoulders. A quick glance at the cable box's digital display announced it was almost five. Realizing she'd slept the day away, she sat up with a startled gasp. Where were the boys? In spite of the fact that they continually asserted their independence by claiming they were old enough to fend for themselves, she still worried about them and their whereabouts when they didn't check in on a regular basis.

"Danny. Davey," she called. A muffled rumble reached her ears. They were either mowing the lawn, which she doubted since she hadn't hounded them about it enough yet, or they were in the garage fiddling around with those darn go-karts.

She followed the sound and found them precisely where she expected; only they weren't alone. They had an accomplice—their father. Now why didn't that surprise her?

Screwdriver at the ready, he was kneeling and leaning over one of the engines, attempting to adjust something or other. Why anything would need adjusting on go-karts that had never left the garage since they were parked there weeks ago was beyond her comprehension. It was obviously a guy thing. They did it because it was there.

Resting her chin in her hands, she leaned on the hood of her Jeep and watched them, grinning at her adorably dirty sons and their regrettably irresistible father. Nick was in his element. And the boys had all the signs of following in his footsteps. They were motor heads, each and every one of them.

"Dad," said Danny, spotting his mother.

"Not now, Dan." Nick leaned further forward.

"Dad!" Danny said again.

"Dad!!!" Danny and Davey shouted in stereophonic harmony. The intensity startled Nick. His grip slipped, pitched him forward, and his head banged against the tubular frame. Maggie winced when hearing the sound of skull meeting metal.

"Geezus!" he yelled, rubbing the bump above his left eye with the heel of his hand, smearing grease across his forehead in the process. "What the fu–"

"Watch it..." Maggie warned, cutting him off in mid swear word. "There are children present."

Looking up, he cast a rueful smile. "Sorry."

Maggie started to tell the boys to get cleaned up, but discovered that they had pulled a disappearing act worthy of Houdini. "There *were* children present a second ago," she said, glancing around and wondering how they had vanished into thin air.

"I guess they didn't want to be around in case you weren't through yelling."

She inhaled deeply and exhaled. "I'm through."

"I changed the oil in your car, checked all the fluids, and replaced the wiper blades. Antifreeze is good to thirty below and your tires still look good too. You should be all set for winter."

It was only early September, but, by god, she was ready for a blizzard. "Thanks," she said, watching Nick pick up a rag and wipe each tool with painstaking precision before returning it to its designated place in the toolbox. She understood his meticulous thoroughness bordering on obsessive. She was the same way with her quilting paraphernalia.

He finished his task and closed the lid, taking much longer than necessary to secure the toolbox latch. Maggie frowned, wondering why Nick was behaving so oddly. He fiddled and fussed with a latch he had probably fastened a thousand times before. Why was it so difficult for him to close it now? Particularly since he possessed the most dexterous hands she'd ever seen on a man, although no one would ever guess it from looking at them.

They were large, long-boned and calloused, hard

working hands, yet she knew how skillfully agile those hands could be, whatever the purpose. Be it a car that badly needed a tune-up or a woman that desperately needed stroking, he could make them both purr with the right tool and a few nimble-fingered maneuvers. Just the thought of those fingers finding their way up her thigh to stroke and pet her, as only he knew how, left her weak in the knees and gasping.

Unable to take her eyes off those magnificent hands, she watched with rapt fascination as he slathered them with waterless, grease-cutting hand soap and work the slick concoction all around with a slow, repetitious, circular, rubbing motion.

"Oh, my," she mouthed, feeling faint and flushed.

Nick eyed her curiously as he reached for clean rag to wipe his hands dry. "You okay?" he asked, sliding the towel up and down and up and down each long, thick finger. Damn the man for being so thorough!

She swallowed hard and licked her dry lips before answering. "I'm fine," she croaked. "Why do you ask?"

"You look a little woozy. I don't want you falling in here again. Your knees probably just healed from the last time." He glanced at her through a thick shock of sun-bleached hair hanging across his grease-streaked forehead.

Coming around the hood of her Jeep, she took the towel from his hand, wrapped a corner around her fingers, and began rubbing the smudge above his eye. Bright emerald green eyes studied his face. He was aging well. The years had been kind to him. He was more handsome now than he was at twenty. The roundness of his youth had given way to features more chiseled and defined. No wonder Mandy Morgan found him an irresistible partner to pair off with in the Chassis commercials.

His fingers wrapped around her wrist. "Does this mean I've been forgiven?" he asked, locking his gaze with hers, their faces barely inches apart and the rest of their bodies equally close. An odd heat generated between them. She felt it course through her body like the sizzling tingle of an electric current.

She shook her head. "I'm not letting you off the hook that easily." Her heart began to beat a little faster. "What it does mean is," she said, letting her cloth-wrapped finger trace the angular curve of his cheekbone and follow the natural bow of his lips. "You have a dirty face."

It started as a sharp expulsion of breath, then a tiny smile tugged at the corners of his mouth, and finally a full-blown laugh exploded. Maggie felt the warm rush of his breath brush past her cheek. The vague, reminiscent scent of Coca-Cola and peppermints teased her nostrils. For as far back as she could remember it was that simple combination of scents she most connected with Nick. Everyone who went into the pits after the races knew they could always count on Nick having a cooler full of Cokes and a stash of Pep-O-Mint Lifesavers. The only thing more predictable was Maggie's presence at his side.

She broke the spell, and turned away. "Where did those boys go?"

Nick curled his fingers around her arm and stopped her retreat. "So what's it going to take to get me out of the doghouse and back in your good graces?"

"Last night was just a small part of what's wrong, Nick. Time. Give me time to figure it all out."

"How much more time do you need?" He sounded more frustrated than angry. "I've already given you four years."

"That's the problem. I don't know."

"Then take all the time you need. I'm not going anywhere." Nick tossed the rag into a bucket and started for the door.

"You can't do that."

He turned on her. "Who says I can't?"

"Me. That's who." She sounded more defiant then she felt. "I don't want you putting your life on hold just because I can't make up my mind."

"And in what capacity are you taking on this authority? Ex-wife? Mother of my children? Friend? Lover? Innocent bystander? What? Tell me, Maggie, because I'd sure as hell like to know where I fit into your life."

She refused to take the bait. This couldn't turn into an argument if she didn't contribute her two cents. A little voice way in the back of her head started singing, "Let It Be." She elected to listen without interruption.

"Tell me what you want and I'll try my damnedest to be whatever it is you want me to be in this relationship?"

He continued without pause. "And like it or not, we do have a relationship, Maggie. Strange and confusing though it might often be, it's still a relationship. But you're going to have to tell me where you want to go with it because I'm getting too many crazy, mixed signals from you lately to make any sense out of your behavior. So until that day comes, I'm still free and considerably over twenty-one, and I'll do anything I damn well want, wherever and for whomever I please."

His response took her by surprise. His behavior was a shade too glib, a tad too casual, and a bit too rational. And what's more he did it all without ever once raising his voice. She expected him to fly off the handle, scream and shout, and walk out. That was his usual way of dealing with her. Just once she'd like him to do what she expected when she expected it! Then it hit her. Joel was right. She did always try to make it Nick's fault.

"Hey, Dad, are we still going tonight?" Davey stood in the doorway, an apple in one hand and an unpeeled banana in the other.

"Going? Where are you going?" Maggie questioned. "And where did you get those clothes?"

"The track and the mall," Davey answered in his typical abbreviated fashion as he sunk his teeth into the shiny red delicious.

"When were you at the mall?" She swiped her thumb across his chin to catch a juice dribble before it found its way to the front of his new shirt.

"Dad took us shopping this afternoon while you were sleeping."

"Shopping? You took the boys shopping? You?" He was full of surprises today.

Nick nodded. "I don't understand what the big deal is. We were done in just a couple of hours."

Maggie held up her hand against his exaggeration. Shopping with the boys was an all day excursion at best. "Two hours? Yeah, right," she guffawed.

"You don't believe me?" He sounded genuinely wounded as he reached into his back pocket and withdrew his wallet. "Here are all the receipts. I'm sure they're time stamped."

He handed Maggie a hefty stack of paper sales slips. She shuffled through them and gasped. It wasn't, however, the time frame that caused her shocked response.

"You paid how much for those sneakers?! And leather Starter jackets? Nick, these are twelve-year-old boys who are growing faster than the speed of sound." She wanted to say more, a lot more, but that little voice started singing again. She couldn't quite tell if it was John or Paul but she definitely recognized the tune. She hoped the answer came sooner than later because she wasn't sure how much more of that song running through her head she could take.

She took a deep, calming breath and handed the receipts back to Nick. She didn't want to look at them. She didn't want to know what the rest of them said. "Have fun at the track."

"How about coming with us?" Nick suggested.

"Me? Go to the track? No. I couldn't. I haven't been to Illiana in years. No. I don't think so. You guys go."

"Come on, Maggie. It'll be fun. I've been thinking about developing a Busch class team and thought what better place to start looking for new talent than where I got my start. I could use your opinion. You always had great instincts."

"Yeah, Mom. Come with us." Danny and Davey stood side-by-side dressed in their designer jeans and signature sneakers, gazing at her with those beautiful blue eyes just like their father's. Damn. She hated it when they double-teamed her like that. She didn't have a chance. She knew it, and what was worse, they knew it.

"All right. I'll go change."

"I need to shower and change too," Nick said.

****

She didn't know how it happened. One minute she was telling Nick he still wasn't off the hook and the next thing she knew he was standing in her bathroom peeling off his clothes. He just walked in while she was brushing her teeth and started stripping.

"What do you think you're doing?" she mumbled through a mouthful of toothpaste foam.

"Taking a shower," he answered as he tossed his shirt on the floor and unzipped his jeans.

She spit and rinsed and reached for a hand towel to wipe her mouth. "What's wrong with showering in the boys' bathroom?"

"Have you seen the boys' bathroom?"

He didn't have to say another word. She knew exactly what he was talking about. Danny and Davey had been known on occasion to leave a bathroom looking like an F5 tornado touched down. "Well, you could at least ask me to leave."

"For what?" He looked at her like she had grown two heads and turned a glaring shade of chartreuse. "It's not like you've never seen me naked."

"That's not the point. It's just that… Well, you know why this isn't…" She could think of a dozen good reasons why he shouldn't be doing what he was doing but couldn't coherently express a single one. She turned and left the room.

His laughter followed her. It was a wonderful husky laugh that tickled and teased and chased her around the bedroom like a mischievous rascal searching for a playmate. Damn the man. Damn the man. Damn the man.

Chapter Twelve

Illiana Motor Speedway hadn't changed all that much over the years. The new owner had made some improvements on the half-mile asphalt track, repaving and adding an infield arc of pavement to create a quarter mile track at one end for turbo stocks and other short track events. A permanent restroom facility with indoor plumbing had also been built to help alleviate the ever-present lines that formed at the modular structure and porta-potties. Indoor plumbing was a major improvement in Maggie's considered opinion. A little paint, a few minor modernizations, but overall the landmark track maintained the same distinctive individuality and exciting atmosphere as it had when she was a kid. She was very glad Nick and the boys had convinced her to come. It was time to face her past.

An overwhelming sense of déjà vu grabbed her the second she climbed out of Nick's truck, and wrapped her in the comfortable familiarity of what had been some of her more pleasant childhood memories. This place had been her playground every Saturday night from April through September.

She and the boys stood off to one side while Nick paid for their admission. The deafening rumble of the stock cars taking their final time trial laps sent welcomed tremors down her spine, and the aromatic mixture of hotdogs, popcorn and fried elephant ears emanating from the concession stands caused a rumbly in her tumbly, as her sons' favorite preschool character Winnie the Pooh would have said.

The carnival like atmosphere running the length of the midway was like stepping into a time machine where she was magically transported to a happier, less complicated time in her life when her biggest problems were what to wear to the track and how to gain Nick's attention once she got there.

97

Smiling like a kid with a fistful of free passes to the circus, Nick joined them and handed each of them a ticket as they headed for the entrance gate.

"Oh, man, does this bring back memories," Nick observed, swinging his arm around her shoulders as if it were the most natural thing for him to do.

Under normal circumstances, Maggie might have moved away or removed his arm but somehow, for at least tonight, it seemed too right to have him do anything else. Tonight they were a family. Tonight they were a couple. Tonight her arm snaked around his waist in an equally acceptable posture. And, in an attempt to keep it there, she hooked her thumb in the belt loop of his jeans while the other digits dangled casually across his denim-clad hip, just as she had done so many years before.

"I'm hungry," Davey announced.

"I'm shocked," Maggie returned.

Nick reached into his front pocket with his free hand and pulled out a stack of folded bills. He thumbed off two twenties and handed them to the boys. They took off toward the concessions before asking either of their parents if they wanted anything. There probably wasn't enough money anyway, she calculated, knowing how much they ate.

"Did you want anything, Boomer?"

"A little later, thanks." Even the dreadful nickname seemed right that night. It was all too perfect, like a well-rehearsed, opening night play. The stage was set, the actors were in their places, all she had to do was stand back and watch the story unfold. The only problem was she wasn't sure if she wanted to be around when the curtain came down on the final act.

"Excuse me," said a little boy of about seven as he tapped Nick on the arm. "My dad says you're Nick Chapparelle the NASCAR guy." The child sounded doubtful.

Nick tousled the child's shiny mop of brown curls and smiled one of his most charming smiles. "Your dad's right." He glanced up and saw the boy's parents standing twenty feet away just inside the entrance gate anxiously awaiting his response. He nodded an acknowledgement and the couple hurried over to join their son.

In anticipation of the forthcoming handshake, Nick removed his arm from around her shoulder. Maggie backed away, preferring to be an out of the way spectator rather than an active participant in the exchange.

"I knew it!" the man exclaimed as he approached. "The minute I saw you come in I told my son who you were." With a grin as bright as the setting sun, the big man grasped Nick's hand and started pumping. "It's a real pleasure, Mr. Chapparelle. I've been following your career since you started out right here at Illiana."

"I appreciate your support, and please, call me Nick."

Maggie watched Nick, her heart swelling with pride. He handled his fame with such ease and self-assurance. There was nothing forced or phony about his demeanor. He appeared genuinely pleased to spend a few minutes with this man and his family and it showed in how they responded to him in return.

Only it wasn't just the one man and his one wife and one son for very long. News of a professional driver on the premises traveled fast. Before she knew it there was a considerable line forming for handshakes, photo ops, and autographs. Nick glanced up between autographs, searching for her through the crowd. When he found her, he tossed her a helpless grin and a quick wink as he reached for the next program to sign.

She backed away further, finding an out of the way niche under the bleachers where she could observe without getting in the way. Bracing her hip against one of the diagonal support beams, she settled in to watch and wait.

She had no idea how popular he'd become. He was becoming a NASCAR favorite, she realized. Since the divorce she hadn't followed his career as closely as she once had for obvious reasons. This was her first eyewitness account of his rising celebrity status. It somehow made it all worthwhile.

"Some things never change, I see—Nick's still hogging the spotlight while poor little Maggie waits for him in the shadows."

Maggie whirled around to the source of the taunting words. She stared into familiar dark eyes. They were older and wiser, and sporting a few more wrinkles, but nevertheless familiar.

"Freddy?" she queried. At his confirming grin, Maggie jumped up and threw her arms around his neck. "Freddy!"

"Good to see you too, Maggie," he said, returning her greeting with an equally enthusiastic hug.

Taking a step back, she took a long, appraising look. Fred Naples had been a member of Nick's original pit crew back in his Illiana days. In fact, way back in the day he was Nick's whole crew, all one of him. He had also been Nick's closest friend and staunchest supporter. Then one Saturday night, shortly after she and Nick eloped, Fred stopped showing up, and Nick refused to discuss his conspicuous absence with anyone, especially Maggie. She always had her suspicions but never any concrete confirmations.

"How long has it been, Freddy?" she gushed.

"Let's see? How long have you and Nick been married?" he countered.

"It would have been twelve and a half years."

"Would have been?"

"We're divorced."

"You know, I heard rumors that you split up, but I figured that's all they were, especially when I spotted the two of you walk in tonight with your hands all over each other just like the old days. I always figured the only way to separate the two of you was with a hydraulic jack and a crow bar. You mind my asking what happened."

She shrugged and tossed her hands in the air in a helpless gesture. "Some people just aren't meant for happily ever after. You do what you got to do, you know?"

"So how long have you been divorced?"

"Four years."

Fred was thoughtful for a moment. "That's just about the same time he started running with the big boys, isn't it?"

She coughed to hide a nervous laugh. "Yeah, I guess it is." She fiddled with the chain around her neck, sliding her fingers back and forth across the delicate herringbone.

"Funny how things like that work out, isn't it, Maggie?"

Knowing if she dared look at him, he'd know in a heartbeat that his assumptions were right on the mark. Her eyes darted all around, searching for something, anything on which to focus.

"Your secret is safe with me, Maggie. His success was all I ever wanted, too." He cast a glance in Nick's direction. "Our lives touch so few truly extraordinary individuals."

Maggie's line of vision followed that of Fred's. "He really is something special," she agreed.

"I wasn't talking about Nick," said Fred, leveling his gaze on her.

Warm green eyes settled on Fred's face as a slow smile lifted the corners of her mouth. The confirmation had finally arrived. "How could he do anything but succeed with both of us in his corner?"

"It seems I owe you a long overdue apology, Maggie."

Before she could ask Fred for further clarification, Danny and Davey abruptly appeared at her side. She wiped dried ketchup from Davey's cheek and brushed bun crumbs from the front of his shirt.

"Fred, these are our sons Danny and Davey. Guys, this is Fred Naples, an old friend of... mine." A minor omission was often easier than a major explanation.

"My god, Maggie, I'd know them anywhere. They're mini Nicks."

Maggie laughed. "In more ways than you can imagine." She turned to Davey. "Go over there and try to speed things along. Maybe seeing you will remind your dad he didn't arrive alone tonight."

Watching Danny and Davey work their way through the crowd, she asked, "So what have you been doing with yourself?"

"I have my own garage just south of Cedar Lake on Route 41." He reached into his wallet and handed her a business card.

"I'll remember that the next time my car needs work." Never one to carry a purse for the simple reason she hated keeping track of it, she slipped the card into the back pocket of her jeans. "Good mechanics are hard to find and you were always one of the best." She caught a brief glimpse of a picture of two little girls as he shut his wallet. "Are they yours?"

He removed the photo from the plastic sleeve and handed it to Maggie. "Sara's eight and Susan's six," he said with an obvious abundance of love and pride. "They live in Michigan with their mother and step dad," he added on a sadder note. "I don't get to see them as often as I'd like."

"They're beautiful, Fred," she said, returning the photo. "Divorce is never easy but it's always worse when there's children involved." What else could she say? Divorce under any circumstance was not an easy subject to discuss.

He forced a weak smile and shrugged. "Like you said, some of us just aren't cut out for happily ever after."

"It's out there, Fred. It just takes some of us longer to find it."

Maggie smiled, casting a wistful glance in Nick's direction. She couldn't help wondering if there was still a happy ending out there for her.

"I should be going. It looks like Nick's fan club is starting to break up. Tell him I said hello."

Maggie touched his arm. "Why don't you stick around and tell him yourself."

He shook his head. "Another time."

"Goodbye, Fred," she said, hugging him again. "It was wonderful seeing you again." He turned and vanished into the crowd as quickly as he had appeared.

"I'm so sorry about that," Nick apologized. "I was really hoping to avoid that whole scenario tonight."

"Maybe you shouldn't have worn that hat." She waggled her finger at the bright red baseball cap perched on his head with the white embroidered 62 trimmed in black emblazoned across the crown.

"That guy coming toward us is wearing number twenty-four on his shirt and hat but I can say with complete certainty he's not Jeff Gordon." Then he pointed to a teenage girl. "Does she bear any resemblance to Mark Martin?" His last example was a woman in her mid sixties. "And she's most definitely not Dale Junior. And that guy over there—"

"All right, all right," she laughed. "Point taken."

"Now, where were we? Oh, yes, now I remember." He

draped his arm around her shoulder after first pulling hers around his waist. A thrilling chill snaked through her. "There," he said. "That feels about right."

More right than he'd ever know.

"Let's go find a seat in the stands and try to salvage what's left of the evening."

Moving his arm to help her up the bleacher steps, his sleeve button caught on her gold herringbone necklace and snapped the delicate chain before either of them realized what happened.

"Damn, Maggie, I'm sorry." He untangled the broken chain from around the button and slipped it into his shirt pocket. "I'll take it to a jeweler on Monday and have it fixed."

"Don't bother," Maggie chuckled. "It's an inexpensive chain I found at a flea market. It'll cost you more to have it fixed than it's worth."

They had barely situated themselves on the wooden bleacher seats located near turn one when the flagman dropped the checkered flag and the announcer declared it was time for a short break between features. Nick and Maggie turned to each other and started to laugh.

"Hey guys, how about getting us something to drink." He handed them another twenty.

"And popcorn," Maggie added as the boys tromped down the bleacher stairs.

She turned to face him, braced her elbow on her knee and rested her chin on her fist, staring at him with an enigmatic smile.

"What?" he questioned, turning to catch her expression. "What's that look for?"

"Has it sunk in yet? You're famous, Nicky. That mob scene earlier confirmed it."

"Yeah, that was pretty wild, wasn't it?" The pride he held in his elevated status in the racing community was apparent, and rightly so, yet she still detected a hint of wonderment and awe in his voice, too.

"Tell me, how many of them encouraged you to reconsider your retirement?"

He shrugged, dismissing her question. "Oh, one or two maybe."

Knowing he was lying, she smiled and waited.

He tried to stare her down. "All right! I lost count."

Wearing a know-it-all grin, she asked, "And how many of those did you promise to reconsider going back next season?"

"A few." He stared straight ahead, showing undue concentration on the currently unoccupied track. "You don't expect me to remember exact numbers, do you?"

She raised a dubious brow and waited for him to overcome this sudden, however temporary, case of amnesia.

"Thirty-seven," he finally blurted.

She started to laugh and jabbed an elbow into his side. "You just made that up."

He tweaked her nose. "You know me too well, Boomer."

"The last time you did that I seem to recall you getting a punch in the gut for your trouble."

Nick threw back his head and laughed. "Fifteen years old and the feistiest green-eyed hellcat I'd ever met. God, you were adorable!" He reached out and tweaked her nose again. "Still are," he added with a wink.

Curling her fingers into a loose fist, she shook it menacingly in his face. "You're asking for it," she warned with a teasing glint belying her threat.

"So are you." He tilted her chin toward him and kissed her. His lips lingered as his tongue played across her lower lip before he drew away. The brief kiss left her breathless and triggered a myriad of other physical responses she chose not to acknowledge.

"Can it get any better than this?" he exclaimed as he held his arms open wide to embrace the night.

Oh, she could think of a few ways, all of them requiring less clothes and more privacy. She wondered if he was up for a historic reenactment of one of their hot and heavy paw and claw sessions behind the pits or under the bleachers.

He propped his feet on the empty seat in front of him and clasped his hands together, resting his elbows on his knees. Rocking his booted feet on the bleacher board with an eager excitement usually reserved for little kids and puppies, Nick watched the cars coming out of pit row and line up behind the pace car for the next race. His unbridled enthusiasm made her grin.

"I can't stand it." Like a man with an itch he couldn't quite reach, Nick rubbed his palms across his knees in an attempt to distract himself from the real irritation. "I want to climb into one of those cars so badly and take a few hot laps."

She'd lost him. The only history that would be repeating itself tonight was her playing second fiddle to the twenty or so drivers jockeying for first place on that half-mile asphalt track stretched out in front of them.

"You really love it, don't you?"

The look on his face was thoughtful and distant. "Yeah, I do. I don't know what ever made me think I could give it up."

"You've already made your decision, haven't you?"

Without taking his eyes off the track, he nodded. "Yeah."

"When?"

"As soon as I tie up some loose ends around here." He looked at her, settling a curious blue gaze over her. "You okay with that?"

"It's your destiny, Nicky." She forced a smile and touched his cheek with fingertips gone cold.

What was it that Fred said—*Something about Nick in the spotlight and her waiting in the shadows?* What a pity. She was getting used to the warmth of the sun on her face again.

Chapter Thirteen

"I ran into an old friend of yours tonight." Except for the glow of the dash lights the truck's interior was dark and she had difficulty judging his reaction when she said, "Fred Naples."

A Chicago station that featured classic rock was playing "Can't Fight the Feeling" by one of Nick's favorite bands, REO Speedwagon. Drumming his thumbs against the steering wheel with the beat of the tune, he continued singing along with the song.

"Nick? Did you hear me? I said I saw Fred tonight."

"I heard you," he said as he turned down the radio. "I just didn't think it required a response."

"What happened between the two of you?"

"Leave it alone, Maggie. It's ancient history."

"He tried to talk you out of marrying me, didn't he?"

"Did Fred tell you that?" There was something she couldn't identify beneath his even tone.

"No," she answered. "That's not what we talked about."

"What did you talk about?" Now he sounded like a detective giving her the third degree.

"You," she answered. "How well you've done. He met our boys. I saw a picture of his daughters. You know, the usual stuff people talk about when they haven't seen each other for years."

He seemed to relax a little. "Oh," was all he said.

"He did say one thing I thought was a little odd. He said he owned me an apology. Do you know why he'd say something like that?" She needed to hear Nick's version.

"I've no idea," Nick answered.

"You and Fred were closer than a lot of brothers. I'm just trying to understand what happened between the two of you. If it wasn't because of me, then what was it?"

"There's nothing to tell, Maggie." His voice was taut and strained again. "He used to be my friend, now he isn't—end of story. People grow apart, they move on with their lives. That's not so difficult to understand, is it?"

"Maybe you should have listened to him," she said on a quiet note. "You might have saved yourself a lot of grief over the years."

"Hey," he said, pulling off the road. The truck came to a gradual stop on the gravel shoulder. Taking her hand, he brought it to his lips and pressed a kiss to her knuckles. "If given the same choices today, I wouldn't do anything differently." He paused for a moment then added, "Except for the divorce. I wouldn't have given in so easily. In fact, I would have fought like hell to keep you."

He unbuckled his seatbelt and leaned across the console. It wasn't what she would call a passionate kiss. It wasn't even a very long kiss. It was warm and undemanding, and so poignant, tender, and loving. It made Maggie weak and brought tears to her eyes. She was desperate for more.

She licked the place on her lips to savor the lingering taste of him. Staring at him through the darkness, the dashboard lights cast an eerie glow across his solemn face. His expression was unfathomable as he watched her tongue glide across her lips.

Two minutes, three minutes, maybe more ticked away. Time became an inconsequential, useless commodity and served no purpose other than to measure the distance between his sweet kisses. As slow as humanly possible he moved nearer, closing the gap between expectant mouths longing to make the next contact. Closer and closer...

"Are we home yet?" Davey asked from the backseat.

As if a giant hand had snatched him by the collar and yanked him back, Nick snapped into his seat with a bouncing thud. He shifted out of park and pulled away from the side of the road with one hand as he refastened his seatbelt with the other.

Maggie turned away and gazed out the window into the passing darkness, torn between loving him and letting him go again. No woman should have to make these choices a second time.

Just as Nick started pulling into the driveway, Maggie unhooked her seatbelt and stretched across the console to shake Danny and Davey awake. No longer small enough to carry, they needed to make their way into the house under their own power.

The truck's suspension bounced and rocked over the curb, throwing her off balance and pitching her against Nick's shoulder. She had to wonder if it was just her imagination or had he intentionally gunned the engine? In a chivalrous, or was it self-serving, attempt to keep her from hitting the steering wheel, he caught a handful of her backside. His hand lingered a bit too long to be considered a mere steadying gesture but didn't stay quite long enough to be called an intentional grope. She took her time righting herself on the seat and cast him a slow, grateful smile. "Sorry about that," she mumbled.

"I'm not," he said with an appreciative sideward glance and a half-cocked dimpled grin as he got out and flipped the driver's seat forward. "Come on, Dan. You too, Dave." He shook each of their legs to rouse them from their slumber. They clambered from the truck and stumbled up the porch and into the house like a pair of zombies.

Within a matter of minutes Maggie helped the boys out of their no longer new looking shirts and jeans. Tugging the shirt over Davey's uncooperative limp arms and lolling head, she realized how way beyond exhausted he must be because neither one had let her help them get ready for bed in several years, and she welcomed this small opportunity to treat them like her little boys again, if only for this one last time. They were dead to the world before she kissed them goodnight and tucked them under their comforters.

In spite of the fact she had slept a good part of the day she was exhausted too and headed down the hall to her bedroom. She didn't have the slightest idea where Nick had disappeared to and at the moment she was too sleepy to give his whereabouts more than a passing thought.

Half naked and just about to slip a wash-softened nightshirt over her head, Maggie heard a light tap on her door. Before she could respond, Nick opened the door and popped his head in.

"I was just wondering if you still wanted this." The

broken chain dangled from his fingers.

Clutching the pale pink cotton to her chest, Maggie stood motionless in the diffused florescent light shining from the bathroom. It reflected off the vanity mirror and cast chunks of distorted light into the adjoining bedroom. Her pupils dilated to gain further clarity in the shadow-riddled room and finally locked with Nick's in silent acquiescence.

Feeling the pulsing rush of blood coursing through her veins, pounding like thunder in her head, she wondered if the entire afternoon and evening had been merely unmitigated foreplay leading to this suspended moment in time. She tried to swallow and licked her dry lips. Nick in turn sucked his lower lip in response.

His eyes turned to deep, dark, unfathomable pools of undisguised desire. She ached with wanton longing, her skin burned from the internal heat working its way to the surface. Shared breathing grew shallow and labored. The nightshirt slipped from her fingers and landed soundlessly to the plush green carpet as he stepped inside and closed the door with a quick, backward kick of his foot.

Coming together, closing the short distance, they reached out for one another. He cupped her face. His fingers caressed her throat as he smothered her with frantic kisses, demanding and possessive. His breathing hissed through his nostrils. Hers ceased for a time then exploded in a heated rush.

All the while he pressed forward, pushing her back, until the edge of the mattress caught behind her knees and toppled them both. Locked in a crazy tangle of arms and legs they tumbled as one onto the bed. Hasty kisses were biting, and sucking, and bruising. Lips and teeth and tongues sought exposed flesh to tease and taunt and tempt.

Maggie's mind reeled, spiraling to glorious new heights of passion and plunging to desperate depths of denied desire. She didn't think it was possible, but she found herself wanting Nick more at that moment than she ever wanted him in all the years before. There was no turning back.

Although compelled by love, their actions were too

frantic, too urgent, too insistent to be defined as making love. It could not be denied. This was unadulterated sex, consensually reduced to its most primitive form—pure and simple and holistically carnal. Needing this man more than life itself, basic instincts dominated her every move and propelled her toward one goal—possessing him completely and forever.

Desperate fingers tore at her lace panties. Rending the flimsy fabric, he tossed the shredded scraps to the floor. Those magnificent, long-fingered hands tangled in the wavy layers of her hair and tugged her head back to expose the flawless flesh of her slender neck, which he attacked with lips moist and searching on his way to more responsive quarry. Heaving breasts quivered with impatient anticipation for the impending assault. The pale mounds danced and trembled beneath his probing lips. He sucked hard, drawing the nipple into his mouth. A thrilling jolt of arousal shot through her as she dug her heels into the mattress to push herself against him.

He released her nipple and began a slow, teasing journey down her body. Moist lips caressed her sensitive flesh as his tongue licked a wet trail down her belly. Hot breath fanned and tickled the sensitive flesh of her inner thigh on the way to his final destination.

Maggie writhed under his oral ministrations, whimpering softly as he gently sucked and licked. She raked her fingers through his hair, clenching handfuls of the thick locks to pull him into her. He clutched her bottom and pulled her against his mouth as she climaxed, rocking her, drawing her deeper, taking each pulsing quiver her body delivered.

The desperate need to touch him, to feel his warm, naked flesh, had her tearing at the buttons of his shirt and tugging at the tails still tucked into his waistband. He half sat and shrugged off the shirt as she unzipped his jeans and released his erection. She drew her fingers down the length of his thick arousal, eliciting a coarse moan as he kicked off his pants and rolled to position himself over her.

Restless and eager, Maggie shifted beneath him, raising her knees and spreading her thighs to bring him that much closer. She felt him slip easily between her folds to rest at her moist opening. She lifted her hips and felt the slight pressure as he entered. Maggie wanted more, craving the full weight of his body pressing her down, crushing her, consuming her.

His initial thrust came hard, but quickly settled into an unrelenting rhythm of smooth, deep strokes, each one bringing her closer and closer to another orgasm. As suddenly as he began though, he paused and withdrew, leaving her to peer at him through the dimness.

She watched him rise to his knees and brace himself against the mattress with thighs spread wide. He loomed over her, a dark, magnificent shadow, his gaze deep and settling as his hands spanned and gripped her hips. Positioning her thighs, he grasped her tightly and lifted, guiding her body upward until he filled her once again.

She braced her palms against the headboard as she welcomed each driving thrust. Each maddening stroke was met with a sharp, ragged gasp until he brought them to an explosive finish. His hoarse cries of ecstasy mingled with those of her throbbing release.

The deed was accomplished with intensity and expediency, and without a single intelligible word passing between them. The harsh reality of their fierce coupling left them breathless, stunned, and speechless. Shoulder-to-shoulder and hip-to-hip, they lay on the bed and stared at the ceiling distorted with ghostly shadows.

Maggie shut her eyes and listened to the lingering sounds of their breathing returning to normalcy. Long minutes stretched into what seemed like eternity until Nick finally shattered the weighty silence.

"What just happened here?" His hoarse words hovered like a late arriving spirit waiting to be acknowledged.

Maggie stretched and rolled to face him, placing an open palm on his damp chest. "You tell me," she purred. Her hand rose and fell with each heavy breath he took.

"I can't begin to explain it." He motioned with a helpless gesture, as if searching for the right words. "Let alone apologize for it."

She shifted her weight and braced herself on an elbow, gazing at him with confusion pinching her features. "Apologize? For what? You've always been a physically demanding lover. Tonight you were just a little more physical than usual."

"Tonight was different. I acted like some feral beast in heat. You should have smacked me on the nose like you would any other horny dog humping your leg."

The image he conjured made her laugh. She collapsed against him, giggling and snorting at the picture in her head.

"Damn it, Maggie! This isn't funny." He pushed her off and jumped to his feet, all the while finding his clothes and dressing. He found his shirt on the floor and put it on. He paced around the room with obvious agitation. "My behavior scared me. It should have scared you too. I could have hurt you."

Maggie was more frightened by this most recent behavior than anything he had done up until then. Fearful, she studied him, watching every move me made.

He raked a shaky hand through his hair. "What's happening to me, Maggie? I feel like I'm losing control. First I knock Joel on his ass this morning and now this. I've heard about this happening to men who participate in competitive sports and suddenly stop. They can become violent and unpredictable when they don't have an outlet for releasing their aggressions."

She scooted to the end of the bed. "Nicky, listen to me. I know you. You're competitive, not bloodthirsty." She scanned the floor for her abandoned nightshirt and started to tug it over her head. It wasn't easy reasoning with an irrational man while still naked. The nightshirt was ripped from her fingers.

Nick stood and stared at her, his eyes darting from one part of her body to another. The color drained from his face, turning him an awful shade of putrid gray, and made him look like he was going to be physically ill.

She glanced down, worried and wondering what had caused this reaction from him. This was not how she wanted him to find out.

The diffused florescent light from the bathroom caused her own skin to take on an unflattering translucent pallor and emphasized the finger sized bruises that were already starting to dapple the surface of her skin. Faint splotches dotted her arms, hips and shoulders. They looked much worse than they felt and she searched for the words to ease his concern.

He reached out and placed his fingers in the pattern spread across her collarbone. The tenderness in his touch was in such sharp contrast to the raw anguish twisting his features.

"My God, Maggie. It looks like I beat you with a ball peen hammer." His eyes filled with tears and he turned away as if he couldn't bear to look at what he'd done.

Maggie snatched the nightshirt from his fingers and covered herself. "This isn't your fault, Nick. You know how easily I bruise. They look a lot worse than they feel. It's nothing, really." Frantic, she wondered what else she could say to convince him.

"Nothing? You call that nothing?" He choked with raw emotion. He turned his back on her and hung his head.

Maybe a less serious approach was the way to go. "Come on, Nicky, you gotta lighten up," she encouraged. Coming up behind him, she wrapped her arms around his waist. Needing to feel the warmth of his body, she slid her hands under his shirt. Her fingertips slipped into the waistband of his jeans and worked their way around to the front. "Half the fun of sex—especially sex with a familiar partner—is going a little crazy now and then." Her fingers fiddled with the brass button. "If you don't like what we did, then we won't do it again." Pop went the button. She slipped her hand inside his jeans and followed the line of hair down his belly.

"That's what scares me the most." He placed a hand over her wrist to keep her from going any further. "I want to do every bit of it again, and then some."

"Then some, huh?" she purred, pressing her cheek against his back. "Whatcha got in mind?"

He flinched as if he'd been burned. "Damn it, Maggie, this is serious." She backed off and stared at him as if she didn't recognize the man standing in front of her. Now he was beginning to scare her.

One more try—straightforward, no nonsense logic this time. There had to be a way to get it through to him. She looked him straight in the eye. "Regardless of what you seem to think, I was never anything less than a willing partner. My guess is you've got a few bruises, bite marks and scratches on you, too." The way he absently rubbed his chest convinced her she was right. "Looks like I must have a proclivity for violence too?"

"Don't be ridiculous." He touched her cheek with the back of his knuckles. "You're the gentlest person I know."

"How can you say that when you said yourself I punched you in the gut fifteen years ago? That sure sounds like I'm establishing a pattern of violent behavior."

"I appreciate what you're trying to do, but nothing you say is going to change the way I feel about what happened here tonight. There's only one thing left for me to do."

This isn't happening, her mind screamed. She couldn't begin to comprehend how a reasonably intelligent man could reach such unreasonable conclusions? "What is it you think you have to do?"

"Leave," he stated. "I need to walk out that door and—" He winced and rubbed his hand across his forehead. "I can't believe I'm saying this..." he murmured. "...not come back until I'm sure this won't happen again."

Maggie half-laughed. "You can't be serious?"

"Do you know of another way?"

"As a matter of fact, I do. It's a simple little word called *no*."

"Come on, Maggie. Do you really think that would have stopped me?"

Maggie stared at him, disbelief warring with outrage. "You arrogant jackass," she sputtered. "If your dick was half as big as your ego I could die a happy woman."

"Wh...what did you say?" he stammered.

"Do you honestly believe I didn't have a choice in any of this? I've got a big news flash for you, Mister NASCAR Big Shot. You ain't all that! So go ahead and walk out of here believing you're doing this for my sake. Just don't expect to find me waiting with open arms when you finally decide it's *safe* to come back." Push was swiftly approaching shove, and Maggie was ready to shove with all her might.

"That's a risk I have to take."

Damn it, he was calling her bluff! "But I'm not." She

gripped his forearm and felt the muscles tense beneath her fingers as he tried to pull away. But she held on, desperate to make him understand. "No, Nick, not this time. Not again. I've risked too much already. If there's any hope of making this work between us we have to stop making these decisions about what's best for each other and start thinking about what's best for *us*."

"What do you mean *again*?" His words were slow and precise, and his tone was chilling as he pried her hand from his arm. "Tell me, Maggie. What have you done? What decision did you make for me?"

She was a coward—a lily-livered, yellow bellied, spineless jellyfish of a coward. She was just a heartbeat away from clamping her mouth shut and not saying another word. Her hands trembled and she clenched them at her side in an effort to steady the tremors.

Nick gripped her by the shoulders. "Tell me, Maggie. What did you do?"

One heartbeat, two, three, four..." She held out longer than she thought she would. "Nothing." She shook her head against his demand. "Nothing," she repeated. "I haven't done anything."

"Fine. Have it your way." Five heartbeats, six, seven... Nick walked out the door, and possibly her life, before her heart had reached the count of ten.

Chapter Fourteen

Whenever there was a problem Maggie wanted to avoid, ignore, or just plain pretend didn't exist, she focused her energies on one of three things: cooking, cleaning, or quilting. In the span of one week the house sparkled from bedrooms to basement, inside and out, she had a freezer stuffed with casseroles, cookies and muffins, and in her workroom there was a special order king-sized quilt top ready for final assembly.

The problem? Nick, of course. It was always Nick. It would forever be Nick. On the super highway of life, Nick was her bump in the road. She might as well have stayed married to him for all the trouble he still caused.

In between the cooking and the cleaning and the quilting, she taught two mid-morning beginner classes at the community center and one in her studio. In her spare time she kept Danny and Davey focused on the straight and narrow—do your homework, clean your room, pick up your clothes, make your bed, take a shower, take out the garbage, mow the lawn, tote that barge, lift that bale, etc. etc. etc. It had gotten to the point where they tried to run and hide whenever she called their names.

They could run, but they couldn't hide, and Maggie entered the family room late one Friday afternoon in search of her sons to find out what they wanted for their movie night dinner. What she found was a room that looked like a hurricane had blown through. Couch cushions were set askew, half empty soda cans and wadded candy wrappers sat on the coffee table next to a tumbled stack of PlayStation disks and DVD movies. How could this have happened from the time they got home from school to now? Maggie shook her head and sighed as she began picking up the mess.

The DVD disk on top was simply labeled, *Chapparelle POV Promo Video*. Although she hadn't paid much attention to the small padded envelope when it arrived in the mail addressed to the boys, she did recall Davey mentioning something or other about a promotional video Nick had made. This was apparently the copy he'd sent to them.

Propelled by a powerful curiosity, Maggie slipped the disk into the player. Lowering herself to the floor, she crossed her legs Indian fashion to watch the television up close as her sons often did.

The helmet cam showed everything from the driver's point of view, as if the viewer were sitting in the cockpit of the racecar. She'd seen camera views from inside cars before—it was pretty standard for every racecar these days—but this was practically virtual reality with its awesome enhancements. It was an incredible experience. She felt like she was the one flipping the starter and ignition switches and giving the crew a thumb's up sign as the car sparked to life with a mighty rumble as it settled into a powerful thundering roar.

"Let's rock this house!" Nick shouted in what had become his signature battle cry as he pulled away. To the high-energy tune of Billy Idol's "Rebel Yell", Nick's hand shifted through the gears as the car accelerated. Fighting 700 plus horsepower with experienced gloved hands gripping the wheel, he whipped around tight, bank-hugging curves and flew like the wind down the straightaway, the signage and empty stands whizzed past in a streaking blur. A view of the speedometer showed speeds in excess of one-ninety. It was over in the time it took the song to play, and then Nick was pulling into pit row and climbing out of the driver's side window. Tugging off his helmet, he tucked it under one arm and smiled into the camera. Her heart and stomach did a little flip flop two-step at the sight of those damn dimples and devastating blue eyes.

"If you think that looked like fun, you ought to try it in bumper to bumper traffic."

A clip of actual race footage zipped across the screen in a blazing streak of brilliant colors and thundering vrooms, zooms and roars.

The colorful NASCAR logo streaked across the screen before it went black.

Maggie stared at the blank screen for an

interminable length of time, her reflection glaring back from the glassy surface. He walked out on her. She was all but ready to take him back, try again, open her heart, but he made the choice to leave this time. If it hadn't been for his reasons, it would have been for hers if she'd confessed her years of deception. Either way, he'd be gone.

Pushing herself off the floor, she busied herself with the part of her life she could control. She headed to the kitchen for a rag and bottle of furniture polish.

There was another part of her self-prescribed busy life she couldn't quite get a grip on—that annoying space between bedtime and dawn. If she wasn't lying awake staring at the ceiling with erotic images swirling in her head she was sound asleep dreaming about them. There were times it got so bad that she couldn't distinguish between the two. Every night for a week she woke up almost as tired as she went to bed.

The next morning wasn't any different and she wondered how much longer she could go on like that. Still sleepy and yawning, she wandered barefoot down the carpeted stairs in a long pink robe. She needed coffee.

"Where do you two think you're going?" Maggie asked her sons who stood dressed and ready to make a getaway out the front door. She couldn't imagine where they were going at seven o'clock on a Saturday morning and told them as much.

"Dad's taking us to the go-kart track," Danny answered. He glanced anxiously past his brother to the outside.

"And when exactly were you planning on telling me about this?"

"We thought you were still asleep. We left you a note."

"A note?" she reiterated. "When did we start communicating through notes around here?"

"We didn't want to disturb you."

"Or ask if our chores were done," Davey mumbled under his breath. He received a scathing look and an elbow in the ribs from his brother.

"*Are* your chores done?" Maggie asked.

"Aw, Mom," Danny exclaimed with obvious exasperation. "You're killing us with all this cleaning. You gotta start talking to dad again!"

"What does one have to do with the other?" She tucked a straggly lock of hair behind her ear and crossed her arms.

He tossed his hands in the air in order to stress the frustration that was clearly written across his youthful features. "All this cleaning isn't normal, Mom. Our friends' rooms smell like the boys' locker room at school."

"You want your room to smell like stinky gym socks and overactive sweat glands?" Was she missing something? There had to be more to it.

"No, but we don't want it smelling like Pledge and Pine Sol all the time either."

"Then tell me what it is you want, Danny." Maggie was trying very hard to understand.

"Stop fighting with Dad. Talk to him."

"Your father and I are not fighting." If the truth were known, she wasn't sure what her current standing was with Nick. She hadn't seen or spoken to him since the night they all went to Illiana. She hadn't even mentioned his name to Danny or Davey. In fact, she'd been trying very hard not to, but he obviously didn't have any trouble discussing her with their sons.

"That's not how he tells it," Danny grumbled. His tone was coated with resentment.

It was bound to come to this sooner or later. It wasn't enough that they looked just like their father, they were now starting to think and act like him too. Damn the man for having such dominate genes!

"I see," was all she said. He and his father obviously shared similar points of view. There wasn't a thing she could do to change that.

Hearing the slamming of a vehicle door, she seriously considered bidding her sons a fond farewell and making a hasty exit while she still had the chance. Confronting Nick was more than she wanted to deal with this early in the morning.

Too late, she realized. The opportunity to retreat had slipped away. The front door swung open and in walked Nick. Visibly perturbed at having been left waiting at the curb, he faced Danny and Davey and asked impatiently, "What's the hold up, guys? Are we going or not?"

Finally noticing her standing at the foot of the stairs, he glanced at her for just a moment, his expression bland and unreadable. Not so much as hello passed his lips before he returned his attention to his sons.

"Mom was just asking about our Saturday chores," Davey explained.

"Is there anything they have to do that can't wait?" Nick questioned, obviously annoyed that it was she who was holding up the show.

"No," she said. She tightened her arms across her chest, her fingers clenched into fists of angry helplessness. Nick was behaving with the same level of hostility as when she had first asked for the divorce. She didn't like dealing with it then any more than she liked dealing with it now. "They're free to go."

The boys slumped with relief.

"You hear that, guys? Let's hit the road." Nick hustled them out in a manner that suggested he was afraid she'd change her mind.

"Have them back no later than two. They have basketball practice at the school gym at two thirty."

I'll see that they get there."

"Fine." She spun around and started toward the kitchen.

Just as he was about to pull the door shut behind him, he hesitated, then turned and said, "You know, it didn't have to be like this, Maggie."

She sighed. "Maybe *this* is all we have left."

His features softened. "You don't really believe that, do you?"

"There are a lot of things I used to believe in that I don't anymore. But, for what it's worth, Nick, I never stopped believing in you."

He choked a coarse laugh. "You sure have a funny way of showing it."

Chapter Fifteen

The invitation proclaimed, *Big Fun Will Be Had By All*! Maggie never doubted it for a minute.

Jen and Ken Walker's parties were legendary. Two or three times a year, depending on their mood or whenever inspiration struck, they hosted spectacular neighborhood bashes. Their themed shindigs went far beyond the typical block party. The invitation Maggie held in her hand was for the Walker's first annual Feast of the Harvest Moon Celebration scheduled for the third Saturday in October—although she couldn't recall there ever being a second annual anything.

The Walker's made sure everyone was included in the evening's festivities. The grownups were invited to a sumptuous, dress-up, adults-only backyard barbeque, weather permitting of course, and all around merrymaking affair. The older children would be whisked away by a horse drawn hay wagon for a supervised overnight campout in nearby Cartwright Woods. The younger kids were ensconced in another neighbor's family room for a games, movies and crafts-filled sleepover.

She had always enjoyed the Walkers' parties in the past, they were the talk of Cartwright Corners for weeks after the event, but this year it actually crossed her mind not to attend. She wasn't sure if she could muster enough genuine enthusiasm to carry her through an entire evening of *Big Fun*.

Not that she had any choice. It wasn't a matter whether she wanted to go or not. She had to go. Fun loving as they were, the Walkers had one very strict, unyielding rule: No children were allowed to attend the planned activities unless their parents attended too. Since turning twelve, Danny and Davey were now classified into the older kids category. They would never forgive her if they had to miss the campout because she was a party pooper.

Maggie tossed the rest of the mail onto the counter and picked up the phone to RSVP. No sense in putting it off.

"Walker Residence," Six-year-old Shanna Walker answered. "Who's calling please?" Precocious as she sounded answering the phone, Maggie knew differently. Shanna had Down's syndrome. She was sweet and loving and the protected darling of Cartwright Corners. Maggie adored the little girl and Shanna returned the affection in triplicate.

"Hi, Shanna Banana!"

"Maggie!"

"May I speak to your mom, please?"

"Sure. She's right here. We're making cookies."

"You are? What kind?"

"Chocolate chip."

"Yum. My favorite!" Maggie enthused.

"Me too!" Shanna wholeheartedly concurred.

"Will you save me one?"

"I will save you two."

"Thank you, Miss Shanna."

"Here's my mom."

"Hi, Maggie," said Jen Walker. "You'd better not be calling to tell me you're not coming to the party."

"Why would I do that?" Maggie asked half-laughing.

"Oh, nothing," Jen hedged. "So I can check you off as a yes? Are you bringing a date?"

"Whoa, not so fast. Something made you think I might decline. Out with it." Maggie heard Jen expel a long, slow breath. In spite of their twenty years age difference, Jen and Maggie had been close friends since the beginning of their friendship. Jen was everything her own mother wasn't.

"Well, Ken ran into Nick at Home Depot a few days ago, they got to talking, one topic led to another and once the subject of the party came up Ken felt obligated to send Nick an invitation. We'd been wrestling with this dilemma for weeks."

"Jen," Maggie tried to interrupt.

"God knows we've had our share of divorces in the neighborhood, spouses have come and gone over the years, but this is a first for Cartwright Corners. We've never had divorced spouses living in different houses in the neighborhood."

"Jen," she tried again with no better luck than the first time. She gave up, knowing Jen would eventually need to come up for air.

"It's not that we don't like Nick or anything like that, but you're like a daughter to us and we've never gotten to know Nick as well as you." She finally stopped and took a breath, giving Maggie a chance to jump in.

"Hey, why wouldn't Nick be invited? He is part of the neighborhood again and has just as much right to be there as I do."

"Well, I just hope it won't be too awkward for you."

In all honesty, the thought that Nick would be there had never crossed Maggie's mind, though she couldn't imagine why it hadn't. Probably because he hadn't attended more than one or two in the years he lived there before. He was rarely home on weekends during racing season. Then again, the last neighborhood party they'd had the opportunity to attend together would have overshadowed any other occasion with all the blackness of a total solar eclipse. She shuddered just thinking about it.

"It's unlikely he'll show up anyway. He only likes crowds when they're cheering him across the finish line."

"He's coming. He hasn't officially RSVP'd yet, but according to Ken, Nick sounded pretty enthusiastic about coming."

"I understand your hesitancy in having us both at one of your parties again. Maybe I should sit this one out and let Nick be the Chapparelle representative this time."

"Don't be ridiculous! I'll uninvite him myself if that's what it takes to get you here."

"I can't speak for Nick, there's no predicting what he's capable of lately, but you have my solemn word that I'll be on my best behavior."

"Really, Maggie, that's not what—"

Maggie interrupted. "If I thought for one minute that there would be a problem I'd be the first to tell you. The last thing I want to do is traumatize your fish again."

Jen chuckled. "You're amazing, you know that. Not many ex-wives would be as understanding."

"Yeah, that's me, Maggie the Amazing," she said.

"Able to overcome tall exes in a single bound."

"So, back to my original question, are you bringing a date?"

"I hadn't given it any thought, but, yeah, sure. I'll bring somebody." Maybe she could convince Joel to be her escort.

As if reading Maggie's thoughts, Jen said, "Why don't you bring that adorable widower friend of yours? Rumor has it that his SUV has been seen in your driveway pretty often lately."

"So glad to hear the neighborhood grapevine is still alive and thriving," Maggie chuckled.

"I'm doing my level best," Jen tossed back with a throaty laugh. "Listen Maggie, I gotta go. The oven timer is going off and Shanna is starting to put on the oven mitts. See you. Bye!"

What an interesting development. Nick was going to the Walker's party. This would be the first time they would be attending the same social function in years and the first time for anything remotely resembling togetherness in weeks. True to his word, Nick had stayed away, severing all contact with her and leaving her wondering what exactly he thought he was accomplishing by doing so. He kept in touch with the boys, and, when he wasn't working on the house, he made a real effort to spend time with them. If nothing else, the evening would be, to say the very least, interesting.

In spite of her denial to the contrary, Jen had every reason to be concerned, Maggie reasoned, remembering the last time she and Nick had attended one of the Walker's parties. She could recall every detail as if the event in question had taken place just the day before. The memory unfolded in her mind like a bad movie.

Arriving home unexpectedly, Nick showed up the morning of the Walker's Midsummer Night's Party after a longer than usual stretch away from home. He'd won his last race in the Busch Grand National the previous week and had just finalized negotiations for a lucrative contract with a major sponsor. While he was riding high on the crest of victory and financial independence, eight and a half months pregnant, Maggie was water retentive and raging on pre-natal hormones, and he had the audacity to call her his beautiful wife the minute he'd walked through the door.

Poor Nick never saw it coming and any attempts on his part to appease her only infuriated her more. Their bickering escalated throughout the day and by the time they'd arrived at the Walkers they were barely civil and hardly speaking. In retrospect, Maggie later realized that not speaking would have been the better course of action. But neither of them knew when to quit or keep their mouths shut.

It was an offhanded, alcohol induced crack she'd overheard Nick make to Ken Walker in reference to the theme of the evening's party that pushed swollen-ankled, big-bellied Maggie right over the edge.

"Our neighborhood is turning into a regular Shakespearean Festival," he'd said. "You've got *A Midsummer Night's Dream* over here while we're in final rehearsal for *Taming of the Shrew* at my house." Nick found himself floating on his back in the middle of the Walker's backyard Koi pond.

The sad part, Maggie realized, was they weren't on any better terms four years later. Not more than a dozen words had passed between them whenever their paths happened to cross over the past weeks. It wasn't that she went out of her way to avoid him; she just never made any effort to be around him either. Most of what she learned about Nick came from information gleaned from conversations with the boys.

Maggie insistently told herself she'd manage to get through one night with him around. She was Maggie the Amazing, after all. Besides it wasn't like they were going to be alone, which was when they seemed to get into the most trouble. There would be dozens of people at this function. What could possibly go wrong? Similar words were probably spoken before the launch of the Titanic too.

She could handle it. She could handle it. She could handle it. If she repeated the mantra long and hard enough she might actually start believing it.

She missed him dreadfully, more so than the first time they separated, probably because it was Nick who initiated the severance this time. Confused beyond rational thought, she couldn't predict what might happen or when. Maybe it was time to extend the olive branch she had just completed—a king sized quilt she'd made for his birthday which was just a few days away. Tonight might be a good time to deliver it, she decided. The boys were going to a preseason Chicago Bulls game with Ken Walker and his sons.

Chapter Sixteen

"Bye, Mom." Davey kissed his mom as he headed out the door to the waiting van in the driveway.

"Behave," she warned, catching a kiss on the run from her other son. She stood on the porch and hugged herself to keep warm as she watched her sons climb into the back of the Walker's van.

The van pulled away and, after watching the taillights fade, she turned and scurried into the house. In a habit she had developed in the weeks that followed Nick buying the Cartwright house, she automatically glanced up the street before closing the door. Only this time she paused longer than was her custom. Except for one small amber-toned light glowing from an upstairs window and the gas lit lamppost that flickered near the front porch, there was nothing much else that would indicate anyone lived there.

Maybe he wasn't home, she reasoned, as if looking for an excuse not to go. No, she argued. If he wasn't home she'd just keep going back until he was. It was time to break the silence.

Maggie approached the wide wrap-around porch of the sprawling Craftsman style bungalow with a nervous stomach. Mindful of keeping it from dragging on the ground, her fingers curled around the handles of the over-sized, tissue paper and ribbon curls embellished gift bag. Suffering from serious second thoughts, unsure how well this unexpected visit would be received, it crossed her mind that maybe she should just leave the package and go. She was about to set the bag by his front door and make a hasty getaway when the heavy oak door swung open, freezing her in her tracks.

"Hi, Maggie," Nick greeted from the doorway.

No man should be allowed to look that good in his stocking feet, loose-fit jeans, and a baggy sweatshirt. A mug of something looking like hot cocoa or milky coffee was clutched in one hand as he held the door open with the other.

"I was wondering when you were going to pay me a visit. Come on in." He stood aside and waved her into the entryway with the hand gripping the stoneware mug. "Your timing is perfect. Ordinarily you'd find me up to my elbows in paint stripper but I'm treating myself to a night off before I start my next project."

Maggie stood in the huge entry hall and looked around. She was astonished. What a remarkable transformation since the first day she'd cringed and shivered in the gloomy, dark foyer. It was now cozy and warm and beautiful.

All the wood, and there was massive quantities of it, had been stripped and refinished. The rich patinas of the varying wood tones gleamed and glowed from the painstaking care it had obviously received, mostly from Nick's skillful hands according to their sons.

"I'm amazed at what you've accomplished in such a short time." Amber stained glass sconces fanned rays of soft light upward to the grid-beamed ceilings and bathed the entire entry in a warm golden ambiance.

"I contracted out the really difficult jobs like the plumbing and re-wiring to the experts. I just did some of the refinishing." He placed the mug on the floor. "Let me take your coat."

Maggie set down the bag and let Nick slip her jacket from her shoulders. Having nowhere else to put it, he draped it over the banister on top of his own Sherpa-lined denim jacket.

"I know better," she said. "I've seen your lights burning late into the night too many times these past weeks to believe that."

"Guilty," he admitted. "It's been fun working with my hands on something other than a car. You might even say it's been a labor of love."

"Well, it shows." She was genuinely impressed.

He eyed the bag at her feet and asked," What've you got there?"

"Oh! I completely forgot the reason I came over. This is for you." She picked up the bag and handed it to Nick. "I know it's a little early, but happy birthday."

"You remembered?" He sounded truly surprised.

She smiled. "Of course."

"Thank you," he said, clearing his throat. "Let's go into the living room."

The living room appeared to be almost finished, but except for a couple of sheet-covered chairs and a very old inlaid occasional table situated between them, it was a blank canvas waiting to be brought to life with color, form and design. Maggie's mind reeled with possibilities but bit her tongue to keep from making unsolicited decorating suggestions as she eyed the pitiful little grouping arranged around the massive wood and stone fireplace. The few pieces of furniture did absolutely nothing to deaden the echo of her footsteps across the beautifully refinished thick planked flooring.

The built-in bookshelves flanking the fireplace glowed rich and warm under the artificial lamplight. There was, however, a big screen television off to the side against one wall, presently with the sound muted. The cast of a popular reality show looked even more ridiculous than usual going through their antics in silence.

Nick picked up the remote and turned it off. "Can I get you something? Coffee, tea?"

She gestured toward the mug on the table. "I'll have whatever you've got there."

"One double mocha hot chocolate coming right up." He placed the gift bag next to the chair that was obviously the one he preferred. "Have a seat, I'll be right back."

TV? Hot chocolate? Maggie was to say the least a little surprised by this side of Nick. In all the years she'd lived with him, this domestic homebody was relatively new and unexpected. When they were married he'd always been so busy, dashing from one commitment to another, he never had time to just relax and watch mindless television. But from all outward appearances, he seemed to adapt remarkably well to the role. A wave of sadness washed over her. Where was this man when she was married to him?

Instead of immediately sitting, Maggie found herself wandering around the room, stepping around ladders and tarps, admiring the defining Craftsman architecture. It was a beautiful house and Nick was faithfully maintaining its original integrity. She passed through the wood pillared archway into the dining room and discovered a tilted drafting table holding a set of blueprints. Flipping through them she came across the architect's color rendition of the kitchen. She was surprised by what she saw.

When they'd built the two-story house she currently lived in she was too young and inexperienced to know what she really wanted. Over the years she'd mentioned features she would add or omit if given the opportunity to design another kitchen. The drawing she stared at was her dream kitchen, right down to the stained glass-paneled doors on the built-in china cabinet and greenhouse window over the sink. She wasn't sure if she should be jealous or flattered. In truth, she was a little of both. Letting the pages drop from her fingers, she moved away and returned to the living room.

Maggie sat on the edge of the seat and folded her hands in her lap. She felt ill at ease and dreadfully uncomfortable. Staring into space, she wondered if coming here had been a mistake. She could just as easily have sent Danny and Davey over with the gift. No, she told herself, she needed to get beyond this and learn to accept Nick's new life.

So absorbed in her thoughts, she didn't hear Nick reenter. Beautifully polished hardwood floors made no sound when walked across in stocking feet. He placed the mug on the table beside her and took his seat.

"Thank you," she said politely, lifting the mug. She carefully sipped the steaming hot cocoa and said, "Mmmm, it's good. What's your secret?"

"Alpine Maiden and hot water," he answered evenly.

"My favorite," she said with a little grin, sipping from the mug again. "What happened to your going back to racing and finishing out the season?"

He shrugged. "I decided to wait and start up again next year. Mandy's keeping me busy," he paused, and then added, "You know, PR stuff."

"It must be difficult to stay away from something you love so much." What she said didn't strike her until the words dangled between them like a yellow caution flag. She wasn't certain if she meant racing or Mandy, but she wasn't about to clarify her statement or ask him to make the distinction. For her, it was more than difficult to keep her distance; it was impossible. She realized that now. She'd never be able to stay away from him completely and resigned herself to the fact that although it might not always be in the manner she wanted, he would always be a part of her life in one way or another.

He looked at her strangely, his eyes narrow and sad. "Yeah, but I'm learning to adjust."

"Are you going to open that?" She gestured with a jerk of her chin toward the gift bag.

Maggie couldn't help smiling as she watched Nick begin the inquisitive process of lifting out the multi-layers of artfully arranged sheets of pastel tissue paper and corkscrew ribbons to get to the carefully folded, tissue wrapped gift inside. His exuberant, childlike expressions twisted Maggie's heart and made her realize she wouldn't have missed this for anything. It was also then she noticed he wasn't wearing his wedding band anymore, not even on his right hand. The tan mark was still visible and seemed to make the ring's absence even more glaringly apparent. Just one more thing, she told herself, to mark the end of their relationship.

He placed the bundle on his lap and slowly peeled the layers of tissues to reveal the prize beneath. "Oh," he breathed, lifting the magnificent quilt by the top edge to allow it to fall open before his eyes.

Maggie waited and watched, looking for some sign as to what he thought about the gift. Nick's earlier statement came to mind. Though heart wrenchingly bittersweet, this, too, had been a labor of love.

"I don't know what to say, Maggie. I'm overwhelmed." His voice was still gripped with untold emotion. "It's exquisite."

"The colors and design were inspired by the stained glass window in the master bedroom," she pointed out in case he couldn't tell.

He nodded. "Yes, I can see that. But I don't understand how? You've never been upstairs."

"That not quite true," she confessed. "I bribed the workmen with a batch of chocolate chip peanut butter cookies one day when you weren't here so I could come in and take some pictures to work from. I've admired that window from a distance for years. I always thought the pattern would translate well into a quilt."

"And you were right." Clutching the quilt to his chest, he leaned forward and brushed a kiss across her cheek. His lips lingered, his chocolaty breath a warm caress. "Thank you so much," he whispered hoarsely in her ear. Returning to his seat he added, "Now all I need is a bed to put it on."

"What have you been sleeping on?"

"One of those inflatable beds. I needed something that was easy to move from room to room. It's actually pretty comfortable. Of course, there were some nights I was so exhausted I could have fallen asleep on the kitchen floor."

"Are you planning on hiring anyone to help decorate the place?"

"I've been meaning to talk to you about that."

"I know of a couple really good decorators in the area. I'll be happy to give you their names and numbers."

"What I'd really like is for you to help me pick out the furniture for the house."

"Why me? I'm not an interior designer."

"But you know my tastes and I trust your judgment. I could really use your help."

Her answer came without pause. "I'm sorry, Nick. I can't."

He shrugged. "I understand. It was just a thought."

"I really should be going." She placed her mug on the table as she stood.

"I'll get your coat," he offered.

Maggie wanted to cry. All this beauty surrounding him, so much of it because of his talents and abilities, yet he was obviously not a happy man. His hands lingered on her shoulders as he helped her into her jacket.

"Jen tells me you're going to their party next week," she said as she slowly buttoned her coat.

"Yeah, it's been a long time since I've been to one of their bashes. It sounds like it might be fun."

"I'll be seeing you there then," she said.

"You can count on it," he said.

They reached for the front door handle together, their

hands touching briefly before Nick pulled his away as if he'd been burned. His fingers flexed and curled against his thigh.

Her chest tightened and she choked a hoarse, "Good night," as she stepped onto the porch.

He leaned his shoulder against the doorjamb, hands in his jean pockets and one stockinged foot on top of the other. "Good night, Mags. Thanks again for the quilt."

"You're welcome," she returned as she hurried down the stairs and across the flagstone walkway. She could feel his eyes following her. She had to tell him—give him another reason to hate her.

Chapter Seventeen

The day of the party arrived with sunshine and optimism, two things of which Maggie could never get enough. When it rained two days straight earlier in the week, she'd had her doubts. Then she awoke to sunshine streaming into her bedroom window and she actually found herself looking forward to the evening's festivities.

She wasn't yet ready to entertain the notion that her growing enthusiasm had anything to do with the fact that Nick was going to be there. But somewhere, sometime between finding out he was on the guest list and getting ready for the evening, Maggie had managed to purchase two new outfits, both of which were lying on her bed under careful consideration.

Standing in bra and panties and nibbling on a hunk of chocolate broken from the king sized Hershey bar lying on the dresser, Maggie cast a deliberating eye on the rich cranberry velveteen pantsuit and pale silver gray silk ruffled blouse. The other garment was a simply designed little black dress made of butter-soft ultra suede.

The suit was certainly more practical considering the event was partly outdoors; but the dress was sexier. Decisions, decisions, decisions. She helped herself to another piece of chocolate.

Her hair was finished. She'd tamed it into a sleek French twist, leaving just a few curling tendrils to frame and soften her face. She was showered, powdered, polished and perfumed, and she kept her makeup to lipstick, blush and mascara.

She reached for her robe when she heard the doorbell and Danny holler, "Mom, it's for you."

Prompt as usual, she thought, casting a quick glance at the bedside clock. Maybe Joel could offer his opinion, or better still, make the decision for her.

"Tell him to come up," she hollered. "I need his help." She hurried into the walk-in closet to get the pumps she planned on wearing with each outfit. Naturally one of the pairs she needed was in a box on the bottom of the stack piled four high on the upper closet shelf. Catching her fingertips under the lip of the lid, she carefully eased the stack forward.

"Looking for help in or out of something?"

She startled at the sound of his voice. The stack teetered and toppled forward, pitching the boxes and their contents all around her head. "Nick!" she exclaimed, annoyed but unharmed. "You're not the help I was expecting."

"Obviously," he drawled.

Kicking the mess out of her way, she found both pairs of shoes then kneeled down to pick up and re-box the rest. "What are you doing here?" she asked.

"Just thought I'd walk over to the party with you, if that's okay."

"Sure, we can go as soon as Joel gets here," she answered, rubbing a stubborn scuffmark with her thumb from the heel of one of the pumps.

Catching her first glimpse of him, her jaw dropped and she stopped dead in her tracks. When was the last time she had seen him dressed like this? Never, she realized. Jeans and tee shirts were his usual everyday garb, with an occasional western cut shirt or sweater replacing the tee when he felt like dressing up. She also recalled seeing him in casual khakis and sport shirts on rare occasion. But never had she ever seen him decked out like this. Even when they got married it was a hasty affair at the local Justice of the Peace with them both in jeans and sneakers. Inauspicious from the very beginning, she realized.

"You look real nice," she croaked, unable to take her eyes off of him. He looked like he'd just stepped off the cover of G.Q. He wore pleated chocolate brown flannel slacks and a fitted matching silk shirt left open at the collar with a tan leather sports jacket. Perfectly polished brown leather loafers peered out from beneath the tailored trouser legs. He was the picture of elegant sophistication and success. How far he'd come from the Newton County good ol' boy she'd fallen in love with half her lifetime ago.

She couldn't help wondering how long it would be before he traded in his heavy-duty 4X4 kick-ass pick-up for a sleek foreign sports car to go with this new image, and new life.

"You like?" he asked, strutting around the room and striking an overly expansive model's pose. "Mandy hooked me up with a fashion stylist when we stopped over in New York on our way back from St. Croix."

Shopping? Mandy got him to go shopping? No wonder he took the boys to the mall. He'd had previous experience.

Casting a critical eye at her comfortable but hardly stylish terrycloth bathrobe, he commented, "Wish I could say the same about your outfit."

"Then use some of your newly acquired fashion sense and tell me what to wear." She gestured toward the bed.

Without hesitation, he made his selection. "Black dress. Definitely. You've got great legs, might as well show them off."

"Dress it is!" She grabbed it from the bed and headed for the bathroom. When she came out she turned her back to him for his assistance with the zipper.

"It's a little snug, don't you think?" he observed, exerting additional pressure on the zipper tab as he tugged it past her waist and up her back.

"It is not!" she hotly denied, whirling too face him. "It's supposed to fit this way."

His eyes grew enormous. "Damn, Maggie! What kind of pushup bra are you wearing?"

"What do you mean?" she asked glancing down at the low cut sweetheart neckline. Not bad. Not bad at all, she had to admit. She definitely appeared fuller than normal and the cut of the neckline only helped emphasize the additional cleavage. Just one of the advantages of her current condition, she reasoned, wondering how much longer she could hide it. She was already pushing her luck and told herself she had to tell Nick soon before it became all too obvious.

"I've told you before that I know every inch of that body and I know for a fact that those are not all yours!" He eyed her narrowly.

"Don't be ridiculous," she admonished, reaching into

her jewelry chest. Pulling out a half-dollar sized black onyx heart on a silver rope chain, she clasped it around her throat. The point of the heart fell just shy of where the cleavage began. She slipped smaller black onyx hearts on French wires through the rarely used holes in her lobes. The only time she wore earrings anymore was when she got dressed up, and those occasions grew fewer and farther apart. She was nothing but a homebody at heart and it wouldn't bother her one iota if she never got dressed up again.

"I've put on a few extra pounds, that's all. Though I must say, it's not very nice of you to notice."

Transferring the black suede three inch heels to one hand, she snatched an oversized gold, fringed challis shawl from the dresser drawer and draped it over one shoulder. The shoes, however, would not be slipped into until she got downstairs. High heels and stairs were a dangerous combination for Maggie and she avoided putting the two together whenever possible. "Now let's get out of here before you say anything else I'm going to regret."

Nick chuckled and Maggie frowned.

"I wonder what's keeping Joel. He's usually Mr. Punctuality," she commented as she paced the foyer. "I'd better call," she said, reaching for the phone.

"Maggie!" Joel said sounding excited and breathless. "I was just about to call you. I've had some trouble with my car. The police are here now."

"Why would you call the police for car trouble?" she questioned, sounding confused, yet knowing there had to be more to the story.

"I do when it's vandalism. Three nails, three tires. Coincidence? I think not."

"Nails?" she questioned, turning to gaze at Nick. He was goofing with the boys at the bottom the stairs and wasn't paying the least bit of attention to her or her conversation with Joel.

"Yeah, those big spike-like things used in construction. The police suspect kids from school. I'm going to be late if I make it at all. I'm really sorry, Maggie. I know you were counting on me to create a buffer between you and Nick tonight."

"It's not your fault. Keep me posted."

Walking with the boys down the street to the Walkers, she cast suspicious sideward glances at Nick the whole time she related Joel's situation.

"That's awful," said Nick, sounding genuinely regretful. "Who'd have ever thought a principal's job could be so hazardous."

Maggie stopped and placed a halting hand on Nick's forearm. Waiting long enough for Danny and Davey to get far enough ahead so as not to let them overhear what she was about to say, she turned to face Nick and whispered, "If I find out you had anything to do with this, so help me, Nick. I'll personally turn you into the police."

"You think I did that to Joel's tires?" He held up one hand and covered his heart with the other. "I swear to God, Maggie, I had nothing to do with it. Messing with a man's car is not my style."

"Well, you can't blame me for suspecting you. You did threaten him once." She began walking again.

"I offered sound advice," Nick corrected, placing a guiding hand on the small of her back as they stepped off the sidewalk into the street.

"Oh, and let's not forget the time you tackled him at his front door."

"That wasn't a tackle, it was more of a jostle."

"Call it whatever you want, I still wouldn't put this past you."

"Your faith in me is under whelming, Maggie," he replied on a droll note. "Besides, I've gotten to know the guy since then. I like him. He's okay."

"Oh, one more thing," she said, stopping again. They were just coming up to the Walker's driveway. "I promised Jen I would behave myself tonight. I hope she can expect the same from you."

"Considering the two biggest contributing factors from that night's fiasco are no longer part of the equation, I feel relatively comfortable in agreeing to that."

"Contributing factors?"

"One," he said, holding up an index finger. "We're no longer married." A second finger joined the first. "And two, you're not pregnant. Since marital disharmony and raging hormones are a volatile combination, elimination of them significantly reduces the risks of anything like that happening again."

She hated it when he was right, well, at least half right, but she was willing to give the handsome devil his due. "When you're right, you're right, Nick." She smiled at him sweetly. "And this time you're absolutely right."

"You're agreeing with me?"

"Does that surprise you?"

"Worries me is more like it."

"Hey, you two, the party's over here." Maggie and Nick turned their heads in unison. They discovered Ken Walker plus more than a dozen neighbors watching them.

"And so is the pond!" A disembodied voice added from the back of the crowd.

"Smile, Nick," she said, forcing a tight smile.

"I'm smiling, I'm smiling..." he said in an equally similar grinning manner.

As they approached the mingling crowd, one of the men piped up, "Hey, Nick, where's Mandy? We were kind of hoping you'd bring her tonight."

"Sorry to disappoint you, fellas, but Mandy has been doing a photo layout in New York all week."

Her teeth-clenching grin never faltered. "*Penthouse* or *Playboy*?" Maggie muttered under her breath.

He returned the tight grin. "Be nice, Maggie darling. We're being watched."

"Right again," she said. "You're two for two."

"Now I'm really worried."

Chapter Eighteen

"Maggie!" Loveable, motherly, exuberant Jen Walker threw her arms around Maggie and hugged her tight. "You look positively radiant."

Maggie grasped Jen's arm and moved with her to an alcove beneath the curved staircase. She glanced furtively at Nick and said, "Enough with the *radiant* comments. Not everyone knows about my condition."

Jen looked appalled. "You haven't told Nick yet?"

Maggie shook her head. "The boys either. The right opportunity has never presented itself."

"Maggie," Jen scolded. "What are you waiting for? This isn't something you can hide forever. You're how far along?"

"About three months," Maggie answered.

"No way!" Jen held her at arms length and glanced up and down Maggie's fuller, curvier, but hardly bulging body with the experienced eye of a woman who'd had five children.

"I've always popped late," Maggie said in an apologetic tone. "Even with the twins. But watch out when I do. It'll happen overnight—boom!"

"I can't believe it. When I was that far along with Shanna the Chicago Bears wanted to rent space on my belly when the Goodyear blimp wasn't available. You, on the other hand, have blossomed into this voluptuous earth mother with a fabulous set of knockers. How fair is that?"

"How fair is what?" Ken Walker queried, poking his head around the corner.

"The price of hemorrhoid cream," Jen said with a seasoned pinch of sarcasm.

"Just tell me it's none of my business, dear," Ken replied with a smile and a peck on her powdered cheek.

"It's none of your business, Ken."

"Was that so hard?" He turned to Maggie. "Hello, dear. You look lovely tonight."

"Thank you. You look pretty spiffy yourself." She eyed the host and hostess decked out in their color-coordinated autumn finery. Jen wore a beautiful floor length burnt orange silk caftan and Ken wore a shirt made from the same rich fabric. What a wonderful couple, Maggie thought with an envious twinge. Thirty years together and they still beamed at each other with loving admiration and mutual respect.

Kissing Ken on his smoothly shaven cheek, Maggie added, "Umm, you smell good, too."

"You like? It's Chassis. Nick sent a bottle to me. In fact he sent the whole neighborhood samples. Didn't you get yours?"

Maggie wrinkled her nose as if she had just smelled something rotten. "Nick wouldn't send anything like that to me. He knows how particular I am about the scents I wear."

Jen touched Maggie's arm in an intentionally distracting manner. "How about coming upstairs with me for a sec. I want to check on Shanna before this shindig gets into full swing."

"Shanna didn't go to Peg's with the rest of the younger kids?" This came as a surprise. Jen never kept Shanna from participating in any of the neighborhood activities.

"She woke up this morning with an upset stomach and the sniffles. I didn't want to risk infecting the whole neighborhood so I kept her home. She's disappointed but seems to understand."

Ascending the staircase, Maggie paused briefly and glanced into the great room from the landing. Catching a glimpse of Nick standing amongst other newly arrived guests, her heart gave a crazy lurch. He appeared so at ease. With one hand in his slacks pocket and the other around a highball glass, his stance was poised and confident. She couldn't help stare at the handsome, sophisticated, elegant man who had once been as big a country hick as she still thought herself to be. He might live just down the block, but in so many other ways he was moving further and further away from the brief life they'd once shared. A contradicting mixture of overwhelming sadness and blatant admiration settled over her features.

"There's something perverse about looking at your ex that way."

Roused from her reverie, Maggie blinked owlishly and forced herself to refocus.

"Huh? I'm sorry, Jen. What did you say?"

Shaking her head, Jen just rolled her eyes and kept on walking.

Approaching the nearest bedroom she heard a combination of giggles and squeals. She discovered Shanna sitting cross-legged on her bed hugging her ever-present sidekick; an over-loved and under-stuffed Tigger. Her older sister, Jackie, was sitting on the floor with her back against the bed for support. They were watching television.

"Jackie graciously volunteered to stay home with Shanna," Jen offered in a way of explaining the older girl's presence.

"Volunteered?" Maggie questioned, seriously doubting the fourteen year old did so without a little arm-twisting, bribery, or both.

Jackie wrinkled her freckled nose. "I'm not that big on camping."

"I'm with you," Maggie agreed. "My idea of roughing it is a hotel without a sauna." She sat on the bed next to Shanna and stroked the little girl's silky blonde hair. "How about the two of you coming to my house for a sleepover? That ought to make up for missing tonight's festivities. We can have our own *big fun*." She kissed the top of Shanna's head and felt she was running a slight fever.

"Will the boys be there?" Jackie asked. Again, the nose crinkled. The nearly two year age difference was just enough for Jackie to think of them as immature pests, which they usually were, exceptionally so, whenever she was around. Maggie suspected it was because Danny and Davey just realized that Jackie was a girl, and it was common knowledge that girls were supposed to be teased and tormented by twelve-year-old boys.

"Nah, I'll ship them off to their dad's for the night. "It'll be just us girls. How does that sound?"

"Great. Will you show me how to quilt this time?"

"You bet!"

"Me too?" Shanna asked.

"You too!" Maggie punctuated her answer with a quick tweak on Shanna's nose. "I'll call your mom in the next few days to arrange a date."

"You won't forget?"

"Are you kidding? I'm the queen of sleepovers. And the queen never forgets."

Rejoining Jen in the hallway, she heard Shanna call her back.

"Maggie, wait!" Shanna hopped off the bed and shuffled in big fuzzy slippers to her dresser.

Maggie could see that Jen was eager to get back to her guests. "You go on ahead," she said, motioning for Jen to leave. "I'll be right down."

She watched Shanna dig around in a drawer and pull out a glittering and gaudy jeweled plastic crown and matching scepter. "A queen needs these," she said, handing the items to Maggie.

Maggie was touched. "Why don't you put it on me?" She kneeled down to Shanna's level and bowed her head. Little fingers placed the bejeweled, filigreed plastic on the top of Maggie's French twist and pressed the combs into her hair. Hiding her discomfort as the prongs dug into her scalp, Maggie flinched without allowing her smile to falter. Standing, she patted her head proudly. "Now it's official. How do I look?"

Shanna beamed. "Pretty."

Jackie giggled as Maggie accepted the proffered scepter.

"I dub thee Princesses Shanna and Jackie," she pronounced, tapping each of them on the shoulder.

Jackie laughed. "Goodnight, Queen Maggie."

"Goodnight, princesses. Sweet dreams." She blew them a kiss as she closed the door. As much as she adored her sons, a daughter would have been nice—someone to share things with that the boys found boring or worse, girly. Her heart wrenched for the little girl she lost.

Before heading downstairs, Maggie made a quick side trip to the bathroom, something she was doing a lot more frequently lately. She may not look all that pregnant but she sure had all the other symptoms that

143

went along with the condition.

Damn, she hadn't thought about having to go down the stairs when she went up. Never having quite mastered the fine art of walking gracefully in high heels, especially down stairs, and realizing it wasn't socially acceptable to come down in her stocking feet or shinny down the banister, she wrapped white knuckles around the polished oak banister as she took each deliberate step slow and sure. She always felt slightly off balance and had to concentrate to walk.

When it came to her preferred choice of footwear, she was more of a sneaker and flip-flop kind of girl. Actually, her very most, all time favorite footwear was nothing at all—barefoot as the day she was born. Here again, not socially acceptable when attending a semi-dressy affair.

Halfway down and feeling reasonably comfortable with her death grip, she looked up to find Nick standing at the foot of the stairs with his arm resting on the stair post watching her. Damn him. He wore the most maddening bemused smirk. First the heels and now Nick—a deadly combination when it came to knocking her off balance.

Upon reaching the final two steps, Maggie felt confident enough to release her death-grip on the banister. Her ankle promptly wobbled and she stumbled, forcing her to catch herself on Nick's outstretched arm.

"Never did quite get the hang of heels, eh, Boomer?" he said, taking her by the hand. His thumb brushed across her knuckles as he gripped her fingers.

"I'm perfectly capable of taking it from here, thank you very much." She tugged her hand away and faced him with as much bravado as she could gather.

He peered at her oddly and suddenly burst out laughing, throwing back his head in a rip snorting, shoulder shaking roar.

"Will you stop that? Everyone is staring." She thumped him on the chest. "Nick, please, cut it out."

"I'm sorry, your highness," he chuckled. "But it seems that your tiara has slipped." His eyes sparkled with amusement.

Reaching up, she felt the plastic crown. It had tipped toward the back of her head and now hung askew over her left ear by only one comb.

Holding her head high with all the haughty demeanor the title bestowed, she declared, "This is not a tiara, it's a crown. I received it at my coronation in Princess Shanna's room." Tugging it loose, the comb tangled in her hair and pulled apart her neatly coifed twist. So much for sophistication, she thought, pulling out the remaining pins that held her hair in place.

"Let me," he said, combing his fingers through her hair to fluff it around her face. His knuckles grazed the curve of her jaw as he drew his hand away. Maggie raised her gaze and found him staring thoughtfully at her. Her lips parted and her breathing grew shallow and rapid. Nick's own breaths, sweet with peppermint, seemed to be equally distressed.

"Hey, Nick. We're waiting to hear more about Brickyard," someone called from a tight knit group of men standing across the room near the fireplace.

"Not me," another man said laughing, his voice husky with liquor and innuendo. "I want to hear more about eye candy Mandy!"

The spell was broken. Hell, it was irreparably shattered. Maggie gestured toward the crowd and said, "You don't want to keep your fans waiting."

"Let's get out of here," Nick suggested in a husky, breathless whisper.

"We can't do that," she said, shaking her head, more against her own inclinations than Nick's suggestion. "Jen and Ken wouldn't understand."

"You're right. I forgot the manners police are monitoring our conduct tonight." He turned and walked away.

Maggie found an out of the way bench located near the open French doors leading to the patio. A tall, potted Ficus dressed for the evening in sparkling gold fairy lights sat like an enchanted sentry in the corner. Situating herself beneath the twinkling branches, she watched Nick with open fascination.

He worked the crowd like a slick politician up for re-election. He shook hands, he patted backs and he laughed in all the right places and at all the wrong jokes. If there had been a single baby around, he would have searched it out and kissed it.

He was, after all, the resident celebrity, the man of the hour, and she couldn't help comparing him to a modern day Lancelot, charming the fair damsels with his dazzling smile and captivating the men with his tales of big league racing, doing battle with not one trusty steed but seven-hundred and fifty horses rumbling under his control.

Growing weary of watching Nick have all the fun, she wandered through the French doors into the backyard. The evening temperature was warm enough for short-term comfort but she detected the crisp snap of autumn hovering close by as an occasional breezy burst rustled through the trees and sent crackling russet leaves to dance across the lawn and stone pathways. She draped her shawl around her shoulders and ventured into the autumnal wonderland.

The Walkers had outdone themselves. Ken must have spent every weekend for the last month getting their backyard ready. Every tree and bush was encrusted with sparkling orange, gold and white fairy lights. Pots and pots of assorted colored mums encircled the stone patio and lined the winding garden paths. Clusters of additional seating were arranged around cozy fire pits for those less than hearty individuals who still wanted to enjoy the cool moonlit evening. The harvest moon was a huge amber globe hanging low in the sky and would have supplied more than sufficient light in spite of the artificial illumination. Maggie was enchanted.

An abundant wait staff wandered from indoors to out, offering tempting hors d'oeuvres and glasses of hard apple cider. Maggie passed when offered something from a drink tray but she did manage to snag a few still warm from the oven cheese puffs and toothpick-speared sweet and sour meatballs.

She stopped to chat with long-standing neighbors and introducing herself to ones she wasn't yet familiar with, welcoming them to Cartwright Corners with a friendly smile and a warm handshake.

One of the hors d'oeuvres she'd eaten made her thirsty, and she headed to the portable bar located beneath the canopied patio. She ordered a diet cola with a twist of lime and helped herself to a mini cheese and spinach quiche from the tray on the bar.

"There you are," said Jen Walker, coming up behind Maggie. "I've been looking all over for you. I was beginning to think my daughters were holding you hostage." Jen ordered her usual vodka and tonic and perched herself on the stool next to Maggie. With her back to the bar, she leaned against it for support.

"I'm sure you have better things to do than worry about my whereabouts." Maggie popped another quiche into her mouth and spun around on the bar stool to face Jen. She nearly choked when she noticed that Gwen Marconi had cornered Nick and was slowly inching herself nearer and nearer with a hungry, predatory look in her eyes.

"Gwen Marconi doesn't live in Cartwright Corners, does she?" Maggie questioned.

"No, but she'd like to. I've heard she's searching for a house in the neighborhood. She finagled a guest invitation through the Rodneys, convincing them she'd be instrumental in introducing them around. Of course I don't think she's spent more than five minutes with them since they arrived." Jen cast a disgusted glance in Gwen's direction. "Its times like this I wish we had formed a homeowners' association so we could veto people like her from moving in."

"I believe that's illegal," Maggie pointed out.

"My husband's a lawyer, and a damn good one. He'd find a way to make it legal." Jen took a long swallow of her drink. "Just look at the way she's got Nick cornered. Shouldn't you go rescue him or something?"

"Nick's a big boy," Maggie laughed, taking a sip of her drink. "He can take care of himself," she assured her friend.

"Harrumph," was Jen's only response, turning to order another drink. "Sure you wouldn't like to accidentally nudge her into the fish pond?" she suggested with an evil chuckle.

Knowing how her friend got after a few vodka and tonics, Maggie laughed again and shook her head. "Not this time. I promised to behave myself, remember?"

"I'd better check on what's keeping the buffet. They

should have started serving twenty minutes ago." Jen tossed back the remainder of her drink and eased herself off the barstool. "See you later, sweetie. Have fun." She pecked the air in the vicinity of Maggie's cheek and headed for the kitchen door on the other side of the patio.

Knowing there were too many guests for a formal sit down dinner, Jen had fully extended the dining room table and turned it into a sumptuous buffet. Barbequed baby back ribs, beef and chicken kabobs, and grilled shrimp were piled high on platters surrounded by one tempting side dish after another. The sideboard was equally decked with multi-tiered trays of individual portions of cheesecake, strawberry tarts, and pumpkin pie. Everything was too tempting to resist.

As far as Maggie could ascertain, there was only one problem with the buffet. Even taking small helpings of less than everything offered, she found her plate fuller than she ever intended. She felt like the third little piggy that had roast beef—as well as ribs, and chicken, and shrimp. But after eyeing the other guests' plates she realized she wasn't in the minority.

Balancing her plate in one hand and gripping a cup of hot apple cider in the other, she glanced around and discovered most of the available seating already filled. Just as she was about to head outdoors in search of a place to sit, she realized her bench under the Ficus was still unoccupied. She settled herself on the polished hardwood and balanced the plate on her lap. After setting her cup of cider on the floor at her feet well out of the way of passersby, Maggie popped a plump shrimp into her mouth. She chewed slowly, savoring the tangy herbed crustacean.

"Are you saving that seat for anyone?" Nick stood in front of her holding an even more heaping plate than her own.

She finished chewing and swallowed. "Uh, no," she answered, picking up the linen-wrapped silverware bundle from the seat beside her. "It all yours," she offered.

He situated himself beside her and glanced at his heaping plate. "I don't know how this happened." He gestured to his plate with a wave of his fork before digging into the bountiful temptations. "A little of this and a little of that and the next thing I know I look like Henry the Eighth at an all-you-can-eat smorgasbord."

"I know what you mean," was all she managed to utter in response to his attempt to draw her into a conversation.

Maggie ate in uncomfortable silence. How could she give the food the attention it deserved when all she could think of was Nick sitting so incredibly close? His slightest movement made her painfully aware of how much she still wanted him. She was finally ready to admit she needed him in her life. Damn the man for not treating her like most men treated their ex-wives, with indifference and total disregard.

When a waiter came around to collect plates, she placed her half eaten fare on the tray. It was hopeless. She couldn't eat another bite.

"Eyes bigger than you stomach, huh?" he teased.

"Yeah," she answered, all the while thinking '*not for long*.' Jen was right. She had to tell him, the sooner the better. She wasn't sure if she was more fearful of telling him or what his reaction would be when she did.

"How about us sharing a piece of that pumpkin pie?" he suggested. "I'm too full to eat a whole slice myself." When he didn't get an answer, he said, "Maggie, you feeling okay?"

"What? Yes, I'm fine. Why do you ask?"

He shrugged. "No reason really, you just seem unusually quiet tonight, that's all."

"I'm fine. Just a little tired. I haven't been sleeping well lately." She folded the napkin on her lap, shook it out and started folding it again.

"There seems to be a lot of that going around." There was a wealth of unspoken meaning behind that offhanded comment. Before he had an opportunity to say anything further, they were interrupted.

"Hey, Nick," a man across the room waved for him to join them. "Could you help us out here? We need another man's opinion."

He smiled congenially and motioned his acknowledgement. "Later, Mags," he said, winking as he turned to join the group.

Maggie watched the animated assembly. It appeared

that Nick's contribution to the conversation only seemed to add yet another dimension to the discussion. When one of the men cupped his hands in front of his chest in the universally understood gesture of a well-endowed female, she rolled her eyes in a commonly interpreted expression of her own. Her jaw dropped to her chest when she saw Nick turn his cupped hands outward, creating a hearty round of laughter from his all male audience. Loosing interest after that, she collected her cup and wandered outdoors.

The wind had shifted and she found fewer people sitting outside. Except for the mixture of men and women clustered around the bar and the three couples on the dance floor, there weren't too many hearty souls left. She looked around wondering what to do next, and hoped her sons were having a better time than she was having. She considered joining Shanna and Jackie for a game of Twister or Monopoly.

In spite of her being a long term resident and knowing the majority of the people present, she felt very much alone and out of place. She didn't belong here. She never did. Her life was built around her sons, her home, her home-based business, and on occasion an exasperating ex-husband. Inasmuch as she loved every aspect of her life, she knew it wasn't very interesting by most people's standards. Nothing could ever change the fact that she was still just Mary Margaret Thornton from the wrong side of everything.

Nick belonged here. Never was that fact more apparent than tonight. People sought him out, they wanted his opinion, regardless of the topic, and they valued his presence. If she hadn't given him his freedom, he would have eventually realized how wrong she was for him and left anyway.

"Hello, pretty lady." Nick's voice penetrated her reverie. "I've been looking for you." The sparkling lights reflected like diamonds in his dazzling blue eyes. "Dance with me?"

Dance? Nick? The music that was playing was slow and sensuous with a definite Latin influence. When did he learn to slow dance? Oh, he could pump his arms and hop around with the best of them when the music was a snappy up-tempo rock tune. But slow dancing with a partner? Was this another Mandy influence? Looks like Nick was being groomed for much bigger and better things.

"Dance?" Maggie echoed.

"I'll take that as a yes." He took her by the hand and led her toward the patio.

"Nick, we've never slow danced together."

"One of many oversights I hope to remedy tonight."

"One of many?" she questioned.

"Watch your step around the Koi pond," he cautioned, guiding her with a solicitous hand. "I've been told it gets very slippery around the stone edges. People have been known to fall in if they're not careful."

Finding an open space, he whirled around to face her and wrapped one arm around her waist. Gripping her hand he tucked it tightly against his chest, which in turn gave her no alternative but to wrap her other hand around his neck. The scent of peppermints and leather mingled with his subtle cologne. She was surprised it wasn't Chassis but grateful that it wasn't.

Ever so slightly he tightened his grip and snugged her hips more tightly against his, leaving no question as to how her nearness affected him.

Then slowly, almost hesitantly, he began to step and rock to the rhythmic beat of the music. She couldn't help but follow his lead and move in sync with every sensuous step.

Nick placed his cheek against her temple and closed his eyes, letting his instincts move his body in responsive harmony with hers. She closed her eyes as well and relaxed against him, allowing her moves to mimic his. Together, their movements could almost be interpreted as vertical foreplay, so in tune was one body with the other. His fingers kneaded the flesh beneath the supple suede at her waist. Muscled thighs and narrow hips thrust and swayed against her. There was just the two of them and the music. Everything else around them faded to black.

Chapter Nineteen

The conversations around the bar ceased as all eyes turned to the couple on the dance floor. Jen and Ken shared a knowing sideward glance and a smile.

My god," one woman sighed. "He's practically making love to her on the dance floor."

"Is that what making love is supposed to look like?" another woman questioned wistfully. She turned to her husband and smacked him on the arm. "Take notes!"

"I'll be more than happy to start acting like Nick Chapparelle when you start looking like Maggie," her husband retorted, reaching for his beer.

****

So many emotions struggled to gain dominance within her. It would be so easy to lose herself in his arms. She opened her eyes and blinked to regain control, forcing herself to stare at the throbbing pulse in the tanned V created by the open collar of his dark shirt.

She managed to finally speak. "What are you doing?"

"I thought I was dancing. But if you have to ask I must be doing something wrong."

"That's not what I mean. I want to know why you're acting like this?"

"Like what?" he whispered against her hair.

"Like we barely know each other."

"Maybe because I want to start over with you, Maggie."

"Start over?" She was confused.

"Uh huh. And in honor of new beginnings, I thought I'd start with a new and improved version of me."

She was curious enough to play along, and asked, "Other than the obvious fact that you dress better, what else makes you new and improved?"

"The clothes are just window dressing, Maggie. The changes I'm talking about have taken place here," he touched the part of his chest where his heart beat below the surface. "And here," he touched his head. "I've been doing some heavy duty thinking these last few weeks. And I've come to some startling conclusions about both of us.

"You were so young when we got married. I shouldn't have rushed you the way I did. I realize that now."

"I didn't give you much choice. I got pregnant. You did what you thought was the right thing to do for me at the time."

"And when you asked for the divorce, weren't you doing what you thought was right for me?"

"It was the right thing to do," she insisted.

"You did it all for me, didn't you? You gave me my freedom and I was so blinded by my own ambition that I never suspected your real motives."

"Nick, don't." She shook her head against his words and tried to get away but he held her tight. "It was wrong from the beginning. Don't you see? I did what I had to do to make it right again."

"Then let's start over from before the beginning." He reached into his jacket pocket. Nestled in the cup of his palm was a small crimson velvet box.

"Look at me, Maggie."

She raised her gaze, visually caressing every familiar feature through a teary blur.

He kneeled down on one knee and took her hand. "Maggie, will you marry me? Again? Please give this Nick a chance to make it right for you this time." Snapping back the velvet lid, he revealed an exquisite diamond marquis solitaire. Its brilliance sparkled and flashed beneath the twinkling lights.

She couldn't speak. She couldn't do anything but stare at the ring and the man holding it as she covered her mouth with trembling fingers. She was roused from her trance-like state by a sudden round of applause followed by cheering hoots and hollers.

"Come on, Maggie. What's it gonna be?"

"Give him your answer, Maggie."

"Yeah, Maggie. Don't keep him waiting."

"Give him another chance, Maggie."

"Marry him, Maggie."

"Yeah, Maggie. Marry him."

"Say yes, Maggie!"

They all started to chant, "Say yes! Say yes! Say yes!"

She glanced from the ring, to Nick, to the expectant faces of the crowd forming around the dance floor. They were all waiting for her to make the next move. But it was the baby inside her that moved first. Not much more than the fluttering of a butterfly wing, but enough to remind her that she was not alone in making this decision.

"I can't, Nick. I can't give you an answer. Not now. The timing still isn't right for us!" She broke free, pushed her way through the crowd, and fled.

The minute she was down the driveway, she stopped and kicked off her shoes, leaving them in the grass where they landed. She could move much quicker without them.

It was only when she reached her front door that she realized she left her black clutch bag with her house keys at the Walkers. She couldn't go back and face them. She'd bust a window if she couldn't find the spare key she'd hidden in a fake rock in the flowerbed.

Crouching, she rummaged through the river rock and mulch, searching for the imposter stone. One rock after another, she lifted and shook, hoping to hear a rattle or feel the weight difference. And one by one she built a pile of disappointing rejects.

"I figured you might need these." Nick dangled her keys in front of her face and tossed her shoes on the grass by her knees. The edge of her small black leather clutch peeked out of his jacket pocket. He tugged it out and handed that to her, too.

"Was it something I said?" he asked.

A startled, nervous laugh burst from her lips. "I don't understand why you're doing this. You're building a wonderful, new life for yourself. Why are you trying to drag me into it?"

"Maggie, I'm trying to build my life around yours, not drag you into mine."

That wasn't the way she saw it. Shifting from one foot to the other, she finally perched on the edge of the glider and planted her feet flat on the concrete to keep from swinging.

"I know the proposal took you by surprise. I don't blame you for not wanting to give me an answer right away. I told you once before. Take all the time you need. I'm not going anywhere."

"Nick, I'm pregnant," she blurted.

"So much for our doing it right the second time," he said under his breath.

"Didn't you hear me? I said I was pregnant."

"I heard you. I've suspected for a while. I was just waiting for confirmation from you."

"You knew?"

"Give me a little credit, Maggie. The boobs, the moods, the bruising, the chocolate bars all over the house. Put them all together they spell Maggie's pregnant. I figure its due about Talladega or maybe Darlington."

Only Nick would determine a due date by the racing schedule. "More like Bristol or Martinsville."

"Those are in April, honey. I figured this baby is due sometime in May."

"I know they're in April, Nick. I was already pregnant when we got back together."

A myriad of emotions rocked his features, shock, despair, disbelief, distress and anguish. Maggie felt them all and wished she could exchange every one of them for just one—understanding. His eyes darted everywhere but never once looked at her.

"Geez," he hissed. "I never saw that one coming."

"Please, Nick, I want to explain." Standing, she took a step toward him then stopped when he backed away, taking two steps back for every one she took toward him. "It's not what you think."

"I'm sure it's exactly what I think."

"It's more complicated than that. I'm having this baby because—"

"Stop! Stop right there. I don't want to hear the details, okay. You don't owe me any explanation."

"I may not owe you one, but I want to give you one just the same."

"Whose is it?"

As if on cue, Joel walked up from the direction of the party. Depending on the point of view, his timing was perfect and awkward. It was to say the least, perfectly awkward.

"There you two are. Ken told me I just missed you.

Better late than never, huh?" He stopped short, glancing from Maggie to Nick, he queried, "Am I interrupting something?"

"You just never learn, do you?" Nick hitched a thumb in Joel's direction. "This one going to marry you too?"

Determined not to cry, Maggie lifted her head high. She'd done nothing wrong. Regardless of the circumstances, this child had been created out of nothing but love.

Joel quietly moved to stand beside her on the porch. He felt an overwhelming obligation to protect her and his child. Placing his arm around her, he said, "I'd be happy to, if she'll have me."

Talk about a bolt from out of the blue. Maggie wasn't sure who was more surprised by the declaration, her or Nick. They both turned and stared at Joel with a mixture of surprise and disbelief.

"There are extenuating circumstances you need to understand," Joel said with a soothing calmness Maggie found reassuring. If anyone could explain the situation, levelheaded Joel could.

"I'll bet," Nick snorted. "But spare me the *we couldn't help ourselves* song and dance. Nobody knows better than me how irresistible she can be." He turned his back on them both and walked away.

"Nicky, wait." Maggie ran after him, desperate to make him listen. She grabbed his arm. "Please," she implored. "Hear me out. You need to know why I'm having this baby—"

"No!" Nick screamed, wrenching his arm free from her grasp as he waved a hand against anything she might try to say. Before she could utter another syllable he broke into a dead run. The heels of his loafers tapped against the asphalt and echoed down the empty street.

Maggie couldn't keep up. A sharp ache clutched her side and caused her to wince against the intruding pain. She stopped in the middle of the street and stared, not sure exactly what she was looking for because Nick had disappeared into the darkness. Not even the glow of the moon could light the dark path on which he ran. "Damn you, Nick Chapparelle," she whispered into the night. "Damn you."

Joel came up behind her and placed his hands on her shoulders. She spun around and buried her face against his chest. He wrapped his arms around her in a gesture of comfort and protection as she sobbed.

Chapter Twenty

Nick couldn't run fast or far enough. When he reached his house he didn't stop. He kept running—past the dilapidated summerhouse, around the abandoned stable and through the overgrown horse track. He didn't stop until he was breathless and sweaty and physically ill. He braced himself against an enormous aged oak and gasped for each breath as he dropped to his knees and wretched.

When the abdominal spasms ceased, he leaned heavily against the oak tree and forced himself to stand. Once realizing there was no place for him to run, he climbed to his feet and headed in the direction of his house.

He'd been sucker punched, blindsided by Maggie's pronouncement. The baby wasn't his. The baby wasn't his. The words kept tumbling around in his brain looking for somewhere to settle for future comprehension. He was having difficulty dealing with it now.

How could he have been so wrong about her? He really believed there had been no one else for her, just as there had been no one else for him. For four long years he'd wandered in and out of her life patiently waiting for her to realize what a mistake the divorce had been. After their night together back in August he really thought he had detected a small glimmer of her contemplating reconciliation—a turning point—in spite of her behavior to the contrary. It had been a turning point all right, all against traffic down a one-way street. Everything he said, or did, after that went from bad to worse.

Once inside, he headed straight for the bedroom to rid himself of his fancy designer duds. The slacks were stained and muddy, and likely beyond salvation. Leaving everything where it dropped, he tugged thick white socks on his feet and dressed in loose fitting jeans and baggy sweatshirt. Might as well be comfortable in his misery, he reasoned.

Casting a cursory glance at the heap of discarded clothes, he eyed the leather sports coat with a twinge of guilt. That jacket had cost more than his first car. Hearing Mandy's stern yet gentle southern reprimand in his head, he dutifully picked it up and hung it in the closet.

And what about Mandy? She'd had such high hopes for him. What was he going to tell her when she asked how his evening went? She'd worked so hard, invested so much time and effort, to help turn him into this man-of-the-world persona, insisting his ex-wife would be swept off her feet by the new improved Nick and land right back in his arms.

Oh, the things he went through at Mandy's insistence were tantamount to taking a weeklong side trip into hell. Shopping, fashion consultants, tailors, dance lessons, etiquette instructions, hair and skin care experts. Who would have guessed he needed exfoliating and moisturizers? Soap and water was all he ever knew. Now he had a bathroom cabinet filled with bottles and jars of skin and hair care products he'd probably never use again, a closet crammed with designer clothes he had no reason to wear, and a head stuffed with useless social dos and don'ts. And for what? What good was being the prize stud in the paddock, as Mandy so eloquently put it, if the filly that curled his fetlocks and shivered his withers was carrying the foal of another stallion? What made it even worse was he actually liked the other guy. Under different circumstances, Joel was the kind of man he'd want as a friend, a good buddy.

He wandered into the living room and slumped into the nearest chair. When did his life get so complicated? He didn't know the answers to very much at the moment, but he knew the answer to that one—fifteen years ago when an adorable waiflike tomboy with huge green eyes named Mary Margaret Thornton bounced into his carefully planned life and rocked his world with a single swish of her strawberry blonde ponytail.

He'd been slightly off kilter ever since with no hope of ever recovering his balance. All that prevented him from making his move the first night he laid eyes on her was the fear of being of accused by his buddies of robbing the cradle, or worse.

She'd appeared with all the unpredictable, electrifying excitement and inexplicable fascination of a sudden summer storm. Her smile struck him like a lightning bolt; her laughter rolled through his brain like distant thunder and those glorious, hellcat green eyes flashed and danced like St. Elmo's fire streaking across the Indiana night sky. Even now, after all that had recently passed between them, the very thought of her made his heart beat a little faster, and his groin ache a little harder.

Unable to distinguish how much of the pain he experienced was actual headache and how much was simply the strain of thinking too much in an effort to make sense out of all of this, he rubbed his forehead and temples in an attempt to ease the throbbing. Either way, he needed something to the dull the sharp pounding taking up residence behind his eyes.

Stepping cautiously through the contractor's maze of aluminum ladders, partially erected scaffolding, and stacks of folded painter's tarps, Nick headed for the kitchen—the last room on the main level still under construction. It required the most extensive floor to ceiling renovations, and he waited until the rest of the downstairs was pretty much completed before undertaking the biggest challenge.

Alcohol or aspirin? Nick gazed into the sparsely stocked walk-in pantry, unable to decide. The aspirin might dull the pain but wouldn't do a thing for numbing the wretched ache in his heart. He reached for the unopened bottle of Jack Daniels—a gift from one of his contractors—and cracked the seal. It wouldn't help the headache but after a few shots he wouldn't care, or better still he wouldn't remember. He carried a glass and the bottle back to the living room and the chair with the shabby upholstery and shot springs and proceeded to anesthetize every part of him that hurt.

****

"Joel, you can't be serious?" Maggie dropped her shoes inside the door and continued down the hall to the kitchen.

Joel closed the door and followed. "It's not that preposterous, Maggie. I really think we could make it work. We're both family oriented, we share similar values and ideals, and we get along reasonably well. Most couples I know don't have that much going for them."

She fixed a pot of coffee, realizing it was going to be a long night, already knowing that elusive companion called sleep wouldn't be joining her again that night. "There's one minor detail you've failed to mention."

"Love?" he said, sounding as if it wasn't worth mentioning in the overall scheme of things. "We've both been down that road and look where's it's gotten us. We're still miserable and alone." He stuffed his hands into his pockets and stood looking out the sliding glass door into the dark yard, the glass reflecting his troubled image.

Maggie remained silent for a very long while. She took her time pouring the aromatic gourmet-flavored brew into stoneware mugs, collecting spoons from a drawer, sugar shaker from an overhead cabinet and creamer carton from the fridge. She carried it all into the adjoining family room and placed the tray on the coffee table as she sat on the sofa.

A splash of cream, a half-teaspoon of sugar, she accomplished each step without conscious effort. Moving methodically, she stirred the mixture with slow, lazy circles. The only sound in the room was the spoon clinking against the sides of the mug and scraping the bottom.

"I can't be a surrogate wife too, Joel," she finally said.

"I know." He turned away from the window and expelled a slow sigh. "I've been standing here wondering what I would do if you actually accepted my spontaneous gesture."

A short laugh burst from her lips. "What are the odds?" she asked, taking her first sip of coffee from the warm spoon. She added a little more cream and tasted again. "Two proposals in one night and I don't accept either one of them." She wrapped her hands around the mug in an attempt to absorb its warmth.

Joel looked at her oddly. "Two proposals?"

"Oh, that's right. You weren't there to witness proposal number one. I gotta tell you, Joel. Your offer to marry me might win in the noble and heartfelt categories, but Nick's wins hands down in every other department. It was a pretty spectacular production—the handsome man, the harvest moon, the romantic music, and a fabulous diamond ring. Oh, you should have seen the ring! It would have knocked your socks off."

"If it was all that, Maggie, why didn't you accept?"

She lost her smile and gave a noncommittal shrug.

"I'm a bit puzzled, Maggie. I can't help wondering why you're not more upset by this whole—" He motioned with his hand, searching for the right word. "Situation," he finally finished.

"I've been wondering about that myself. Weird, isn't it?" She handed him his coffee. "With or without Nick, this is my life. I don't have the luxury of curling myself into a little corner and cease living until when or if Nick and I resolve our differences. I have two sons that count on me to be here for them. If we're meant to get back together, it'll happen when the time is right. And it won't take moonlight or diamonds to do it either."

"Beth and I would never have asked you to do this if we had thought it would cause you one second of grief. You know that, don't you?"

"In the first place, you didn't ask, I offered and you accepted. And in the second place, if Nick had bothered to stick around long enough to hear me out, there wouldn't be any need for this conversation."

"You want me to talk to him?"

She shook her head. "I figure that right about now he's sleeping off an alcohol induced coma. I'll go over there in the morning while he's still too hung over to run or interrupt and tell him the whole story. We'll see what happens after that."

****

There was something sickening and demanding fighting for attention in his head. Nick groaned and winced as he pulled his feet off the threadbare ottoman and attempted to push himself upright. The wingback chair he had fallen asleep in was a sagging remnant of bygone days that came with the house, as was all the furniture still in the room. The springs were shot and the stuffing had compacted and shifted over the years into varying depths of lumps and bumps. His spine cracked and rebelled as he shifted forward and gripped his pounding head between his hands.

"Aaaarrgh," he grimaced, reaching for the jangling source of his immense discomfort. He fumbled for the annoying cell phone with uncooperative fingers.

"Hello." His voice sounded like fried sand.

"Good morning, sugah!" The sweet feminine Texas drawl greeted him. "I sincerely hope I'm interrupting something."

"Mandy," he breathed.

"My, my, you sound like you had a good time last night. Celebrating, I assume?"

"Oh, yeah," Nick groaned. "It was a night I won't likely forget any time soon."

"Don't tell me she didn't like the ring?"

"It left her speechless. Until she found the words to turn me down, that is."

"Oh, honey, I'm so sorry. I was sure you'd have that filly eating peaches right out of your hand after last night. Tell Mandy what happened and don't leave anything out."

He gave her an abbreviated version of the previous night's events. "Look, Mandy. I'm in desperate need of a bathroom, a hot shower, and a gallon of black coffee so could we continue this conversation a little later? Are you still in New York?" That was the problem with cell phones. A person could be calling from anywhere in the world and you wouldn't know unless you asked.

"I'm at the house in Houston. I flew in late last night. Daddy and I have a board meeting first thing Monday morning."

"I need to get away from here. Would you mind if I camp out at your place in St. Croix for a little while?"

"Of course not, sugah. Stay as long as you like. I'll call the staff and let them know you're coming."

"Thanks, Mandy."

"You're welcome, sugah. The Lear will be waiting for you at Midway."

"You don't need to send the plane. I'll fly commercial."

"Y'all know my daddy taught me to never take no for an answer."

"Fine. I'm in no shape to argue."

"Y'all be sure to call me if there's anything else you need, okay? Bye bye for now."

"Bye, Mandy. Thanks again." He punched the disconnect button and immediately dialed information for the number of a local limo service. He was also in no condition to drive to the airport.

Chapter Twenty-One

Maggie was waiting for the boys when they returned home the next morning. Now that Nick was aware of her condition, she had to tell Danny and Davey. She didn't want them hearing the news from anyone other than herself.

Looking happy, scruffy, and tired, they tromped into the house, dumping their backpacks and camping gear on the kitchen floor as they made a beeline for the fridge.

"Didn't you eat the hardy chuck wagon breakfast that was served this morning?" She watched them unload the refrigerator and cabinets with the all the necessities two growing boys needed to sustain them until their next scheduled feeding.

"Sure, and it was real good too, but a guy gets hungry walking all the way from Cartwright Woods." Davey hauled a Jethro-sized bowl from the cabinet and filled it with Cheerios and milk.

"I can certainly understand how that mile trek could work up quite an appetite. I don't know how you managed to make it all the way home without stopping at a few neighbors along the way." Maggie screwed the cap back on the milk jug and returned it to the fridge. Now was as good a time as any to tell them. They might be more receptive with full stomachs.

"Sit down, guys. There's something important I need to discuss with you."

Are we in trouble for something?" Danny asked. A peanut butter and jelly on toast hovered halfway between the paper plate and his mouth.

She briefly considered the worried sideward glances the boys exchanged. Under normal circumstances she would have pursued the silent looks that passed between them. But a more pressing matter urged her to remain focused and she dismissed their behavior as a twelve year old's perpetually guilty conscious. At this age they were always doing something or other to get themselves into trouble with their mother.

"No. This is about me. Remember the talk we had about where babies come from?"

Davey stopped chewing long enough to ask, "Is this another talk about sex?"

Finally, Maggie thought, she finally found something that took Davey's attention from food. This wasn't exactly what she had in mind, however.

"In a way, yes, it's another sex talk. I'm pregnant."

"You and dad are having another baby?" Danny exclaimed. "That's so cool."

Now came the difficult part. Maggie placed her hands on the table and clutched them tightly. "Your dad isn't the father. In fact, it's not my baby either."

"Come on Mom, even I know a girl can't use 'it's not mine' as an excuse." Danny was adamant on that point.

"Ordinarily, no, I couldn't. But the circumstances surrounding this pregnancy are a little unusual." She could see now that she had their undivided attention. Confusion pinched their young faces in almost identical expressions, and their food sat half eaten and ignored on the table. They stared at her, waiting for her to go on.

"You remember Beth Hubbard, don't you?" They nodded solemnly.

"Your friend who had cancer and died," Davey recalled.

"That's right. Well, Beth and Joel wanted children very much but Beth couldn't get pregnant. They were going through a process called in vitro fertilization when the doctor discovered she had breast cancer. That's when I offered to carry their baby for them."

"You got pregnant without having sex?" Danny seemed exceptionally curious about that particular detail.

"That's right. Beth's eggs had already been harvested through a medical procedure in preparation for the in vitro process. They were joined with Joel's sperm in a laboratory and when the eggs became fertilized they were implanted inside my uterus during another medical procedure. So you see—this is their baby. I'm only supplying a safe place for it to grow and develop until it's ready to be born. It has none of my genetics, only Beth and Joel's."

"Does dad know?"

"Yes. I told him last night."

Danny scowled. "Is this baby the reason why you're not wearing the ring dad got you?"

Maggie was stunned. His reasoning was amazingly on the mark. "You knew about the ring?"

"Uh huh. We helped dad pick it out. Didn't you think it was pretty?"

"It was the most beautiful ring I'd ever seen." She wanted to weep. She felt as if she had refused her sons as well as Nick.

"Then why aren't you wearing it? Don't you want to marry him again? You love him, don't you?" His questions appeared to be rhetorical, as if he really didn't want to hear her answers.

"Sweetheart," she began, cupping his chin. "As difficult as this is for you and your brother to understand, this is something your dad and I have to work out on our own. This has nothing to do with the two of you."

Danny recoiled from her touch. Leaping to his feet, he screamed, "How could you do this? This baby is ruining everything!" Angry tears streamed down his face, and he swiped at them with the back of his hand. "Dad loves you!"

"Danny," she gasped. "I'm not doing this to hurt you guys, or your dad. I'm doing this for Joel. This baby is all he has left since Beth died."

"I knew it. I knew I should have tried harder to stop him from coming around." He ran from the room and stormed up the stairs.

Chilling speculation seeped into her consciousness. She turned to Davey who sat scrunched down in his chair, quietly taking it all in but offering no opinion of his own.

"What did your brother mean by that?"

Davey hung his head.

"Davey..." she said. "Tell me."

His voice was barely audible. "We put the nails in Mr. Hubbard's tires."

She closed her eyes against his confession and buried her face in her hands. After giving herself a minute to process the information, she lifted her head and said, "Go to your room. I want you and your brother to stay there and think about what you've done until I figure out what your punishment is going to be for this act of vandalism."

Without a word in his own defense, Davey slogged up the stairs looking as if he were being sent to live out the remainder of his natural life in solitary confinement.

She couldn't believe her sons had done something like this. They weren't bad boys. She wanted to believe they were simply acting out against her involvement with another man. Regardless of how platonic the relationship was they obviously considered Joel a threat even before they knew about the baby. She needed to discuss this with Nick. Even if he didn't want anything more to do with her, he was still their father and needed to be involved in their discipline, especially when it involved something as serious as this.

She grabbed a jacket from the coat tree on her way out the door and headed down the street. Considering the lateness of the morning, the neighborhood was unusually quiet. One and all had obviously had very *Big Fun* the previous night and were recovering by sleeping in.

As she approached the Craftsman house, she caught a glimpse of his blue truck sitting in the gravel drive near the back entrance. That was a good sign. He hadn't pulled one of his famous disappearing acts yet.

Just as she approached the brick pillared entrance to the property, a sleek black stretch limo passed her on the street and turned into the driveway, stopping in front of the wraparound porch nearest the front door. She slipped between the brick column and an overgrown yew bush and watched Nick's other life unfold before her eyes. Out he dashed dressed casually in loose fitting jeans, black t-shirt and denim jacket, baseball cap and sunglasses, with a tan leather weekender swinging loosely in his hand. The driver held open the rear door as Nick tossed the bag into the back and ducked in after it.

An overly active imagination was a terrible thing to waste and impossible to ignore, and Maggie's was working overtime. The tinted windows made it impossible to determine if there was anyone else in the car, but she couldn't help picturing Mandy in the limo, ready, willing and able to offer him another dose of T.L.C. Or maybe

Mandy was already waiting at a pre-arranged destination? Her mind whirled with possibilities, all of which involved some form of debauchery. The limo was long gone before Maggie moved from behind the shrub.

Looks like determining the boys' punishment had fallen solely onto her shoulders. She couldn't very well tell them to *"wait until your father gets home"* when she didn't have the slightest idea as to where he'd gone or when he'd be back. Damn the man for never being around when she needed him.

****

The private jet touched down and jostled him awake. Suffering from what he passed off as a drumming hangover, Nick dozed on and off for most of the long flight from Chicago to St. Croix. He grabbed his carry-on bag, the only luggage he brought, and waited at the door for the plane to taxi to a stop. He then jogged down the steps and across the sun-baked tarmac to the open Renegade and waiting driver. He recognized the driver and full-time caretaker, Tomas, and the memorable classic yellow Jeep from his previous visit.

Tomas cast him a broad smile as he approached. "Hello, Mr. Nick, nice to see you again." He reached for Nick's bag, but Nick waved him off and tossed it into the back before climbing into the passenger seat by gripping the overhead roll bar and swinging his legs into the doorless vehicle with agility not much different than when he crawled into his racecar.

He strapped himself in and smacked the dash with an open palm. "Let's go."

In spite of the breathtaking scenery, Nick scrunched down, leaned back against the seat and closed his eyes behind wraparound sunglasses. The flight left him with a queasy, unsettled stomach and made him wonder if he was coming down with something more than just an acute reaction to the Tennessee sour mash he'd ingested the night before.

He was shown to a different bedroom than he'd used on his last visit. This one was bigger and had a spectacular view of the bay from the wall of glass leading to the terrace. Simply designed and decorated in relaxing pastel yellow and cool shades of green typically associated with the tropics, he realized he was staying in the master suite, although there were no personal touches or belongings that would indicate that the room was ever occupied by the villa's owner, Elliot Morgan. Though functional and beautifully appointed, all he could see at the moment was the king-sized polished chrome version of a four-poster bed and the fluffy oversized pillows that would soon be cradling his aching head.

After instructing Tomas to leave him to his own devices during this stay, he showered, swallowed more over-the-counter pain medication, and slipped between the smooth, cool green sheets to escape into the blissful depths of mindless slumber where his dreams were more pleasant and painless than his current reality.

It was more than twelve hours later when he finally awoke, actually feeling almost human again. The headache he'd suffered with for the last two days still lingered, though it had settled into a less intense, more tolerable thrumming behind his eyes.

He showered again, however brief, remembering about the limited fresh water supply on the island, and dressed in frayed denim cutoffs and a faded black NASCAR tee shirt he had long since ripped the sleeves off. He looked more like a vagrant beach bum than a houseguest of the Morgan's, but he wasn't there to impress anybody and didn't care what he looked like. All he wanted was comfortable and familiar.

Mandy, of course, would have never allowed him to get away with dressing like that if she'd been there. She would have had a Texas-size tantrum and lectured him on the importance of dressing for success.

Success. What a colossal hoot. What good was the fame and fortune without someone to share it with? At this low point in his life he really didn't care how he looked so it was a good thing for him that Mandy wasn't there to see how far he had strayed from her careful tutelage.

Feeling the pangs of real hunger, he rubbed his empty stomach as he wandered from the upper bedroom level. He snooped and poked around the immaculate pastel peach and creamy white kitchen looking for something he wanted to eat, or rather something that didn't require too much effort on his part to fix. He discovered a cache of fresh, buttery croissants, which he slathered with creamy peanut butter and strawberry jam—international cuisine at its finest.

More leaning than sitting, he perched himself against a white wrought iron stool at the tumbled marble counter and munched on the flaky croissant, trying to think back as to the last time he'd eaten anything more significant than the cheese Danish and coffee he'd grabbed at the airport while he waited for the Lear to refuel. It was then he realized it was at the Walker's buffet almost two days before. That explained why he hadn't been hungry until now. He'd stuffed his face with enough food that night to sustain him on a long and winding trek through the Sahara.

"Can I fix you anything, Mr. Nick?"

Still chewing, he smiled and shook his head as he took a long swallow of milk to wash down the peanut butter. "No thanks, Dahlia. This is fine." He took another bite of the croissant. "I told Tomas I didn't want to be waited on while I'm here."

"It's no trouble, really. That's why I'm here." Dahlia started to pick up, screwing the lids back on the jars and resealing the container of croissants.

"I would have cleaned up after myself," he teased. "Honest."

"Then your mama, she taught you right." She spoke with the charming inflections of an island native.

"More like my wife."

"You married, Mr. Nick?" She frowned and narrowed her gaze, silently expressing her opinion that a married man had no business being there without his spouse.

"Not any more. I meant ex-wife," he corrected, practically choking on the term. He'd never get used to calling Maggie that. Regardless of her future marital status, he'd resigned himself to the simple fact that she'd be his wife forever, if only in his heart.

"Divorce is such a bad thing," the housekeeper stated. "It makes for many unhappy, lonely people in the world." She loaded the dishwasher and cast an impatient glance at his unfinished milk glass.

He quickly downed the last swallows and handed her

the glass, wiping his mouth with the back of his hand—a dreadful habit he realized he'd picked up from his sons.

"I couldn't agree with you more. Tell me something, Dahlia. How long have you and Tomas been married?"

"It was thirty-eight years this past April."

"Wow. Thirty-eight years. That's wonderful." He sounded truly awed at the prospect. He didn't know anyone who stayed married that long anymore. "Any children?"

"Oh yes," she said proudly. "We have six—three boys and three girls."

"Six!" Nick exclaimed.

"And seven grandchildren with another due any day."

"I always wanted a big family."

What about you, Mr. Nick? Did your marriage produce any children before the divorce?"

He nodded. "Twin sons. They're twelve now." He hesitated then added, "We had a daughter too, but she died when she was just an infant." A puzzled frown creased his brow. He didn't know why he mentioned Megan. He never talked about her. He'd buried the memories of her so deeply that there were times when he almost forgot he and Maggie had ever had another child. It was a time in his life he didn't like thinking about. Her death had been the beginning of the end for him and his marriage. Everything he accomplished after that was meaningless without his family to share it. Why couldn't Maggie understand that?

"I am so sorry for your loss, Mr. Nick. I can see her death is still painful for you."

"It was a long time ago, Dahlia." He rubbed his eye with the back of his knuckle as if there were an annoying itch that refused to be ignored.

"Whether it is the death of a child or the end of a marriage, grieving must finally be set free. When I look at you I do not see a man who has let go of either one." She wiped the counter in front of him with a sponge and scooped the crumbs off the edge into her palm, which she dusted into the sink by swiping her hands back and forth. Then she rinsed the sink and wiped it dry with a towel. "There is a lovely fresh tuna steak marinating in the refrigerator waiting to be grilled. I would be happy to come back later tonight and fix you dinner."

"I can manage, thanks. Go," he motioned to the door.
"Enjoy the evening with your husband. He's a lucky man."

"We are both the lucky ones, I think."

"Yes," he agreed, envious of the simple life this
woman shared for so many years with her husband. "You
are." He almost smiled envisioning an older version of
himself and Maggie sitting on a porch in a pair of
matching rockers with grandchildren scurrying all
around. An older looking Joel entered the picture and
turned his almost smile into a definite scowl. He shook his
head to clear the disturbing images and promptly left the
kitchen. The pounding was beginning to return.

Pouring a tall glass of pineapple-mango juice over ice
from the mini fridge behind the teakwood bar, he added a
generous splash of locally produced Cruzan rum and
reached for the remote that controlled the satellite radio.
What was he in the mood for, he asked himself as he
flipped through the channels? Classical? No. Opera? No!
Country? Not tonight. He was depressed enough. Jazz?
He hesitated when hearing Dave Koz, knowing this was
one of Maggie's favorite artists. No, nothing that
reminded him of her either. Eventually, he stopped when
finding something very Caribbean flavored—calypso and
steel drums. When in Rome, he reasoned with a resigned
sigh as the playful music bounced around the room from
the multitude of inconspicuously arranged speakers. In
spite of the lively tempo, the snappy beat couldn't muster
enough enthusiasm to so much as cause a solitary toe to
twitch in rhythm with the music.

Grabbing a handful of assorted nuts from the carved
wooden dish on the bar, he popped them into his mouth
and wandered through the open French doors and onto
the terrace overlooking the turquoise bay. The ever-
present island breeze greeted him, touching his face like a
lover's caress.

Leaning on the balustrade, he watched the activity
on the beach and water below. A shapely strawberry
blonde in a skimpy string bikini waved from a passing
speedboat. He returned the wave. She had the same build
and body type and similar hair but it wasn't Maggie. No
sense in pretending it was. Another woman jogging on the

beach looked familiar too. Damn. How could he ever purge her from his thoughts when he saw her everywhere he turned?

Where did he go from here, he wondered, flopping onto the thick padded chaise lounge as he peered into the bright blue Caribbean sky. Nowhere at the moment, he decided as he slid the sunglasses from the top of his head to shield his eyes from the glaring sun. He chose to cut himself off from the outside world, in particular that little corner of Indiana he called home.

After only a few miserable days of wallowing in self-pity and self-indulgence Nick realized he wasn't cut out for the lifestyle he was trying to live. It was just taking things from bad to worse.

When the headaches worsened, leaving him fatigued and nauseous, he looked for excuses and blamed it on stress, lack of activity, poor diet, and excessive drinking.

After examining his recent conduct, he decided to change his behavior and started with eating healthier. He eliminated alcohol from his daily routine and forced himself to relax. He started exercising regularly again, too, jogging on the beach every morning and swimming laps in the pool every afternoon.

Nick hoisted himself out of the deep end of pool instead of using the stairs or ladder. His back and shoulder muscles strained and bulged against the added exertion. He couldn't believe how easily he had fallen out of shape and sincerely hoped he could get back to his fighting weight with just as little effort.

Grabbing a towel, he dried off and draped it around his neck as he took the stone steps leading from the pool two at a time and entered the house to get himself a glass of juice. He'd grown extremely fond of the tropical fruit mixture blended fresh daily by Dahlia.

"You look like you're feeling better today, Mr. Nick," the housekeeper stated as she polished the marble-topped table in the dining area.

He looked at her, his eyebrows drawing together. "What makes you think I haven't been feeling well?"

"Too much pain medication for a man who is feeling good," she stated.

Of course, it dawned on him, the wastebasket in his

bathroom. He wasn't used to having people clean up after him. In spite of his repeated efforts to stop Dahlia and her husband from waiting on him, he realized it was futile to keep them from doing what they considered to be their job.

He smiled. Her concern touched him. "Just a pesky headache that I can't seem to shake. Nothing serious."

Nick turned his attention to a portrait of Mandy hanging over a teak credenza. It portrayed her in a lush tropical setting very similar in style and form to post-impressionist Paul Gauguin. Draped in a white gauzy sarong, she stood like a proud, pale moon goddess amid the pure, bright primitive colors. The stark contrast between her ethereal beauty and the colorful background was startling and haunting.

He absently rubbed his chest where a dull, empty ache began to radiate. Maybe he'd reached a turning point. Maybe it was time to move on so Maggie could do the same.

"Have you given any thought to what you would like for dinner tonight?" Dahlia asked, jarring Nick back to reality. "I've noticed you're trying to eat a little healthier lately. Tomas picked up some shrimp at the market this morning. I could grill them with some fresh herbs and vegetables."

"I'm never going to get you to stop waiting on me, am I?" He sipped his juice and peered at her from over the rim of chunky stemmed goblet.

"Tomas and I have been working for the Morgan family for more than twenty years. It has been both a pleasure and a privilege to serve them and their guests." Her response had been brief and to the point. "Now, how about those shrimp?"

"Thank you, Dahlia. The shrimp sound delicious." All this talk of shrimp made him think of his sons. Danny and Davey loved shrimp, especially deep-fried and dipped in a barrel of tangy cocktail sauce.

A pang of raw, unvarnished guilt niggled at him for never getting in touch with the boys since he left, and they couldn't reach him if they tried because his cell phone didn't work this far from the mainland. But somehow he knew he could explain his hasty disappearance to them when he returned. They'd understand even if no one else would.

He had grown extremely close to Danny and Davey in recent months, and it crossed his mind to ask for custody when Maggie remarried. She was starting a new family. She might actually be relieved to have him take the boys off her hands once the baby was born. Yeah, right. Like that would ever happen. If she was nothing else, she was a devoted mother who loved her sons more than life itself. She'd never give them up without a monumental fight, and he'd never put her through a custody battle.

Maggie. His lips mouthed her name. When would the mere thought of her stop causing such wretched pain in his heart? Would he ever be able to get on with his life or was he destined to live the remainder of his days on this earth loving a woman he'd never have? He clenched his teeth and gripped his head, massaging his fingers against his temples and forehead.

The headache was back in force and with it an overwhelming wave of nausea and dizziness. He hastened to the quiet darkness of his room and fumbled for the bottle of prescription pain meds he kept on the nightstand. After considerable searching he'd found a doctor on the island that prescribed the medication with only a cursory examination and a promise from Nick to follow up with his own doctor when he returned home.

The prescription drug at least dulled the pain to tolerable. He leaned against the pillows and covered his eyes with his forearm, concentrating on deep breathing and relaxing. It was time to stop fooling himself and admit there might be something more serious causing the symptoms. It was time to stop speculating and see a doctor. Soon, he told himself. He would go home soon. As tempting as it was to stay in this tropical paradise forever, he knew it was time to end this self-imposed exile. Just a few more days, he told himself as he slipped from awareness into dreamless sleep.

Chapter Twenty-Two

Reclined on the thick cushioned chaise, Nick lifted his head and sipped from the glass in his hand. The sweating tumbler dripped on his bare chest and he swiped the beads of water with a flick of his fingers before letting his head drop back against the tufted turquoise head support. Nick re-crossed his ankles and closed his sad blue eyes, raising his face to absorb the soothing warmth of the late afternoon sun. From behind his closed eyelids, he detected a change in the sun's intensity and figured a cloud was passing, offering a brief respite from the glaring brightness.

"Ooofff!" Something large, flat and heavy landed on his recumbent abdomen. Startled, he opened his eyes. It wasn't a cloud after all, it was Mandy. She stood at the foot of the lounge blocking his direct sun. At least he assumed it was Mandy. She was nothing more than a shapely dark silhouette framed by a brilliant solar aura.

Squinting and shading his eyes, he focused on her face and asked, "What's this?"

"The final draft of the merger contracts."

He sat up, balancing the hefty bundle in his palm. "All this for one little merger?"

"The board of directors is very thorough," she said with a laugh. "As are our lawyers."

Dressed in a tailored navy power suit and hint of pink blouse, Mandy Morgan looked trim and professional—a poster perfect image of the consummate businesswoman. It was sure a far cry from the barely there string bikini she wore the last time they occupied the same space on the terrace months earlier.

"Any problems?" Nick questioned, tossing the weighty manila envelope to the stone patio. It landed with a significant thud. He was ready to get out from under the financial burden. Morgan Enterprises had the resources to expand and grow the business far beyond anything he could have ever managed. The impending merger would be the best of both worlds for him and his team. He could now concentrate on building the cars he wanted and developing a racing team capable of challenging the best of the best without always worrying about how to pay the bills or make payroll.

"I don't foresee any. It's basically down to final approval from you and our lawyers taking it from there. There are a few additional contractual obligations the board insists you fulfill, but otherwise it's all pretty much what we discussed previously. Read it over and we'll go from there."

"What additional obligations?" Nick queried. "I've already agreed to drive for another three seasons."

"Commercials, public appearances, you know, PR stuff." She dismissed his concerns with a wave of a well-manicured hand.

Nick's spine stiffened. "Oh no," he protested. "I will not do another Chassis commercial."

"What's wrong with another Chassis commercial?" Mandy inquired with an innocent roll of her big brown eyes.

"I'd rather parade down Michigan Avenue in the middle of winter with thirty weight motor oil smeared all over my body and Morgan spark plugs shoved up my nose than go through that again. How come the other drivers get to do commercials for manly products like beer and razors and tools?"

Mandy laughed, her chocolate brown eyes crinkling with impish humor. "In spite of the fact that Chassis sales jumped by nearly thirty-seven percent in the weeks following that ad campaign, you won't be required to make any more Chassis ads. Besides, we couldn't possibly top that one. It's an industry classic. You're now exclusive spokesperson for Morgan Motor Parts. Period. Is that manly enough for you?"

"Yeah, "he said, sounding pleased at the prospect. "I can live with that."

She kicked off her sensible navy heels and removed her suit jacket, carelessly tossing it across the arm of the companion lounge as she encouraged him to scoot over with a pat on his thigh so she could sit beside him.

She studied his face. "You're looking rested," Mandy commented.

He half-laughed. "I should. I've been sleeping about twelve hours out of every twenty-four."

She lifted the glass from his fingers and took a long swallow. "What is this?" Her mouth expressed repulsive surprise.

"Dahlia said it was a blend of pineapple and mango."

"And...?"

"Ice."

"No Cruzan, no vodka, no gin?"

"Straight up juice."

She looked at him, as if seeing him in a whole new light, and smiled. "So you're presently stone cold sober?"

"As a judge."

Her gaze traveled down his body until it landed on the worn, faded denim cutoffs. "What may I ask are these?" She played with the raggedy strings hanging from the frayed edges and twisted them around her slender fingers.

"These have been my favorite shorts for years," he defended. "I've had them since college."

"Yes, I can see they've been around for a while." She chuckled, letting her pink manicured fingertips slip beneath the frayed edges to stroke the firm hair-roughened inner thigh beneath. "Don't you think it's time they finally graduated to a rag bag?" Higher and higher her fingers traveled.

Gripping her wrist with a gentle restraint, he queried with husky suspicion, "Mandy, what are you doing?"

Pressing her fingertips against his lips, she quieted his half-hearted protests. "Maybe it's time to kick this relationship up a notch and turn tabloid innuendo into reality. Public opinion already has us guilty. We might as well take advantage of the situation and enjoy ourselves. Let's really give 'em something to talk about, sugah." Limpid brown eyes visually caressed his surprised face.

"I've been patient and I think I've been a good girl long enough." A naughty but nice smile brightened her full, pouty lips. "Although I gotta tell you, Nick honey, I'm better when I'm bad."

Her voice dripped sweet and thick, like honey from a

sterling spoon. It coated his brain, soothing his pain and numbing his conscience. His broken heart longed to be comforted and begin the process of healing. This act could be the ultimate defiance—the final severance—and if not for the sugar Mandy supplied to help the medicine go down, a much bitterer pill to swallow. He was a free man. There wasn't anything holding him back. He mulled her proposition over and over in his head and had to admit he was tempted.

His hesitant silence forced her to continue her pitch. "I'm not lookin' for a lifetime, sugah. No promises, no commitments. Just you and me in that fabulous four-poster upstairs. What possible harm is there in that?"

She scooted closer and splayed her hands on his naked chest, massaging the hard, developed pectorals as she leaned forward and kissed him with practiced lips. Nick closed his eyes and allowed her the tentative exploration.

After unfastening the top pearly buttons of her shirt, she lifted his motionless hand and slipped it beneath the silky fabric, pressing it to her ample breast. His fingers flexed and felt the supple fullness covered in satin and lace. Mandy arched her back and pressed herself deeper into his grasp, moaning with obvious pleasure.

"All you need is a little of Mandy's special brand of southern hospitality," she purred, letting her hand wander down his stomach to explore the region below his waist beneath the thin, soft denim.

It would be so easy to surrender—to let this beautiful, sexy woman ease his battered spirit and soothe his broken heart. Relenting, he shifted to his side and lifted her petite frame to stretch the length of his taut, tanned body. A husky moan of approval escaped from his lips as his hands ran down her firm hips and thighs. Finding the hem of the prim dark blue skirt, he pushed it up and caressed the smooth expanse of perfect flesh beneath. It would be so easy. Who would know? Who would care?

He smiled when flashing green eyes looked back at him—big, beautiful, glorious green eyes. His heavy lids lifted slowly, and he leveled his gaze on her lovely face. A wave of sheer panic clutched at him when realizing

Mandy's eyes were brown!

"No!" He pushed away and rolled backwards off the lounge. Catching himself in a stumbling crouch, he scrambled to his feet.

"Oh, my god, Mandy. Oh, my god." Stunned, he stared unblinking, searching for some sort of reaction. He couldn't tell from her posture or expression what was going through that beautiful pale blond head.

"That response is normally reserved for during the act, sugah," Mandy muttered. She stared at him, her head tilted, her expression bland and indefinable.

"Mandy, please, I want you to know this has nothing to do with you. You are a beautiful, desirable woman and I'm probably going to kick myself in the morning, but I've never made love to another woman since Maggie. And until I know there isn't a snowball's chance in hell that we'll ever be together again, I can't do this. I thought I could, I really did, but I can't. I'm sorry."

Pushing down her skirt and buttoning her blouse, Mandy started to laugh. "I was this close," she drawled, gesturing with thumb and forefinger spaced barely an inch apart.

"You were closer than that," he admitted.

"I don't think so, sugah," she said, smoothing her mussed hair. "There was still an important part that wasn't quite as cooperative as the rest of you. And if the girls here can't get a rise out of you I don't think anything could have coaxed you to do otherwise." Though obviously disappointed, Mandy shrugged with resignation.

"I'm so very, very sorry, Mandy," Nick apologized. "I won't blame you if you take that contract and tear it into a million pieces."

"Now why in the name of sweet Sam Houston would I do a thing like that? Daddy taught me a long time ago to never confuse business with pleasure. I know a good thing when I see it, Nick, honey. And business-wise you are a very good thing. You are, however, if you don't mind my saying so, sorely lacking in the pleasure-wise department."

He rubbed his forehead in an attempt to wipe the sheepish look off his face and mumbled, "You can take the boy out of Indiana..." He paused. "Well, you know the rest."

"Yes, unfortunately, I'm afraid I do," she said, swinging her feet to stand. She smoothed her skirt with several long swipes of her polished fingers and slipped into the abandoned pumps.

"I guess what I'm trying to say is there aren't enough lessons, or fashion consultants, or even money in the world to change the way I feel. Maggie means everything to me. For fifteen years she's been the only woman in my life. It's her face I see at the beginning of every dream and the end of every finish line. As long as there's even a small chance I can be a little part of her life, I have to take it." He tossed his hands up in a helpless gesture.

"Don't waste those pretty words on me, honey. Forget the fancy clothes, and all that other stuff I thought you needed to get her back. Just tell her what's in that overgrown country boy heart of yours and don't give up until you hit the devil square in the eye with that snowball!"

"Yeah?" For the first time in innumerable days a glimmer of hope sparked and flickered in his eyes and challenged the lingering pain for supremacy. Mandy was right. He never accepted defeat so readily before. Why was he giving up so easily this time when the stakes were higher and more valuable than anything he'd ever been challenged for in the past? "You're absolutely right, Mandy. I'm going back and fighting for what's mine!"

"Yea!" Mandy cheered. "So why, are y'all still standing here?"

Chapter Twenty-Three

"Danny, Davey," Maggie hollered from the kitchen. "Get a move on. Your bus is going to be here any second." She grabbed their lunches from the counter and waited for them at the front door.

Sounding like a stampeding herd with very large feet, they flew down the stairs, jackets flapping, high tops untied and hair disheveled. She was at least grateful that their faces were clean and their flies were zipped, but it was time for haircuts, Maggie noted.

As a longstanding mother, she was prepared for a number of last minute emergencies. Maggie dug around in her robe pocket and produced a comb. She also had safety pins, nail clippers, shoestrings, Band-aids, individually wrapped wet wipes and a purse size pack of tissues. She found it was easier to have them at the ready then search for any one of the items when they were needed. As she swiped the comb across each of their heads, she said, "Zip your coats and tie your shoes."

Without argument, they dropped their book bags and complied. Since the incident with Joel's tires, Maggie rarely found it necessary to tell them anything more than once. They were in the process of working off a very large debt and she found it more effective when she added to what they owed whenever they misbehaved to a point where she found it necessary to raise her voice. They were learning a very valuable lesson—accountability for their actions.

Danny was still sullen and moody and Maggie wasn't sure at whom he was angrier—her for obvious reasons or Nick for disappearing without so much as an adios. Davey, on the other hand, wasn't nearly so easy to read. He didn't wear his heart on his sleeve like his brother and, as long as she continued to feed him regularly, gave all outward appearances of being his usual happy, even-tempered self. She wasn't sure which son she was more concerned about, Danny who openly displayed his resentment or Davey who kept everything bottled up inside.

"Still no word from your dad?" she asked Danny, smoothing a last errant lock of hair from his forehead.

"No," he answered gruffly, jerking away.

She understood her son's hostility, and she grew increasingly peeved at Nick with each passing day he remained incommunicado. To give her the cold shoulder was one thing; to ignore his sons was inexcusable.

"Maybe he was abducted by aliens," Davey suggested, his quirky tone attempting to lighten his brother's gloomy mood. "Or disappeared over the Bermuda Triangle!"

Sighing dramatically, Danny cast his brother a disbelieving eye roll. "I think your brain was abducted by aliens. You know, close encounters with the dumbest kind."

"They took mine only because they couldn't find yours." Davey countered with a wicked laugh and a backhanded smack on his brother's jacket sleeve.

Maggie intervened and situated herself between them before Danny had a chance to retaliate. She placed a restraining grip on Danny's arm and held them apart. "That's enough," she warned.

"Try to have a good day," she interjected, kissing each in turn on the top of their unruly blond heads as she scooted them out the door. Watching them trudge down the drive, she'd swear they had grown again, and made her realize it wouldn't be long before they were looking down at her and kissing her on the top of the head. They were going to be every inch as tall as their father. They were already every bit as good looking.

Just as she shut the door, she heard the bus' brakes squeal to a stop at the end of the cul-de-sac. They were cutting it closer and closer every day and, as she wondered what it was that delayed them, made a mental note to monitor their morning routine more closely.

After pouring a tall orange juice, Maggie moseyed into her workroom with glass in hand to plan her day. Glancing at the appointment calendar lying open on the desk, she was more than a little surprised to see the day's date. It was the first time in four years she hadn't dreaded its coming, and she couldn't stop the wave of guilt she felt for not remembering.

Then she recalled what the grief counselor had told her—the final step in the grieving process was acceptance. Her healing was obviously nearing its completion. Although Megan would never be far from her thoughts, Maggie realized the crushing sadness that had once overwhelmed her wasn't there anymore. She was finally coming to terms with the death of the infant daughter whose little wriggling body she'd cuddled and nursed and changed for such a short time. As Megan's mother she'd had the special privilege of holding her sweet child every day of her brief life from her first robust wail to her last silent breath.

Smiling through tears, Maggie stroked her expanding belly. Just as she had predicted, she popped suddenly, looking like someone had inflated her with an air compressor while she slept. Practically overnight she looked round and very pregnant.

A series of abrupt fetal movements made her laugh out loud. This precious child was indeed a joyous affirmation that the cycle of life goes on. She'd become a surrogate for herself every bit as much as for Beth and Joel. It was this simple act of giving life that had brought her closure when nothing else had. If only Nick had given her the opportunity to explain the concept. It made her wonder when she ever would have the chance. He'd been gone so long this time, almost two weeks without any contact, and she missed him more than she ever thought possible.

From a bottom desk drawer Maggie withdrew a silver-framed photo of Nick holding Megan taken the day they'd brought her home from the hospital. With a heavy heart, Maggie stared at the photo through a teary blur. It was one of the rare and wonderful pictures she had of the two of them. She had plenty of photos of Megan alone or with her big brothers, but precious few with just her father. Unaware of the camera or anything thing else but the newborn he cradled in his arms, Nick gazed at the sleeping, downy-haired infant wrapped in a puffy quilted cloud of pink and white. She wondered where he was as she set the photo on her desk where it belonged.

A second glance at her date book confirmed she didn't have a workshop scheduled until one. Not that the ladies coming in that afternoon needed an instructor. They knew every bit as much about quilting as Maggie. These bi-weekly dates were more of a social gathering for them than a learning experience. Every other week they scheduled their block of time, showed up faithfully, creating one beautiful quilt after another, all of which were donated to a pre-selected charity for raffle or auction. To date these women had raised thousands of dollars for good causes doing something they loved.

Glancing at the delicate china desk clock her sons had presented her on her twenty-fifth birthday, Maggie figured she had plenty of time to do what she wanted before the Quilting B's arrived, and she hurried up the stairs to dress.

The early November morning appeared sunny and mild when Maggie stepped out of the house and inhaled. The air was crisp and cold and carried with it the distinct scent of an early snowfall, and she was glad she dressed in warm layers of wool and corduroy. The nippy air chilled her lungs and made her shiver in spite of her adequate attire.

The wind was brisk and stinging, quickly chapping her lips and pinching a rosy blush into her cheeks as she pulled up the hood of her jacket and tightened the blue cable knit scarf around her neck. Stuffing her mitten-clad hands deep into her pockets, her breaths creating puffy clouds of misty vapor, she stepped off the curb and began a vigorous pace down the street toward Cartwright Woods. Tucked in the crook of one arm she carried a clay pot full of hearty gold and rusty red mums.

Thanksgiving was just around the corner and she could practically smell the sweet spices and pungent herbs that helped create the memorable scents of the traditional family oriented holiday. Pumpkins and scarecrows, bundled dried cornstalks and potted mums decorated porches and yards along her route. Picture windows displayed colorful cardboard cutouts of turkeys, cornucopias and autumn leaves.

Most of the Cartwright Corners residents were big on decorating for holidays, her home being no exception. She couldn't wait to see the neighborhood lit up for Christmas. That holiday more than any other brought out the ghost of good-natured competition, and every year the streets looked like Broadway on opening night.

Pine Arbor Cemetery was well within walking distance when she took the shortcut where the cemetery's back property line butted up against the far side of Cartwright Woods. There was a permanent break in the old chain link fence where the residents of Cartwright Corners cut through the cemetery to get to the town's main drag. Old man Cartwright never enforced the "Private Property" signs he had posted decades earlier. As long as folks respected the woods and left it in the same condition as they found it, he'd always said, they were welcome to enjoy nature's bounty. It suddenly occurred to Maggie that Nick now owned the property she hiked across. The pasture and woods were all part of the acreage surrounding the house he'd bought.

As she neared the six-foot high stone fence that encircled the sprawling bungalow and surrounding yard, she slowed her pace and hesitated for only a second before stretching on tiptoes to grip the decorative iron scrollwork that topped the wall. As she wedged the toes of her boots into naturally created projections, she pulled herself up and peered across the cobblestone wall.

Glancing around for some sign that Nick had returned, her heart plummeted when finding his truck covered with a thick layer of undisturbed construction dust. Crushing disappointment shadowed her weather-chapped features as she lowered herself.

The only activity she had witnessed that morning was a local plumbing firm unloading new bathroom fixtures from the back of a fire engine red box van. On a less serious note, she had to admit she was pleased to see the old-fashion styled claw-footed tub and pedestal sink being carried into the house, and was eager to see the progress Nick had accomplished on the house's restoration since her one and only visit. She couldn't help wonder if she would ever be welcome there again.

Maggie forced herself not to dwell on the possibility of him sharing the house with someone else. All she ever wanted was to make things right for him and all she ever seemed to do was make things worse for her.

Fallen leaves crunched and rustled as her brown leather ankle boots waded through leafy drifts arranged in piles by the blustery wind. The underlying ground was still soft from recent rains and she occasionally felt her feet sink into the boggy, rotting layers of leaves and mushy earth.

The woods were teaming with activity. A half dozen white-bellied brown squirrels scurried up and down gnarly barked oaks, leaping from branch to branch with acorns clutched in their tiny jaws, while a pair of blue jays squawked and flew from a leafless maple into the secluded protection of a towering blue spruce.

At the sound of something much bigger than a squirrel crashing through the brush, Maggie startled and whirled around just in time to see two white-tailed deer disappear into a dense cluster of pungent pines and spruce. Captivated, Maggie couldn't help smiling at the bustling wildlife preparing for the forthcoming winter as she climbed through the opening in the fence and slipped from a place where life abounded into another world where the pall of death resided.

Megan's gravesite was located near the center of the cemetery in a section specifically designated for babies and children. As depressing as it sounded, Maggie found the place a peaceful retreat and comforting interlude. She often went there to sit and reflect on what might have been, not so much in a maudlin way of hanging on but more as a way of letting go. The cluster of tiny headstones and grave markers were surrounded by a secluded arbor bordered on three sides by a line of tall evergreens. Two larger-than-life granite angels stood sentry on either side of the hedged entrance, maintaining an ever-present vigil on their eternally young charges.

The grassy ground was soft and spongy as she approached the area. She came up short when realizing she wasn't alone. Fifty feet up the path she spotted a man wearing a heavy Sherpa-trimmed denim jacket and black Stetson walking away from her toward the same area she was heading. There was something so haunting about the solitary figure. She stood transfixed until the cold and heartache penetrated her faraway thoughts and caused her to shiver. Maintaining a fair distance, she followed the path and kept a close eye on the lone form ahead.

He walked slowly, as if uncertain to where he was going, pausing occasionally to kick away leaves in order to read an engraved plaque or headstone. Hunched against the wind with hands shoved deep in side pockets and collar turned up, he finally stopped and crouched down, removing his hat as he lowered his frame. He brushed away the remaining debris covering the recessed headstone as he balanced on the balls of his booted feet. The wind whipped his hair around his bowed head as he braced his elbows on his knees, gripping the brim of his hat in his fingers. Deep in thought or prayer, he never heard her approach.

Maggie's heart lurched and twisted as unbidden tears sprang to her eyes. She covered her mouth with her mittened hand and closed her eyes against the painful image of a grieving father.

Gripped by the stark realization of what she witnessed, she cried harder. She'd been so overwhelmed by her own heartache when Megan died, she hadn't given his sorrow a second thought. Nick had moved through the wake and funeral with such stoic reserve, it hadn't occurred to her that he'd never allowed himself the opportunity to properly mourn his child's death. While she was nearing the end of her grieving period, it appeared that Nick was just beginning his, and it came to her with startling clarity that she alone was responsible for this tragic turn of events. Asking for the divorce so soon after Megan's death had short-circuited his mourning. She'd been so consumed with doing what was best for his career she'd completely ignored his needs as a father. She buried her face in her hands, deeply ashamed and confused.

How could she ever forgive herself for what she'd done? A better question was how could he? She approached slowly. Hesitant to intrude, yet compelled to comfort, she reached out a tentative hand and touched his shoulder.

Nick drew a ragged breath and turned to face her. His eyes were red and puffy, his features strained and drawn. Upon seeing her, he quickly lowered his head and turned away.

Kneeling beside him, she placed the pot of mums near the grave marker. She grasped and tugged at the scraggly weeds growing around the granite plaque and tossed them aside.

She sat back on her heels placed a hand on his back. "I know we have some unresolved issues, Nick. Please don't ever let this child we created be one of them. She was our little girl, our baby." When his only response was a deep, shuddering sigh, Maggie chose to back off and leave him alone.

Breaking off a handful of the potted mums, Maggie took the smaller bouquet and retreated, walking a short distance down a different path away from Angel's Gate. After placing the flowers in the brass vase attached to the simple granite headstone, she sat on the concrete bench positioned near the foot of Beth's grave.

Steeped deeply in fond memories of her dear friend, Maggie never heard Nick come up behind her.

"Elizabeth Hubbard?" he questioned.

"You knew her as Beth Mahoney," Maggie clarified.

Recognition twisted his features. "The cute little red head you used to hang around with in high school?"

Maggie nodded.

"My god, Maggie, she's your age. What happened?" He sat next to her, their shoulders barely touching. He scooted a little closer until their hips and thighs touched too. "Was it an accident?"

"Breast cancer," Maggie answered. Feeling the warmth he generated, she fought against the impulse to lean into him and forced herself to inch away. Could she trust him to be there if she leaned too hard? Or would he disappear if things got ugly again?

"I thought only older women got breast cancer."

"That's what a lot of people think, including a few doctors. In Beth's case it simply wasn't diagnosed early enough because no one took the lump seriously. Not even Beth or her husband."

"Hubbard? Hubbard?" Nick reiterated under his breath. "Why do I know that name?"

Without saying another word, Maggie stood and swept away the leaves with her foot from the lower portion of the granite headstone to reveal what was engraved there: BELOVED WIFE OF JOEL.

Chapter Twenty-Four

She heard his startled intake of breath. "Now that I finally have your attention, you need to know something about this baby I'm carrying." She watched his gaze drop to the swelling protrusion beneath her jacket. "It's theirs—Beth and Joel's. I'm their surrogate." Maggie went on and briefly explained to Nick the same details she had given the boys.

"Why didn't you tell me this before?"

"The right time just never seemed to present itself. The longer I put it off the harder it got to tell you. And that night after the party, well, you know how well that went. When I went to your house the next morning, you were gone."

Nick covered his face with his hands and drew them down with a long, disturbed sigh. "Do you have any idea how excited I was when I thought we were going to have another baby? This was our second chance. When you told me the baby wasn't mine I felt like I'd been punched in the gut with a baseball bat. I couldn't breathe, I couldn't think, and I sure as hell wasn't interested in hearing anything else you had to say." His voice grated with a rawness she could almost feel. "Even now, knowing the circumstances, it still hurts knowing you're carrying another man's child."

"I know," she said against the burning tightness clutching at her own throat. "Hurting you is all I seem to do." She leaned against his shoulder, and rubbed his arm with the back of her mittened hand. "I'm so sorry for everything, Nicky. My only hope is that someday you'll find it in your heart to forgive me for the mess I've made of your life." She stood and started to leave.

"Maggie, don't go." Nick placed a restraining hand on her arm. "There's nothing to forgive."

"How can you say that?" She sounded truly bewildered, and looked at him with aching regret and deep sadness. She tugged off a mitten and touched his cheek with warm fingers, felt the place where his dimple would be if he were smiling. "I don't want to hurt you any more. I think it's my turn to put some distance between us."

He frowned, his mouth turning down at the corners, and his eyes narrowed to squinting slits. "For how long?" He pulled a pair of wraparound sunglasses from the inside pocket of his jacket and slipped them on.

She hadn't expected him to ask for a specific timeframe. "I don't know. Let's see what happens after the baby is born."

"That's still months away," he stated, as if that fact alone dismissed her suggestion. He shook his head against the very idea. "No. I won't agree to that."

"Nick, please, I need the time to concentrate on delivering a healthy baby. I owe it to Beth."

"Fine," he answered tersely without another moment's pause. "Whatever you think." His jaw muscle popped and twitched.

"Thank you for understanding, Nick."

"Don't ever confuse my capitulating for understanding, Maggie." He stared at her through the smoky lenses. "I simply don't have the energy to argue with you."

Nick not have the energy to argue? She studied his face. He looked tired, almost haggard, and his forehead puckered with deep furrowed ridges.

"Did Beth know?" he asked. "Did she know you were pregnant before she died?"

Maggie shook her head. "No."

Maggie reached into her jacket pocket and pulled out a crumpled but reasonably clean tissue. She smoothed it between her fingers and blew her runny nose. "She took a turn for the worse and died shortly after I was implanted with the embryos." She choked on the words.

The Presbyterian Church located a mile down the road from the cemetery rang its tower bells every day at noon. Upon hearing them toll, Maggie's eyes grew enormous with surprise. "I've got a group of ladies coming to the house at one. I've got to get back."

"Mind if I walk with you?" Nick asked.

"Of course not," she answered.

"I only asked because I don't want to be accused later of breaking a rule or anything." He clenched his cold fists and jammed them deep into the slash pockets of his coat.

Ignoring his sarcasm, she replied, "Let's just take each day as it comes, okay?" She hastened her pace and he dropped into step beside her.

"Is it safe to assume these plans of yours don't include marrying Joel?"

She shook her head. "No."

He stopped in his tracks. "No?" He sounded horrified.

"I don't mean no, as in it's not safe to assume, I mean no, I don't plan to marry Joel," she clarified, sounding as if the prospect was absurd. "He was just being chivalrous and overprotective that night. Joel is a dear, sweet friend and he's going to make a wonderful, loving father, but that's all." She gave a little shudder. "Marrying my dead friend's husband... That's just too weird to even think about, let alone consider."

"I'm glad to hear that." Nick sounded happy and relieved. "So what are your thoughts about marrying your ex-husband?" He took her mitten-covered hand and wrapped it in his own. "The offer still stands, you know."

"I feel very optimistic about the possibility."

"Do you think you could be a bit more specific?" he prompted.

She stopped and turned to face him. Placing her hands on his chest, she said, "We rushed into marriage the first time, Nicky. Let's not make that same mistakes again, okay?"

He nudged the brim of his hat off his face with the tip of his thumb. "Take all the time you need, little lady, but keep in mind I'd like to get married again before I'm offered the AARP discount on the honeymoon suite."

She stifled a laugh. "Well..." she drawled, deliberately drawing out the word. "Considering your advanced years, I'd better hurry and give you an answer before you forget what the honeymoon suite is for."

"I'll show you what it's for—" he growled, whirling her into a tight embrace. The kiss was slow and deep, filled with endless longing and tender promises. He forced a slow, lazy smile, hoping to hide the painful drumming in his head. "How's that?"

"More than I deserve," she said as she closed her eyes and pressed her cheek against his chest. "I love you," she said with a breathless whisper. "And I plan on spending the rest of my life proving it to you."

Nick tightened his embrace. Closing his eyes, he lifted his face to the sun with an expression awash with poignant relief and gratitude. He was nearing the finish line of the most important race he'd ever run. "No arguments from me." He took her hand and brought it to his lips as they started walking again.

"You know, Nicky, on my way over here this morning it occurred to me that these are Chapparelle Woods now."

"They will always be Cartwright Woods."

"Will you continue to let people cut across the property on their way to town?"

"To be honest I've never given it any thought." The pain in his head made it difficult for him to concentrate. It made him nauseous and turned him irritable and cranky. At times like this the hurt in his head was almost too excruciating to endure, and he forced himself to take deep, slow breaths to maintain control.

"Well, will you?"

"Will I what?" he asked. Though feeling an overwhelming peace within, his head pounded relentlessly. However hard he fought for control, he teetered on the brink of civility.

"Are you going to leave the property accessible to the neighborhood?"

"Sure, why the hell not?" he snapped. "The whole damn friggin' world can traipse all over it for all I care."

Maggie cast him a startled sideward glance, wondering why he sounded so annoyed. Was she treading into an area he didn't want to discuss? Did he have plans for the property he didn't want her to know about? She watched him rip off his sunglasses with one hand as he rubbed his eyes and forehead with the other. His fingers were tense and trembling.

Placing a gentle hand on his arm, she asked, "You okay?"

"Yeah, I'm fine," he said. "Just tired." He sighed and looked at her with heavy-lidded eyes and dilated pupils.

"I'm sorry, honey. I didn't mean to snap like that." He absently rubbed his temples.

"I've got just the thing to perk you up. A nice cup of hot chocolate smothered with whipped cream and sprinkles," she enthused as they approached her front porch. "How does that sound?"

"Sounds okay," he said. "But I'd rather have you smothered in whipped cream and sprinkles." To hell with the pain, he thought. Nothing was going to stop him from enjoying every minute of this monumental turning point in their lives.

"Hmmm," she purred and giggled, slipping the key into the door lock. "I'll see what I can do."

"To hell with the whipped cream," he growled as the door closed behind them. Nick wasted no time in pulling her into his arms. She raised her face to accept his kisses. "This is where you belong," he whispered against her hair. "It's where you've always belonged."

"I never wanted to let myself believe it. I was convinced you were better off without me." She unbuttoned his jacket and slipped her arms around his waist. He felt lean and taut beneath the soft chamois shirt.

"And what about now?" The brim of his Stetson cast a distorted shadow across his handsome face and further deepened an already dark tan. "What more do I have to do to prove to you that I can't live without you?"

Maggie studied him with a thoughtful gaze. The suspicion started small, just an annoying inkling that refused to be disregarded, no differently she imagined, than an irritating pebble shifting in the sole of a shoe until she was finally forced to acknowledge it. It rubbed and aggravated until she couldn't stand it anymore.

"It looks like you've faired pretty well without me these last couple weeks." In spite of wanting to keep her tone nonjudgmental, she couldn't keep the accusatory pitch from rising in her voice. "Where was it this time, Nick? Mexico? The Rivera? Hawaii? Wait, don't tell me. You were in St. Croix again, weren't you?" She sounded like a jealous, resentful shrew. "While you were funning and sunning in the Virgin Islands again, your wife and sons were freezing and wheezing in Northwest Indiana wondering where in the hell you were."

There was only one word out of her entire tirade that caught his attention. "My wife? When did you start considering yourself my wife again?"

"That's not what I said."

"Yes it is."

"Well, it's not what I meant," she insisted.

"Yes it is." He gripped her by the shoulders and forced her to look at him. "You've never stopped thinking of me as your husband anymore than I stopped thinking of you as my wife. The divorce, the last four years, all your arguments to the contrary, haven't changed one thing, have they, Maggie?"

She gave his question careful consideration then started to laugh. "No. It doesn't seem so. I'm still the pregnant shrew and you still think you're going to tame me!" Her hearty laughter filled the hallway; it glistened in her emerald eyes and filled her face with pure joy. "Fighting seems to be every bit as much a part of our relationship as the loving."

Nick's husky laugh bubbled up and burst from his lips like a gusher spouting from deep within the earth. "God, how I love you! Make no mistake about that." He reached for her. Maggie didn't need any prompting. She settled into his embrace finally knowing Nick was right. This was where she belonged.

"I'm sorry, Nicky. I didn't mean to accuse you of things I know you're incapable of doing."

"Yeah, well, that was another lifetime ago. Let's put the past behind us and focus on our future life together." He absently rubbed his forehead.

"Is that your way of telling me you spent another life with someone else?" She began to get the horrible feeling that his hesitance meant that more happened than he was willing to admit. "Nick?"

Stepping back, he placed a short distance between them and lowered his head. "I can't lie to you, Maggie. I was miserable, and hurting. I thought we were through for good this time and she was very available. I came close. I almost let myself get carried away."

She swallowed hard. "Almost?" A sharp stab of irrefutable jealously pierced her heart. Inasmuch as she'd never tell him, she wouldn't have blamed him for getting carried away, as he put it. But she sure as hell didn't have to like it if he had.

"I just couldn't do it. As beautiful and sexy and willing as she was, I couldn't do it."

Maggie swallowed hard. "What stopped you?"

"I just told you." He sounded exasperated. "I couldn't do it."

The realization wasn't like a cartoon light bulb popping over her head. It was more of a gradual brightening like a rheostat bringing the evidence into focus from fuzzy dimness to crystal brilliance. "Oh!" Maggie exclaimed. "You couldn't *do* it." She collapsed against him, giddy with relief. "I'm so glad!"

"This is not ordinarily something a man likes to celebrate, honey. But just this once I'll make an exception."

"You who!" Betty Folger poked her head inside the door then walked in. Her friends followed close behind their fearless leader. "Hello, Maggie dear." Upon noticing Nick, she glanced questioningly at Maggie. "You were expecting us, weren't you?"

"Yes, of course, Betty." Maggie wiggled out of Nick's stronghold and gestured toward the workroom. "Go on in, ladies. I'll be with you in just a few minutes."

"Looks like our Maggie has found herself a new beau," Betty stage whispered to the others, who all offered their nodding agreement. Betty glanced over her shoulder and smiled her approval.

Nick respectfully removed his hat. "It's a pleasure to meet you ladies." Hat in hand, he flashed them a dazzling toothpaste commercial smile with dimples so deep Betty could have parked her Volvo in their charming depths.

Maggie cast him an almost shy, loving glance. "Dinner tonight?"

"You bet."

"It's movie night."

"Whose turn?"

"Mine."

"Aw, Maggie," he whined, slapping his hat against his thigh. "Please, not a night of sappy chick flicks."

"I'll make you a deal. I'll let you pick the movie if you

tell me everything, and I do mean *everything*, about your stay is St. Croix."

"So what'll it be?" he said straight-faced. "*Steel Magnolias* or *The Way We Were*?"

"You rat!" she chuckled, poking him in the ribs. "Get whatever you want at the video store. Just don't think for a minute you're off the hook. You've still got some serious splainin' to do, mister."

"I'll pick the boys up from school, too. I suspect I've got some serious splainin' to do to them too."

"You bet your sweet Stetson, you do!"

Chapter Twenty-Five

"Looks like you're going to finish up today, ladies." Maggie circled the quilting frame that held the pastel masterpiece and gave each member of the quilting club a congratulatory pat on the back for their extraordinary efforts. She paused when she reached Betty Folger and allowed her hand to rest on the woman's shoulder.

"Have you given any thought to your next project?"

"No, not yet," the woman on Betty's left answered.

"Would you mind if I suggest a design I've been working on?"

"Of course not, dear," said Betty.

Maggie hurried to her desk and pulled out a sketch from a folder. "Keep in mind that it's only a rough draft, but if you give me the okay I'll have it scaled out and the pattern ready by your next scheduled day."

She laid the preliminary drawing on the quilt the women were finishing and held her breath as each of them took their turn studying the drawing before passing it on to the next for similar scrutiny.

"Maggie, dear," said Betty as she removed her half lens magnifying glasses and let them dangle from a pearly beaded chain against her bosom. "Considering the personal significance of this design, are you sure you don't want to do this quilt yourself?"

Maggie's heart plummeted. "You don't like it." It was a statement not a question.

"On the contrary, it's beautiful and by far one of the best patterns you've ever designed. But wouldn't you like to be the one to make it?"

"With the holidays and all I'm on deadline for several special order projects at the moment. I'm really anxious to get this one started as soon as possible. I was hoping to have it ready for a breast cancer fundraiser held in February. I would not only consider it a huge favor but a significant honor if you ladies would do the work for me.

My contribution to the project will be all the fabric and supplies."

Betty glanced at the ladies seated around the quilting frame and received a nod of approval from each of her surrounding cohorts. "It's unanimous."

The only thing brighter than her grateful tears was the brilliance of her smile. "Thank you all so much," she gushed, working her way around the frame to give each woman an appreciative hug. "You ladies are the best!" A hearty kick punctuated her statement. She clutched her stomach and laughed. "I think someone else it trying to say thank you, too!"

Maggie started to work on the final design the minute The Quilting B's walked out the door with a solemn promise they'd be back the following week ready to start their newest project. Another unanimous vote by the group decided to work more frequently to assure the quilt was completed in time for the charity auction.

Once she had all the pattern pieces drawn to scale and converted into templates, Maggie would start the most difficult part of the process—selecting the perfect fabrics. She scanned the shelves of stacked bolts already on hand and pulled several down for further consideration, but she definitely needed to go shopping.

She was still working on cutting and fitting the templates when Nick and the boys came stomping into the house. A glance at the desk clock told her it was nearly seven. The boys had gotten out of school hours ago. It made her to wonder what the three of them had been up to all afternoon. Nick's 'splainin'' must have taken longer than she thought it would. She hoped the boys weren't too hard on him, although she also hoped they didn't let him off the hook too easily either.

Turning from her task, Maggie found the boys flanking Nick in the middle. They filled the archway of her workroom wearing identical Cheshire grins and staring at her with the same intense blue gazes. Visually caressing each handsome face, she asked herself if this was what she had to look forward to living with the three of them again? Oh, dear Lord, she hoped so.

"What's going on, guys?" she asked, setting down her cutting tool and removing the glasses she only wore for extended close work.

"Nothing," Danny answered.

"Yeah, nothing," Davey parroted.

"Absolutely nothing," Nick emphasized.

"Three nothings from you guys always add up to a big something."

It's nothing, Mom," Danny assured her. "Honest. We're just happy to see you, that's all." The three of them surrounded her and kissed her in turn, one son on each cheek and Nick on her lips.

"Yeah, happy," said Davey.

"Very happy," Nick whispered.

Maggie shifted her wary gaze from left to middle to right and back again. "Okay, fine." Electing to ignore them, she began the necessary task of straightening her worktable and putting away the tools of her craft. Everything was carefully returned to its designated storage compartment. "I'm not going to let the three of you drive me crazy. Not tonight, anyway. I've got dinner to get started." She turned off the gooseneck lamp, pushed away from the worktable and left the room, leaving her troublesome trio laughing in the dark.

So completely wrapped up with working on the quilt design all afternoon, she hadn't given dinner a passing thought. Maggie stood in the middle of the kitchen and pondered what to fix that wouldn't take much time or effort. Where was all the miraculous assistance from animated hands and talking refrigerators the commercial moms always got when dinner was down to the wire? She opened the freezer and stared intently through the misty condensation swirling from the frosty cavity. Nothing remotely interesting captured her attention.

"It's too late to start something now, Mags. Why don't I pick something up?" Nick suggested.

Slamming the freezer door shut, she answered without giving his suggestion a second thought. "Chinese. I want Chinese." Her tone allowed for no substitutions.

"Now why doesn't that surprise me?" He shook his head and laughed. "Chinese and chocolate. Some things never change."

"Okay, Mr. Know-It-All, what do I want from The Golden Buddha?" It had been a long time since they'd had

Chinese food together. He couldn't possibly remember what she liked.

"Egg rolls, hot and sour soup, crab Rangoon and shrimp lo mien."

She smiled smugly thinking he didn't know her as well as he thought. "Close but no cigar for the man in the black Stetson."

"With sweet and sour sauce for the egg rolls and almond cookies for dessert," he added. "But I'll pick up a couple of double chocolate hot fudge sundaes from Dairy Queen just to be on the safe side."

Correct on all counts—right down to the hot fudge sundae! If she didn't have this sudden, uncontrollable craving for every single, delectable, MSG-free morsel he ticked off, she would have requested something entirely different like Peking duck and moo goo gai pan just to prove him wrong.

"Lucky guess," she grumbled.

"Yeah, that must be it," he conceded. "Come on guys. Let's go get your mother's lucky guess dinner before she tries to change her order just to prove me wrong." He laughed all the way out the door.

****

What was taking them so long? Maggie wondered, feeling her empty stomach growl for the umpteenth time. Already starving and swiftly approaching nauseous, she dug around in the pantry and pulled out a box of crackers. Nibbling on a dry saltine and clutching an additional stack between her fingers, she wandered to the front door and glanced out the pebbled glass sidelight. Nick and the boys were taking an unusually long time in picking up dinner from a carryout restaurant less than three miles away. She could have walked there and back faster.

However hard she tried to convince herself otherwise, she couldn't shake the uneasy feeling that crept into her consciousness until it finally refused to be ignored. She hoped that her hormonally stimulated imagination was just working overtime and she was just being worrisome for nothing.

She sighed with relief when spotting the high headlights of a truck turn into their cul-de-sac, which she recognized as the F-250 as it neared the house. It bounced

203

and jostled as it took the curb with excessive speed and came to abrupt, cab-jerking, tire-screeching stop just inches from the garage. Maggie waited at the rear door ready to tell him in no uncertain terms to save that kind of driving for the track, especially when their children were in the vehicle.

As he entered through the sliding glass door, Nick cast her a *don't-even-go-there* look that made her hold her tongue. Highly agitated, he plunked the carryout bags on the island counter and paced the length of the kitchen like a restless tiger. Beneath the tan, his face and neck were flushed with anger. The boys seemed only slightly less disturbed than their father.

"What took so long? I was getting worried." Maggie looked to the boys for answers since Nick didn't appear to be in any mood to explain anything. He continued to pace the floor, occasionally pounding the counter with the side of his fist.

She'd never seen him like this before. Maggie gestured and mouthed, "What happened?" to the twins.

Danny and Davey glanced at each other before Danny answered. "There was kind of an accident."

"Accident? That was no accident," Nick fumed. "An accident is something that happens without any previous knowledge of it occurring. I knew exactly what was going to happen to that friggin' idiot."

"What happened?" Maggie asked aloud this time.

"Some loud mouth jackass in the restaurant recognized me when the clerk called my name for our order. He started going on and on and on to the guy sitting next to him, loud enough for me to hear of course, about Brickyard and how I deserved what happened to me considering the way I was driving that day and how amazed he was that somebody didn't try to put me in the wall a lot sooner than lap one-twenty.

"I really tried to ignore the idiot, Maggie. I calmly paid our check and we left. I figured it was all over when he climbed into his car."

Maggie watched in amazement as Nick's entire demeanor suddenly shifted gears from irritated to envious. "And what a car, Maggie, you should have seen it—a mint condition '69 Camaro Z28 Coupe. It was a beauty—Lemans blue, rally stripes, chrome wheels..."

"Nick," said Maggie, in an attempt to get his attention. "You're digressing." Not to mention drooling, she noted as she snapped her fingers to bring him back from the land of hot muscle cars and big block engines.

He shook his head and blinked. "Anyway, he gunned his engine like he was challenging me or something. I made the mistake of laughing and must have looked at him like he was crazy because he popped the clutch and jumped out of the parking spot next to us like a jackrabbit on fire. He nearly hit Davey!"

"What?" Maggie exclaimed, horrified. "Are you alright?" she asked her son as she placed her arm around him and did a visual and physical inventory of his visible parts.

"That's when I lost it, Maggie. I'm used to disgruntled fans blowing off steam because they think I did this or that to their favorite driver. Hell, it goes with the job. I've learned over the years to turn a deaf ear to their rantings. But I can't ignore some asshole that endangers one of my kids."

Maggie was almost afraid to ask. "What did you do?"

"The sonofabitch's car is in a ditch off Route 30. Needless to say his Camaro isn't so cherry anymore."

"Nick, you didn't? Please tell me you didn't run him off the road."

"That's the beauty of it, Maggie. I never touched the jerk. I didn't have to. Too much horsepower and too little brains is a dangerous combination. The second the chicken shit thought I was coming after him he stomped on the gas and took off. He lost control all by himself. The car's rear end started coming around on him when he accelerated, he over compensated, and flipped into the ditch."

"Was he hurt?" she asked.

"Nah. You know what they say about drunks and children.

"I called the cops from my cell and waited until they showed up. I told them what happened and lucky for me so did several other good Samaritans who witnessed the accident and stopped. When they inspected my truck and didn't find a scratch on it, they took my statement and let me go. The other guy, however, was unsuccessfully attempting to pass a field sobriety test when we left."

He took long, deliberate strides into the family room and hunkered onto the sofa. After tugging off his boots, he rested his head against the cushions and closed his eyes. "My guess is he's sitting behind bars even as I speak facing reckless driving charges and a DUI."

"I'm just glad that nobody got hurt." Maggie attempted to divert everyone's attention to a more pleasant subject, like food. The farther along in this pregnancy she got the more she sounded and acted like Davey. "Let's eat. I'm starved."

Never opening his eyes, Nick murmured, "You go ahead. I'm not hungry."

"So, what racing movie did you guys get this time?" Maggie asked, unpacking the numerous white cardboard cartons onto the island counter. The emanating smells were making her ravenous.

"We got a classic double feature, Mom—*Stroker Ace* and *Six Pack*." Davey answered, then paused and turned to her with a curious frown. "How'd you know we'd get racing movies?"

"Because you always get racing movies," she said. "Or some other form of action movie dealing with speeding, crashing, chasing, zooming or flying." Maggie bit into a crunchy Rangoon and savored the creamy crab filling. She licked her fingers then loaded her plate with all her favorites while the boys did the same. As much as she always teased and complained about their movie selections, she honestly didn't care what they got. It was the time they spent together as a family that was most important to her. She would have been just as happy with static and a test pattern.

"How about my fixing you a plate, Nick?" she offered.

"Not now," he answered tersely, resting his forearm across his eyes.

Maggie carried an egg roll into the family room and waved it under his nose, certain he'd perk up the minute he smelled his favorite Chinese appetizer. He barely opened his eyes and pushed her hand away. "I said I wasn't hungry," he snapped. Maggie jumped back with surprise and dropped the egg roll. It landed on the carpet beside her foot. Without a word she bent and picked it up.

He sat up and slouched forward, clutching his head in his hands. "Honey, I'm sorry. I've got this bitch of a headache I just can't seem to shake and it's making me idle a little rough."

"How long has this been going on?" She sat beside him and rubbed his neck where his hair was beginning to curl at the nape. Looks like her sons weren't the only ones who needed a haircut.

"I don't know...two, three weeks maybe."

"Three weeks?" she repeated. "Have you seen a doctor?" She was more concerned than she let on. Nick was the healthiest person she knew. He never got as much as a cold.

He nodded. "I saw one in St. Croix when over-the-counter pain meds weren't working anymore."

"And what did he say?"

"Nothing conclusive. He told me to follow up with my own doctor."

"Have you made an appointment to see Doctor Fields?"

"I've already seen him."

"And what did he say?" She felt like she was struggling to drag every word out of him.

"Nothing. He's waiting for the test results."

Tests? What tests?"

"EEG, brain scan, MRI, blood work for starters."

"Those tests take time. How long have you been back? Your truck didn't look like it had been moved as of this morning."

A sly, pleased smile tugged at the corners of his mouth. "Been checking up on me?"

"Don't stray from the subject? How long have you been home?"

"I flew in late Wednesday. I stayed at a hotel near the airport then rented a car and drove directly to the doctor's the next morning. He sent me to the neurologist down the hall from his office and that doctor sent me for the tests."

"Did the neurologist give you any idea what might be wrong?"

Nick shook his head. "You know doctors don't work

that way." Squinting against the glare from the table lamp situated behind her, he looked at her through pain-glazed eyes and managed a smile. "I missed having you care bout me."

She smiled and rested her chin on his shoulder. "I never stopped caring, Nicky. I just didn't always let you know how much."

Chapter Twenty-Six

The medication he'd taken earlier started to work and Nick began to feel better by the time Maggie and the boys finished eating. He picked at the leftovers, knowing he had to eat something or risk getting sick from taking the pills on an empty stomach. It was a vicious cycle he knew he couldn't keep repeating. It was wearing him down. In spite of his growing concerns, he wanted answers. How could he plan a future when he didn't know if he had one?

After eating as much as he possibly could, he clapped his hands and rubbed them together, and said, "So what's it going to be, guys? Burt Reynolds or Kenny Rogers?"

"*Six Pack*," Davey said, grabbing the DVD case from the table.

Maggie was already in her usual spot on the sofa, curled in one corner against the padded arm with one leg stretched out the length of the couch and the other tucked under her. Nick didn't waste any time in snuggling his back into the curve of her legs. She draped her arms over his shoulders and kissed the top of his head as they settled into a comfortable position to watch the movie.

By the beginning of the second feature, Maggie found herself falling asleep. Nick had stretched out the length of the couch and had his head resting in her lap. She eased herself out from under him, kissing him on the forehead as she did so, and slipped a throw pillow into the spot she recently vacated.

"I'm heading to bed," she announced. "Don't forget to turn everything off and lock up. Goodnight, guys."

She immediately fell into a deep, dreamless sleep and when she awoke a few hours later she felt like she had slept much longer than the clock dictated. Shifting her weight, she realized she wasn't alone. Nick was lying curled up beside her. Her bladder urged her to hasten to the bathroom and when she returned she found him half-sitting with pillows propped behind his head.

"I'm sorry I woke you," she said softly as she slipped under the covers. "But when nature calls, I've got to answer." She eased over and rested her head against his chest. His arm curled around her shoulder and pulled her closer.

"You didn't wake me. I've been watching you."

She breathed a little chuckle and snuggled more deeply into his embrace. "What were you watching? I was asleep." Her hand splayed across his chest. Everywhere her hand wandered, her fingers caressed his warm flesh in a manner that suggested she couldn't quite believe he was real. There had been too many nights her arms had reached out for Nick and all she found was the same emptiness she felt in her heart.

"I was watching you sleep." he explained as he played with her hair, repeatedly running the silken strand through his fingers. "Do you remember the first time we slept together?"

"How could I ever forget?" she chuckled. "It was on a leaky air mattress in the back of your pickup parked behind your uncle's barn."

"Not the first time we made love, although that, too, brings back fond memories. I mean the first time we actually slept together, all night, wrapped in each other's arms."

"It was November, right around this same time of year actually. My folks were out of town and you drove up from Purdue to be with me. We spent the weekend playing house and making babies, as I recall."

"That was the first time I watched you sleep. I knew then and there that you were the woman I wanted to share a bed with for the rest of my life. Watching you tonight with your fist tucked under your cheek took me back to that first night. Whenever I had trouble falling asleep these past couple years, I'd picture you like that in my mind and I'd drift right off. Those images of you were like a shining light at the end of a very long and dark tunnel."

"I was holding you back," Maggie murmured in defense of her past actions. "You have to know I only did what I thought was best for you."

"I do know that, Boomer. I'll never agree with your methods, but I've come to understand your motives. Life has a funny way of taking us down paths we'd never choose to travel on our own. You pushed me down one of those roads. Although I would have preferred to make the journey with you, I won't deny the last four years has been one helluva an exciting ride. I am, however, relieved to know my days of traveling solo are over."

When she didn't respond, he asked, "They are over, right?"

"Yes, Nicky. They're over. I won't make the same mistake again." She pressed a reassuring kiss to his chest. "I'm never going anywhere without you." She felt him tense and tighten his grip, as if he couldn't pull her close enough.

"I'm not planning on going anywhere either, but what if the decision isn't ours to make this time? What if this journey is out of both of our hands?" His voice cracked and broke.

Icy fingers chilled her blood to a point where she felt it creep sluggishly through her veins, and she shivered against him. She didn't like the direction this conversation was heading. "What do you mean?" She needed further clarification.

He hesitated, as if loath to further the discussion, but he continued, knowing it had to be said. "What if these headaches are a just a symptom of something more serious? It might have been easier for you if I'd left things the way they were."

"No," she said. Her heart crashed and fluttered against her ribs. "Don't talk like that." She couldn't, she wouldn't, believe there was anything wrong with this warm, vital man whose heart she felt and heard beating within his chest.

"If this road turns out to be a dead-end for me, I want you to know that you and the boys will be well provided for—I've seen to that. I've made some very profitable investments, and my contract with Morgan Enterprises has a hefty death benefit even if it's not racing related."

"Will you stop? Talk to me about investments and death benefits when you're ninety, okay?" Maggie pushed away and climbed out of her snug, secure place beside him. She didn't want to be warm and protected or safe because she wasn't feeling any of those things at the moment. She felt threatened and frightened. Hugging herself from the unnatural cold that penetrated every pore, she trembled and cried.

Wearing only a pair of flannel boxers, he swung his legs to the floor, and came to where she was standing. Coming up behind her, he wrapped her into the shelter of his arms. "I don't like talking about this any more than you do. I'm scared too, but we have to be practical. Not talking about it isn't going to change the fact that there might be something seriously wrong with me."

"I don't want to be practical!" She choked on her tears. "Damn it, Nick. This isn't fair!" Turning in his arms, she buried her face against his chest, once again finding reassurance in the steady thumping of his heart. "I just got you back. I'm not letting you go that easily. You've got more races to win and we've got more babies to make."

"I like the sound of your priorities, honey, but we're getting ahead of ourselves. Let's wait and see what the doctor has to say. Okay?" He chucked her under the chin and kissed her. His lips were tender and warm as he whispered the depth his love in low, husky tones, sharing his most intimate thoughts with heartfelt eloquence and breathless sighs.

Maggie clung to him, wanting to keep him close, as if she had been blessed with the ability to protect him and keep him safe as long as she never let him go. Leading him back to bed, she pulled the covers over them and tucked him tightly against her. Nothing was going to take him away from her without one hell of a fight.

****

Some time during the wee hours of the morning they had shifted into the nestled spoons position with Nick curved tightly behind her. There was something comforting in finding herself wrapped within the arms of the man she loved. Snuggling deeper into the bend of his long legs, she asked herself how she had ever managed to survive those years without him.

A loud knock and an even louder, "Mom! Dad!" shouted from the hall made her raise her head from the pillow and respond to their demanding children.

The door swung open and in they bounded. "It's snowing!" Danny announced.

Nick gave a sleepy groan against the nape of her neck. "Tell them to come back in the spring," he mumbled, snuggling deeper under the blankets against her back.

Under the covers and out of sight, his hand slipped under her nightgown. Maggie shifted under his wandering touch until he found her breast, which he began to knead gently, rolling the nipple between his thumb and forefinger until it blossomed under his relentless attention. Loose flannel wasn't nearly as restrictive as tight denim. She felt him grow hard and press against the back of her thigh with an urgency she found hard to ignore. Her own growing need made it difficult for her to concentrate on what the boys were saying.

"Dad, you promised we could take the snowmobiles out the first snowfall, remember?" Danny stated.

Nick sighed. "I did, didn't I?" He shifted to give himself a little more room to expand.

"Uh huh," Davey confirmed.

"How about getting the coffee started and we'll be down in a few minutes," Maggie told the boys as she moved restlessly under the wandering explorations of Nick's talented fingers.

"Sure," Danny said, eyeing his cuddling parents who showed no signs of getting up. As he left the room he added, "Uh, Dad, you might as well take your time and do it right. The snow's not going anywhere."

Nick collapsed against her chuckling, his warm breath tickling her neck. "We're going to have our hands full with that one."

"You already seem to have your hands full," Maggie said, moving and stretching against him like a contented house cat as she rolled to face him.

"Well, so I do," he said in mock surprise.

She wiggled her fingers beneath the elastic band of his boxers. "Now so do I."

****

The once pristine, snow covered pasture behind the old house was now zigzagged and crisscrossed with

213

snowmobile tracks. Maggie focused her camera and snapped repeatedly as Davey whizzed past with Nick bouncing on the back. She wanted pictures—lots and lots of pictures.

Danny followed close behind on a second sled and she snapped again. The three of them were having the time of their lives. She detected broad grins on all three faces in spite of the clunky helmets they wore. On their second pass Davey stopped just long enough to let Nick hop off before zooming away to join his brother for another lap around the field.

It was a perfect early snowfall. The sun was shining with enough cloud cover to keep it from glaring off the snow and blinding anyone venturing into the great outdoors. The wind was non-existent, and the temperature was just cold enough to keep the snow from turning to sloppy slush.

"Do they ever give up?" Nick asked, tugging off his helmet. "A five hundred mile race isn't this exhausting." He plunked himself on the snow-covered ground and sat with his legs outstretched.

He patted the snow next to him and flashed an alluring smile. "Come sit by me."

Maggie aimed her camera at him and snapped the last picture on the roll. "No way. I'm cold enough without parking my butt in the snow." She slipped the camera into the pocket of her parka and secured the Velcro closure. "I'm not wearing snow pants like you."

He patted his lap. "This is warmer. Could be downright hot if you give it a chance."

"Tempting as it sounds, I'm going to pass. I've had enough outdoorsy activity for today. You and the boys will have to finish this bonding experience without me. I'm heading to a nice dry, climate-controlled mall, get these pictures developed, and hunt for fabric. "Have fun." She bent down and kissed him. "I love you."

He wrapped his arms around her and tugged her down. She landed on top of him and Nick rolled over, pinning her under him. It was such a curious sensation having the back half of her body chilled from lying in the snow and her front half warm and toasty from his body covering hers.

Grabbing a handful of snow from over her head she whipped it at him. It fell short of its mark and the majority of the wet stuff landed in her face.

He laughed. "Lucky for me you throw like a girl." Slow and meticulously he began the process of kissing away each little clump of snowflakes from her face with warm, caressing lips.

"Get a room!" Danny shouted as he whizzed past.

"That's it!" Nick leaped to his feet, pulling her up with him. "I'm locking that one in his room until he's twenty-one."

"Oh, Nicky..." Maggie called.

"What?" He turned and caught a loosely packed snowball square in the chest.

"Who throws like a girl, huh?" she shouted, running as fast as her snow boots and cumbersome pregnant body would carry her. She wasn't about to stick around to find out how well he could retaliate.

Chapter Twenty-Seven

Some people had an affinity for bookstores, others had a penchant for antiques, and there were even those who enjoyed roaming office supply stores in search of the perfect pen or binder. For Maggie it was wandering through aisles of fabric bolts at *Material World*.

Hunting for fabrics was always a near spiritual experience for Maggie. She couldn't explain why she was such a perfectionist when it came to choosing the fabrics for her designs, it was simply part of her—an activity she so thoroughly enjoyed it often took hours to find just one perfect piece of cloth.

The selection process was never complete until she touched the cloth, caressed it, let it slip through her fingers. The texture and finish was every bit as important and the color. She paused and caressed a beautiful length of Egyptian cotton that caught her experienced eye. The finish was smooth as silk and the colors were deep and rich.

"Hi, Maggie."

The cloth dropped from her hand as she turned and discovered Jen Walker clutching an assortment of colorful calicos and coordinating solids. "Hi, Jen. What's with all the fabric? Don't tell me you're taking up quilting after all these years?"

"No, but my daughters have been bitten by the bug. Ever since their sleepover at your house they have become quite the quilting fanatics. Jackie pours over pattern books and quilting magazines with Shanna. They're not accomplishing much yet, but it's keeping them busy and they're sure having fun in the process."

"That's wonderful!" Maggie exclaimed. "It's an activity they can share and enjoy for a lifetime. My grandma always said if you pass the passion on to just one person the craft will never die."

"What's wonderful is they've found a common

interest and I think it's brought them closer because of it. I want to thank you for taking the time to work with them, especially Shanna. Not everyone is so patient and understanding."

"We had so much fun that night. I enjoyed every minute. You tell them to call me or come over if they have any questions or need help."

Jen reached out and patted Maggie's forearm. "I know you really mean that, and I appreciate it." She gasped when seeing her youngest daughter approaching with another bolt of fabric clutched in her chubby arms. "Oh, Shanna, not more fabric."

"I really like this one, Mommy!" She held up the neon hot pink cotton stamped with purple and yellow daisies. It was bright and gaudy and undeniably eye-catching, and just the thing any child would select if given the chance. "Do you like it, Maggie?"

"All that matters is that you like it, Shanna Banana. It will make very pretty throw pillows for your bed."

"And quite possibly a nightlight." Jen chuckled, shielding her eyes from the glare.

"Dual purpose—all the better," said Maggie.

"Please, Mommy," Shanna begged.

"All right, but that's the last piece," Jen relented and instructed the clerk to measure off two yards of the flashy pink fabric then turned to Maggie. "I see Nick is back."

"Uh huh." Maggie nodded and absently fingered a spool of sparkly black and orange Halloween ribbon from the seasonal notions sale bin.

"So how long will his truck be parked in your driveway this time?" Jen's voice was understandably skeptical.

"For as long as we both shall live." However long that might be.

Jen's eyes grew wide with surprise. "Are you saying what I think you're saying? You're back together? Really? For good?"

"Sorta looks that way."

"For ever and ever?"

"Yes, Jen!" Maggie exclaimed, exasperated. "For ever and ever. Amen already."

"Halleluiah! So when are you going to make it

official? You realize, of course, this calls for a party—a reception with all the trimmings." Jen's enthusiasm bubbled over like an uncorked bottle of champagne. "Just give me a date and I'll take it from there. You won't have to do a thing but show up with the groom. Consider it our wedding present."

"Slow down, Jen. We haven't gotten that far yet."

"What are you waiting for? You're not kids this time around."

"There's another matter that needs to be taken care of first." A cloud of seriousness settled over her face.

"What's wrong? Oh, no. Don't tell me he married that buxom blonde Texan on the rebound and now you've got a messy annulment to deal with? You know where to come if you need legal advice."

Maggie shook her head. "No, no, it's nothing like that, Jen, but I really can't talk about it right now." She wasn't ready to share this fragment of her life with anyone yet, not even her dear friend who knew just about everything else there was to know about her. She was still trying to get a handle on it herself, feeling very much like she'd just been handed an unstable bomb and one false move would cause the thing to blow up in her face. Maggie knew she was being irrational and superstitious, but she couldn't bring herself to voice Nick's health crisis aloud.

"You know I'm always there for you, Maggie, whenever you're ready to talk."

Maggie nodded and her mouth formed a grateful smile. "Thanks," was all she said, suddenly overcome by an overwhelming desire to be with Nick. She needed to hear the resonant timbre of his voice, feel his warm, supple flesh beneath her hands, and caress his strong, handsome face with loving green eyes. She wanted to wrap her arms around him and never let go. Mumbling her goodbyes, she fled the place that had once carried with it fonder memories and hurried home.

****

Maggie walked in the house and nearly killed herself on the mountain of boots, helmets, gloves, snow pants and jackets heaped just inside the door. Everything was lying in puddles of melted snow.

She kicked her way through yelling, "Danny, Davey, Nick!"

"Dad's sleeping. He wasn't feeling good," Davey responded. He carried a box of vanilla wafers in one hand and a quart of chocolate milk in the other. Ordinarily she would have lectured Davey for a good five minutes on the disgusting, unsanitary practice of drinking from the carton, but in the overall scheme of recent events it didn't seem important enough to mention. Talk about getting a crash course in the art of putting things into proper perspective.

"What do you mean he wasn't feeling good?" She kicked the nearest helmet out of her way. It skittered and spun across the entry and stopped only when it struck the opposite hall wall and left a small, but nonetheless noticeable gouge in the plaster—another meaningless matter not to get upset about.

Watching the helmet, he answered, "He said he felt nauseous, like he was getting the flu or something."

"You and Danny get this mess picked up and put away where it belongs." She stepped over the last pair of wet boots. "Where's your dad?"

"Upstairs."

When she walked into the bedroom she found it almost as dark and silent as the middle of a moonless night. The blinds were down and the drapes were drawn. Nick was lying on his side with his back to the door wrapped in the old quilt of her grandmother's she kept on the rocker in her workroom. Overwhelmed by the desire to see him more clearly, she pulled back a drapery panel and raised one of the blinds to give the room just enough natural light to illuminate the darkness.

She sat on the edge of the bed and rubbed his back. "Nicky?" She hated seeing him this way and felt helpless knowing there was nothing in her power to make it better.

He lifted his head and turned toward the sound her voice. His eyes were glazed and unfocused yet he smiled when seeing her. "Hi," he whispered.

"Davey said you were sick."

"It was the weirdest thing," he said as he rolled over and sat up. After propping pillows against the headboard, he leaned against them. Every move he made seemed to be an effort. "I was just standing there watching the boys, and all of a sudden I got dizzy and nauseous. I never actually threw up or anything, but it sure felt like I was going to for a while."

"I don't like the sound of that. I think you should go to the emergency room."

He shook his head. "No. I'm not going anywhere. I took some pills. It's starting to ease up."

"They can run more tests. The sooner the doctors know what's wrong the sooner they can fix it."

"Maggie, honey, listen to me." He sat up and rested his forearm across an up drawn knee. His hand waved in an expressive manner in an attempt to make his point. "It's Saturday afternoon. Unless it's a chest clutching, bone crushing, or blood spurting emergency they're just going to tell me there's nothing they can do until they get the test results."

"You don't know that for sure." He was probably right but she didn't like giving up so easily.

"Yeah, I do. Please, just let me enjoy the rest of this weekend with my family."

"All right. But first thing Monday morning we're calling for those results. Agreed?" She shook her finger at him to stress the importance of what she was saying.

"Agreed. So what wonderful fabrics did you find today?" He leaned against the pillows and tucked his hands behind his head, waiting for her to regale him with her fabulous discoveries.

Maggie shrugged and shook her head. "I didn't find anything."

He studied her for a moment." I feel like I'm keeping you from something that's important."

"It's just a quilt, Nick. It's not that important."

"I saw the design on your desk. It is that important." He reached across the bed and picked something up from the nightstand. "I also found this." It was too dark to tell what it was until he handed it to her. It was the silver-framed photo of him holding Megan.

"Isn't it beautiful?" She caressed it with her fingertips.

Nick took it back and gazed at it. "Did you mean

what you said last night, about our having more babies?"

Maggie nodded and smiled. "Absolutely. Just as soon as I deliver this one safely into Joel's arms, we'll start on more of our own. We'll create our own racing dynasty and give that Petty family a run for their money."

"That's going to mean a bigger house with a lot more bedrooms, you know."

She grinned. "Got a particular place in mind?"

"I might," he said, reaching for her. She crawled across the bed and curled up beside him, resting her head in the curve of his shoulder. "I'm on intimate terms with the owner. I might be able to work out a deal with her."

"Her?"

"It's all yours, Maggie—the house, the woods, the pasture, everything. The deed is in your name. I told you that the restoration was a labor of love." Wrapping his arms around her, he pulled her more tightly against him.

"Just how many bedrooms are we talking about?" she asked, stretching herself to better fit the length of his body with a satisfied smile and a slow contented sigh.

"Only five, but we can always add on."

"Sounds like we've got our work cut out for us." She closed her eyes and snuggled deeper into his embrace. Like a rare, delicate flower that blooms after only so many years of dormancy, Maggie felt herself beginning to come to life again.

Curling his fingers under her chin, he lifted her face and gazed at her. His thumb slipped lightly across her lower lip. Gripping his hand, she pressed a kiss into the palm then cradled it against her cheek as her eyes fluttered open and cast upon him a look of love so sweet and unconditional that it took his breath away. He lowered his head to accept the kiss that beckoned to him from her waiting lips.

"Sheesh! You guys are at it again? Would you please get married so you can start acting like regular parents?" Danny gave one of his famous eye rolls and tossed his hands in the air, vanishing as suddenly as he had appeared and mumbling something that neither Nick nor Maggie could understand.

"Promise me we won't have any more like him?" Nick chuckled under his breath.

"No guarantees unless we find someone else to father them."

"If that's the only option you're giving me then I guess we'll just have to take our chances and hope for the best."

If she were forced to inventory her current priorities, hoping for the best was most definitely at the top of her list, right below praying for a miracle.

****

"Post Concussion Syndrome?" Nick repeated the diagnosis and looked at the neurologist for further clarification. He finally had a name for what was wrong with him, and it didn't sound nearly as ominous as tumor or aneurysm.

"It's not uncommon for this to happen after sustaining a head injury," the doctor explained. "The symptoms you've been experiencing are a collective reaction to the concussion you suffered from months ago."

Dressed in only a drafty back-tied paper gown and whatever was left of his dignity, Nick braced his palms against the cold vinyl examination table and wrapped anxious fingers around the edge, and asked, "Is it serious?" The doctor had put him through a thorough physical before handing down this final diagnosis. The paper cover crinkled and creased as he shifted his weight.

"No, not really. That's not to say you shouldn't take it easy. I wouldn't recommend putting yourself into any high-risk situations that could cause further head trauma for a while. Although these symptoms can linger for months, you've probably been through the worst already. The anxiety of expecting the worst in all likelihood exacerbated the condition. Stress and tension only seem to make the symptoms worse. My guess is you'll be feeling better in a matter of days. If you don't feel better already."

"As a matter of fact, I do. Just knowing I'm not going to die from this has me wanting to run ninety-nine yards for the game winning touchdown, spike the football in the end zone and do a little victory dance." Assuming a wide grin, he waved his hands over his head in a gesture he normally reserved for victory lane.

The doctor laughed. "I'm going to give you some literature on relaxation techniques to help ease the headaches when they do occur. I'm also giving you a prescription for the pain but I only want you to take it as a last resort. I don't want you getting dependent."

"Will this effect my driving?"

If you're talking about ordinary day-to-day driving, no, it shouldn't affect that at all. I think you already know your limitations. But I don't imagine that's what you're asking me, is it?"

"You know it's not, doc. How about it? Will I be able to race again?"

"I see no reason to think otherwise, Nick. Considering the fact that you haven't exhibited more than a handful of the symptoms associated with the syndrome you seem to have a mild case. You should be good to go by Daytona."

Nick looked a little surprised. "You a racing fan, doc?"

"Not really, but my two teenage sons are huge NASCAR fans. I feel silly asking, but if it isn't too much of an imposition, I'd sure appreciate a couple autographs."

"All things considered, doc, I think I can do better than a couple of autographs. Name the race and I'll get you and your sons passes."

"I don't ordinarily accept these offers of patient gratitude, but I don't see how I can refuse this one. My boys would never forgive me if I did otherwise." The doctor seemed almost embarrassed by his admission. "The nurse will be back with the script and literature."

"Thanks again for everything, doc." Nick extended his hand.

"It's always a pleasure giving good news to a patient. Good luck to you."

Nick hopped off the table and reached for his clothes. He couldn't wait to get home to tell Maggie the news. Inasmuch as she had fiercely argued that she wanted to go with him, he argued just as strongly against the idea. Good news or bad, he told her, he wanted to be the one to tell her. They would deal with it together in the privacy of their home, not in the sterile surroundings of an impersonal stainless steel and slick-tiled clinic. She'd finally relented, though he'd won the debate by only a narrow margin. The last thing he said to her before he left that morning was, "Everything is going to be okay." Optimism had always been his greatest ally.

****

Clutching a bouquet of the deepest red, longest stemmed, sweetest smelling roses he could find, Nick burst through the door and shouted, "Maggie, I'm home!" Home...the word wrapped around him like one of her exquisite quilts.

Maggie ran to him. He didn't have to say another word. The heart stopping, dimpled smile said it all. She threw herself into his outstretched arms with such force that it knocked the flowers right out of his hand. Roses rained down and scattered all around them.

"Didn't I tell you that everything was going to be okay?"

"Yes, you did!" Damn the man for being such a know it all and bless him for being right this time.

Damn him, love him, bless him, curse him—the heart of the matter was it all came from the same place and there was nothing that would ever stop her from experiencing those feelings about him again and again and again.

Epilogue

The birthing room was a flurry of last minute preparation.

"Hee-hee-hee-hee-hee," Maggie panted.

"You're almost there, Maggie," the doctor reassured and encouraged.

"How's he doing?" Maggie managed to query before the next contraction hit.

"Not much longer," said Joel. "It's almost over."

"Here comes another one," Maggie grimaced.

"And look, here he comes," Joel sounded positively ecstatic.

"I can't see. What's happening now?"

"One more push, Maggie," said the doctor.

"Joel, tell me what's happening...hee-hee-hee..."

"He's hanging in there."

"Maggie," the doctor exasperated. "I could really use your cooperation. Push."

She scrunched her face and gave it all she had. "Tell me what's going on," she strained.

"Oh my God." Joel sounded positively astounded. "I don't believe what he's doing."

"What! What?" Maggie exclaimed.

"Push, Maggie!" The doctor interrupted.

"This is unbelievable." Joel slapped his forehead with the palm of his hand.

"Push."

"I can't take much more," Maggie groaned through clenched teeth.

"He's coming around on the outside," Joel exclaimed.

"He's what?"

"Maggie, push!"

She braced her palms against the bed. "Arrrrrrrrgh!"

"Just a little more. That's it. You can do it. A little more, a little more."

"Push!"

"Now give me everything you've got."

Maggie threw herself forward and strained. "Arrrrrrrrgh!"

"Yes!" Joel whooped with joy. "Nick did it!" He turned away from the television just in time to see the doctor deliver his child.

"It's a girl!" the doctor announced.

Nick winning at Martinsville suddenly paled by comparison. He watched in awe as the doctor suctioned the mucus from the baby's mouth and he gasped as his daughter took her first crying breath. Tears blurred his vision as he glanced from Maggie to the baby. "Maggie, you did it," he said in an awed, reverent whisper.

"We did it." Maggie collapsed against the bed. "Looks like me and Nick crossed the finish line together."

"Would you like to hold the baby?" The nurse began to hand Maggie the blanket wrapped infant.

Maggie shook her head. "That honor goes to her father."

Smiling knowingly, the nurse placed the mewling bundle into Joel's waiting arms.

"What name did you finally decide on?" Maggie questioned as she ran a fingertip across the infant's downy head.

"Mary Elizabeth Nicole, after both her mothers, *and* the winner of today's race."

Maggie glanced at the photo of Beth she'd placed on the bedside table and smiled through tender tears. "I think she would be pleased."

"There's no doubt about it. Mary has her mother's birthmark. Look." Joel folded back the blanket and exposed the baby's left shoulder. High on her back just above the shoulder blade was a small, rosy pink birthmark in the unmistakable shape of a kiss—an angel's kiss.

Maggie glanced at the television and watched the post race craziness with an expression that defied description. They had all been somehow touched by that angel.